ACCLAIM FOR

MALICE DOMESTIC 1

"Elizabeth Peters has coaxed from a baker's dozen of interesting authors the 'traditional' short stories. . . . Witty, cheeky, sardonic, deliciously sarcastic."
—*Buffalo News*

MALICE DOMESTIC 2

"The second very solid volume in the series of mystery short stories offers ample evidence that a skillful writer can deliver a worthwhile read in pared-down prose."

—*Publishers Weekly*

MALICE DOMESTIC 3

"Another solid anthology of original short stories from some of today's leading authors."
—*The Purloined Letter*

Elizabeth Peters Presents *Malice Domestic 1*
Mary Higgins Clark Presents *Malice Domestic 2*
Nancy Pickard Presents *Malice Domestic 3*
Carolyn G. Hart Presents *Malice Domestic 4*
Phyllis A. Whitney Presents *Malice Domestic 5*

Published by POCKET BOOKS

PHYLLIS A. WHITNEY

presents

MALICE DOMESTIC 5

An Anthology of Original Traditional Mystery Stories

POCKET BOOKS

New York London Toronto Sydney Tokyo Singapore

An *Original* Publication of POCKET BOOKS

POCKET BOOKS, a division of Simon & Schuster Inc.
1230 Avenue of the Americas, New York, NY 10020

Copyright © 1996 by Malice Domestic, Ltd.

ISBN: 0-671-89632-6

First Pocket Books printing May 1996

10 9 8 7 6 5 4 3 2 1

POCKET and colophon are registered trademarks of
Simon & Schuster Inc.

Cover art by John Zielinski

Printed in the U.S.A.

Copyright Notices

Contents

Contents

Mysteries of Manners, Labors of Love

Phyllis A. Whitney

———

When I first heard the name *Malice Domestic*® proposed for a new mystery fans' group that was forming, I expressed dismay. "Malice" was fine, but I wasn't sure about "domestic." I doubt whether any of my heroines has ever made a bed or vacuumed a rug, so I felt doubtful. However, nothing else surfaced in the way of a title. "Soft-boiled" and "cozy" please me even less. Then someone explained to me kindly that "domestic" didn't, in this case, mean household chores. It referred to mystery stories that concerned themselves with family-and-friends events, wherein, after all, most crimes are committed.

Now, of course, *Malice Domestic* thrives and is accepted and respected as a means of celebrating mysteries that are not in the hard-boiled territory. The name trips from our tongues easily, and sometimes we just call it "Malice" affectionately.

It is a unique, very different sort of literary organization, with a hardworking board of directors and many able volunteers. Once a year a convention is held—a lovely bash with imaginative panels of experts (I served on one called "Things That Go Bump in the Night"), a Ghost of Honor, and various unexpected happenings.

Malice Domestic has fun. In a way, it reminds me of the Mystery Writers of America's early days, when numerous skits were put on by the members, and there was a bit of clowning to be expected at the annual dinners. Now MWA is so successful and dignified that no such romps are possible. *Malice Domestic* is still young and obstreperous, and anything can happen.

There is a platform—sort of. Our novels indulge in less gore and explicit sex, and are closer to Mary Roberts Rinehart than Raymond Chandler (looking back).

One achievement that *Malice Domestic* can be especially satisfied with is the annual publication of an anthology of short stories written by some of the mystery field's most gifted writers. When I look at the contents pages of these books, I am filled with awe, respect, and not a little envy. Envy because I cannot, for the life of me, write a short story (so my name never appears on the contents page).

Long, long ago, when the century and I were young, I wrote short stories for the pulp paper magazines. It was a painful time, though very good training for a beginning writer. If you can write a salable short story, you will never write a boring novel. I must have written three hundred short stories, about two hundred of which went into the wastebasket, with less than one hundred published. I collected a large number of rejection slips and suffered a great deal.

Finally, in despair, I wrote a book. Eureka! I discovered that I really wasn't a short story writer, and no more rejections have been received. My early books weren't mysteries. Mystery writing is the most difficult of all to do well, and I had to learn my craft. Once I hit my stride with mysteries, I never looked back or wanted to write any other kind of novel.

The quality of writing in these *Malice Domestic* anthologies is high, and I am happy to be presenting this volume— even though I can't make the contents page with a short story.

Salutations, *Malice Domestic!* We are proud of you.

Phyllis A. Whitney

A living legend in the mystery field at the age of 93, Phyllis A. Whitney has published over seventy bestselling novels, the most recent being *Daughter of the Stars* (1994). In 1990 she was honored with the Malice Domestic Award for Lifetime Achievement. Equally proficient in writing for both adults and young people, she won two Edgars for juvenile mysteries for *The Mystery of the Haunted Pool* (1961) and *The Mystery of the Hidden Hand* (1964). A past president of the Mystery Writers of America, Whitney received MWA's Grand Master Award in 1988.

MALICE DOMESTIC 5

Conventual Spirit

Sharan Newman

June 1137, the convent of the Paraclete, France

"Pride, Catherine! Evil, wicked pride! It will be your damnation, girl!"

Sister Bertrada glared at Catherine, their faces an inch apart. "You'll never be allowed to become one of us unless you learn some humility," the old nun continued. "How dare you try to lecture me on the blessed St. Jerome! Do you think you've received a vision of the Truth?"

Catherine bit her tongue.

"No, Sister," she said.

Even those two words sounded impudent to Sister Bertrada, who considered the student novices under her care to be her own private purgatory. And Catherine LeVendeur, with her ready tongue and sharp mind, was her special bane.

"Abbess Heloise has a soft spot for you, though I can't see why," Bertrada went on. "I don't find your glib attempts at rhetoric endearing at all."

"No, Sister." Catherine tried to back up, but Sister

1

Bertrada had her wedged into a corner of the refectory and there was no farther back to go.

"What you need is some serious manual labor."

Catherine stifled a groan. Sister Bertrada did not consider sitting for hours hunched over a table laboriously copying a Psalter to be real work. Never mind that her fingers cramped, her back ached, and her eyes burned at the end of the day. Now she tried to look meek and obliging as she awaited Sister Bertrada's orders.

She succeeded about as well as most sixteen-year-old girls would.

Sister Bertrada had eyes like the Archangel Michael, which glowed with righteousness and ferreted out the most deeply hidden sins. Her cane tapped the wooden floor with ominous thumps as she considered an appropriate penance.

"Go find Sister Felicitia," she told Catherine at last. "Ask her to give you a bucket and a brush. The transept of the oratory has mud all over the floor. You can easily finish scrubbing it before Vespers, if you give the labor the same passion you use to defy me."

Catherine bowed her head, hopefully in outward submission. Sister Bertrada snorted to show that she wasn't fooled in the least, then turned and marched out, leaving Catherine once again defeated by spiritual superiority.

Outside, she was met by her friend and fellow student, Emilie. Emilie took one look at Catherine's face and started laughing.

"Why in the world did you feel you had to tell Sister Bertrada that St. Jerome nagged poor St. Paula to death?"

Catherine shrugged. "I was only quoting from a letter of St. Ambrose. I thought it was interesting that even the saints had their quarrels."

Emilie shook her head in wonder. "You've been here a year and you still have no sense about when to speak and when to keep silent. Sister Melisande would find it amusing, so would Mother Heloise, but Sister Bertrada . . . !"

"I agree," Catherine said sadly. "And now I'm to pay for it on my knees, as usual."

"And proper." Emilie smiled at her fondly. "Oh, Catherine, you do make lessons interesting, if more volatile. I'm so glad you came here."

Catherine sighed. "So am I. Now if only Sister Bertrada could share our happiness."

If meekness were the only test for judging the worthiness of a soul, then Sister Felicitia should have inherited the earth long ago. She was the only daughter of a noble family, who ought to have had to do nothing more than sing the hours, sew, and copy manuscripts. Her only distinction was that her face was marred by deep scars on both sides, running from temple to jaw. Catherine had never heard how she came by them, but assumed that this disfigurement was the reason she was in the convent instead of married to some lord. Although for the dowry Felicitia commanded, it was surprising that no one was willing to take her, no matter what she looked like.

Felicitia certainly didn't behave like a pampered noblewoman. She always volunteered when the most disagreeable tasks were being assigned. She scrubbed out the reredorter, even leaning into the holes in the seats above the river to scrub the filth from the inside. She hauled wood and dug vegetables. She never lifted her eyes from the job she was doing. She never raised her voice in dispute.

Catherine didn't know what to make of her.

"I'll need the bucket later this evening," Sister Felicitia said when Catherine stated her orders. "I'd help you, of course, but I'm dyeing today."

Catherine had noticed. The woman's hands were stained blue with woad. It would be days before it all washed off. Sister Felicitia didn't appear concerned by this. Nor did she seem aware that the day was soft and bright and that the other women were all sitting in the cloister, sewing and chatting softly while soaking up the June sunshine.

"Sister Bertrada wants me to do this alone, anyway," Catherine said, picking up the bucket and brush. Sister Felicitia nodded without looking up. She did not indulge in unnecessary conversation.

* * *

3

Catherine spilled half the water tripping over the door-stop to the oratory. Coming in from the sunlight, it seemed to her that there were bright doves fluttering before her eyes. So she missed her step in the darkness, and then mopped up the puddles before spending the better part of the afternoon scrubbing the stone floor. But, true to Sister Bertrada's prediction, she did indeed have the job finished in time for Vespers, although her robes were still damp and stained at the hem, unsuitable attire for the Divine Office.

And that was how she knew that there had been no muddy footprints on the oratory floor when the nuns retired to the dormitory that evening.

Of course, Sister Bertrada didn't believe her.

"This time, do it properly," she told Catherine as she handed her the bucket the next day.

Catherine fervently wanted to protest. She had scrubbed the floor thoroughly, half of it with her own skirts. It had been clean. Perhaps one of the nuns had forgotten and worn her wooden clogs to prayers instead of her slippers. It wasn't her fault.

But Catherine knew that she would never be allowed to remain here at the Paraclete if she contradicted Sister Bertrada every time she opened her mouth, and she wanted to stay at the convent more than anything else in the world. So she took the proffered bucket and returned to the dark oratory.

She propped the door open to let the light in and knelt to begin the task.

"That's odd," she said as she started on the marks.

"That's *very* odd," she added as she went on to the next ones.

These had to have been made recently, after Compline, when all the women had retired for the night. They were in the shape of footprints, starting at the door and running across the transept to the chapter room, stopping at the bottom of the staircase to the nuns' dormitory. The marks were smudged, perhaps by the slippers of the nuns when they came down just before dawn for Vigils and Lauds. But the muddy prints had certainly been made by bare feet. And they were still damp.

4

Who could have entered the oratory secretly in the middle of the night?

Catherine wondered about it all the while she was scrubbing. When she had finished, she went to the prioress, Astane, for an explanation.

"These footprints," Astane asked. "You already removed them?"

"Sister Bertrada told me to," Catherine explained.

The prioress nodded. "Very good, child. You are learning."

"But I know they weren't there yesterday evening," Catherine insisted. "I did clean the floor carefully the first time. Someone was in the oratory after we went to bed."

"That seems unlikely." Astane did not appear alarmed by Catherine's statement. "The door is barred on the inside, after all."

"Then how did the footprints get there?" Catherine persisted.

The prioress raised her eyebrows. "That is not your concern, my dear."

"It is if I have to wipe them up," Catherine muttered under her breath.

Not far enough under. Astane's hand gripped her chin tightly and tilted her face upward.

"I presume you were praying just then," the prioress said.

Catherine marveled at the strength in these old women. Sister Bertrada, Prioress Astane; they both must be nearly seventy, but with hands as firm and steady as a blacksmith's. And eyes that saw the smallest lie.

"No, Sister," Catherine said. "But I am now. *Domine, noli me arguere in ira tua* "

The prioress's lip twitched and her sharp glance softened. "'Lord, do not rebuke me in your anger . . .'" she translated. "Catherine, dear, I'm not angry with you and I hope and trust that our Lord isn't, either."

She paused. "Sister Bertrada, on the other hand . . ."

Catherine needed no further warning. She resolved not to mention the footprints in the oratory again.

* * *

But the next morning, everyone saw them.

The light of early dawn slanted through the narrow windows of the chapter, illuminating the clumps of damp earth, a few fresh stalks still clinging to them, forming a clear trail of footprints across the room.

"How did those get there?" Emilie whispered to Catherine, peering down the stairs over the shoulders of the choir nuns.

"They're exactly the same as yesterday," Catherine whispered back. "But I'm sure I cleaned it all. I know I did."

Sister Bertrada and Sister Felicitia walked through the marks, apparently without noticing, but the other women stopped. They looked at each other in confusion, pointing at the footprints, starting at the barred door to the garden, going through the oratory and ending at the steps to their sleeping room.

Sister Ursula shuddered. "Something is coming for us!" she shrieked. "A wild man of the woods has invaded the convent!"

A few of the others gave startled cries, but Emilie giggled, putting a hand over her mouth to stifle the sound. Behind her, Sister Bietriz bent over her shoulder.

"What is it?" she whispered.

Emilie swallowed her laughter. "'Wild man' indeed!" she whispered back. "Maybe Sister Bertrada has a secret lover!"

Bietriz and Catherine exploded in most unseemly mirth.

"Quiet!" The object of their speculation raised her cane in warning.

They composed themselves as quickly as possible, knowing that the matter would not be forgotten, but hoping to alleviate the punishment.

"Catherine," Sister Bertrada continued. "Since you and Emilie find this mess so amusing, you may clean it. Bietriz, you will help them."

Catherine opened her mouth to object that she had already removed the marks twice and it had done no good. Just as she inhaled to speak, Emilie stepped on her toe.

"Yie . . . yes, Sister," Catherine said instead.

Privately, she agreed with both Ursula and Emilie. The

marks must have been made by a wild man from the forest. For who else could become enamored of Sister Bertrada?

"I agree that there is something very strange about this," Emilie told Catherine as they scrubbed. "Who could be getting in here every night? And why doesn't Mother Heloise say something about it? Do you think she knows who it is?"

Catherine wrung out the washrag. Bietriz, whose family was too exalted for floors, leaned against the wall and pointed out spots they had missed.

"Mother Heloise probably doesn't think this worth commenting on," she said. "Perhaps she thinks someone is playing a trick and doesn't want them encouraged. You don't really believe one of us is letting a man in, do you?"

"Who?" Emilie asked. "Sister Bertrada? She and Sister Felicitia would be the most logical suspects. Since they sleep on either side of the door, they have the best chance of leaving at night without being noticed."

Catherine tried to imagine either woman tiptoeing down the steps to let in a secret lover. In Sister Bertrada's case her imagination didn't stretch far enough.

She laughed. "I would find it easier to believe in a monster."

"It's not so preposterous," Emilie continued. "Sister Felicitia is really quite beautiful, even now. I've heard that she had a number of men eager to marry her, but she refused them all. Her father was furious when she announced that she would only wed Christ."

Catherine leaned back on her heels and considered. "I suppose she might have changed her mind," she said. "Perhaps one of them continued to pursue her even here and convinced her that he wanted her despite her looks and had no interest in her property."

Bietriz shook her head. "I don't think so, Catherine. Felicitia made those scars herself, with the knife she used to cut embroidery thread. She sliced right through her cheeks, purposely, so that no one would desire her. That was how her father was finally convinced to let her come here."

Catherine sat back in shock, knocking over the bucket of soapy water.

"How do you know this?" she asked.

"It was common knowledge at the time," Bietriz answered. "I was about twelve then. I remember how upset my mother was about it. Felicitia threatened to cut off her own nose next. It's dreadful, but I benefited from her example. When I said I wanted to come to the Paraclete, no one dared oppose me. Mother even refused to let me have my sewing basket unless she was present, just in case."

"I see." Catherine was once again reminded that she was only a merchant's daughter, at the Paraclete by virtue of her quick mind and her father's money. Bietriz was from one of the best families in Champagne, related in some way even to the count. Bietriz knew all about the life of a noblewoman and all the gossip she herself would not normally be privy to. At the Paraclete they could be sisters in Christ, but not in the world.

"Very well," Catherine said. "I will accept that Sister Felicitia is not likely to be letting a man in. But I don't see how any of the rest of us could do it without waking someone."

"Nor do I," Emilie agreed. "In which case we might have to consider Ursula's theory."

"That some half-human creature came in from the forest?" Catherine snorted.

Emilie stood, shaking out her skirts. Bietriz picked up the bucket, her contribution to the labor.

"Of course not," Emilie said. "Even a half-human creature would have to unbar the door. But Satan can pass through bars and locks, if someone summons him. And it's said that he often appears as a beautiful young man."

Bietriz was skeptical. "So we should demand to know who has been having dreams of seduction lately? Who will admit to that?"

Catherine felt a chill run down her spine. Was it possible that one of them could be inviting Evil into the convent, perhaps unwittingly? It was well known that the devil used dreams to lure and confuse the innocent into sin. She tried to remember her dreams of the past few nights. The memories were dim, so it was likely that she had only had dreams of *ventris inanitate,* those deriving from an empty stomach and of no relevance.

They walked out into the sunlight and Catherine felt the fear diminish. While it was true that Satan used dreams to tempt weak humans, sin could only occur when one was awake. Tertullian said so. We can no more be condemned for dreaming we are sinners than rewarded for dreaming we are saints.

"And why would the devil leave footprints?" she continued the thought aloud. "That doesn't seem very subtle."

Emilie didn't want to give up her demon lover theory.

"There is a rock near my home with a dent in it that everyone says is the devil's toe print," she told Catherine. "So why not the whole foot? Satan is known to be devious. Perhaps he doesn't just want one soul. He may be trying to cause dissension among us so that he may take us all."

Bietriz had moved on to another worry. "Why is it that the feet are only coming in?" she asked them. "How does this intruder get out?"

"Perhaps he turns into something else," Emilie answered. "Satan can do that, too."

She seemed delighted with her conclusions, and her expression dared them to come up with a refutation.

Catherine looked at her. Was she serious? Did she now believe they were being visited by the devil as shape-changer? Emilie was usually scornful of such tales. Why was she so eager to assign a supernatural explanation to this? An answer leaped unbidden to her mind.

Emilie's bed wasn't that far from the door.

Catherine tried to suppress the thought as unworthy, but it wouldn't be put down. Emilie was blond, beautiful, and also from a noble family. Perhaps she wasn't as happy in the convent as she pretended. It entailed a much smaller stretch of the imagination to see Emilie unbarring the door for a lover than Sister Felicitia.

But that explanation didn't satisfy her, either. It wasn't

like Emilie. And Catherine was sure Mother Heloise and Prioress Astane didn't believe that one of the nuns had a secret lover, human or demon. If they did, then Brother Baldwin and the other lay brothers who lived nearby would have been set to guard the oratory entrance.

She was missing something. Catherine hated to leave a puzzle unsolved. She had to find out who was doing this. She sighed. It was either that or spend the rest of her life scrubbing the oratory floor.

It was nearly midsummer. The days were long and busy. Apart from reciting the Divine Office seven times a day, the nuns all performed manual labor. They studied, copied manuscripts for the convent library, sewed both church vestments and their own clothing, as well as doing the daily round of cleaning, cooking, and gardening necessary to keep themselves alive.

Catherine meant to stay awake that night, but after the long day, she fell asleep as soon as she lay down and didn't wake until the bell rang for Vigils.

Even in the dim light of the lamp carried by Sister Felicitia, they could all see the fresh footprints at the bottom of the stairs.

Sister Ursula retreated back up the stairs, whimpering, and had to be ordered to continue to the oratory. The others obeyed as well, but with obvious reluctance.

Mother Heloise and Prioress Astane were already waiting in the chapel. Their presence reassured the women and reminded them of their duty to pray. But Catherine was not the only one who looked to see that the bar was still across the garden door.

"Satan won't distract me," Emilie whispered virtuously as they filed into their places. "He can't get you while you're praying."

Catherine wasn't so confident. Whatever was doing this had thoroughly distracted her. She missed the antiphon more than once and knew that bowing her apology to God would not save her from Sister Bertrada's rebuke.

There was an explanation for this, either natural or

supernatural. Catherine didn't care which it was. She only wanted to know the truth.

The next day was the eve of the feast of the Nativity of St. John the Baptist. There would be a special vigil that night. It was also midsummer's eve, a time of spirits crossing between worlds, a fearsome long twilight. A good Christian could be driven mad or worse by the things that walked this night. These beliefs were officially denied and forbidden, but children learned the folk tales before they were weaned and such stories were hard to uproot. The shimmering sunlight of the morning was not bright enough to dispel fear.

Each afternoon while they worked in the cloister, the women were permitted some edifying conversation. Today, the usual gentle murmurs and soft laughter had become a buzzing of wonderment, anger, and fear.

"What if this thing doesn't stop tonight at the bottom of the stairs?" Sister Ursula said, her eyes round with terror and anticipation. "What if it climbs right up and into our beds?"

"All of ours, or just yours?" Bietriz asked.

Ursula reddened with anger. "What are you implying?" she demanded. "I would never bring scandal upon us. How dare you even suggest such a thing!"

Bietriz sighed and put down her sewing. She went over to Ursula and took her gently by the shoulders.

"I apologize," she said. "It was not a kind joke. I make no accusations. I believe you have become overwrought by these happenings. Perhaps you could sleep with Sister Melisande in the infirmary tonight."

"Perhaps I will," Ursula muttered. "Better than being slandered by my sisters or murdered by demons in the dortor."

Sister Felicitia was seated on the grass, her stained hands weaving softened reeds to mend a basket. She looked up.

"There are no demons here," she said firmly.

They all stared at her. It would have been more surprising if a sheep in the meadow had spouted philosophy.

"How do you know?" Ursula asked.

"Mother Heloise promised me," Felicitia answered. "The demons won't come for me here."

She bent again to her work. The others were silent.

"Well," Ursula said finally. "Perhaps I will stay in the dortor. But if anything attacks me, I'll scream so loud you'll think Judgment Day has come."

"If you wake me," Emilie warned, "you'll wish it had."

Before Vespers the Abbess Heloise gathered all the women together in the chapter room. There was a collective sigh of relief as they assembled. Finally, all would be explained.

The abbess smiled at them all fondly. Her large brown eyes studied them, and Catherine felt that Mother Heloise knew just what each of them was thinking and feeling.

"It has been brought to my attention," she began, "that some of you have been concerned about some mud stains in the oratory and chapel. I fear that you have allowed these queries to go beyond normal curiosity to unwholesome speculation. This saddens me greatly. If something so natural and common as wet earth can cause you to imagine demons and suspect each other of scandalous behavior, then I have not done my duty as your mentor or your mother."

There was a rustle of surprise and denial. Heloise held up her hand for silence. There was silence.

"Therefore," she continued, "I apologize to you all for not providing the proper spiritual guidance. I will endeavor to do so in the future and will ask our founder, Master Abelard, for advice on how this may best be done. I hope you will forgive me."

That was all. Heloise signaled the chantress to lead them in for Vespers.

They followed in bewildered obedience. Catherine and Emilie stared at each other, shaking their heads. As far as Catherine could see, they had just been told that the intruder in the convent was none of their business. It made no sense.

Mindful of her earlier mistakes, Catherine tried desperately to keep her mind on the service for St. John's Eve, despite the turmoil in her mind.

"Ecce, mitto angelum meum . . ." Behold, I send my angel, who will prepare the way for you before my coming. *"Vox clamitis in deserto . . ."* A voice crying in the wilderness.

She tried to concentrate on St. John. It was hard to imagine him as a baby, leaping for joy in his mother's womb as they visited the Virgin Mary. She always saw him as the gaunt man of the desert, living naked on a diet of locusts and honey. People must have thought him mad, preaching a savior no one had heard of.

"Ecce, mitto angelum meum . . ."

All at once Catherine realized what she had been doing. She had looked at the problem from one direction only. Mother Heloise knew the answer. That was why she wasn't worried. When one turned the proposition around, it made perfect sense. Now, if only she could stay awake tonight to prove her theory.

The night, usually too brief, seemed to stretch on forever. Catherine was beginning to believe that she had made an error in her logic.

There was a rustling from the other end of the room. Someone was getting up. Catherine waited. Whoever it was could be coming this way, to use the reredorter. No one passed her bed. She heard a creak from the end of the room, as if someone else were also awake. She peered over the blanket. It was too dark to tell. There were no more sounds. Perhaps it had only been someone tossing about with a nightmare. Perhaps. But she had to know.

Carefully, Catherine eased out of bed. They all slept fully dressed, even to their slippers, so as to be ready for the Night Office. Catherine looked up and down the rows on either side of the room. In the dim light everyone appeared to be accounted for and asleep. Slowly, fearing even to breathe, Catherine moved down the room to the door. It was open.

All the tales of monsters and demons came rushing suddenly into her mind. Anything could be at the foot of those stairs. Who would protect her if she encountered them against orders, because of her arrogant curiosity?

She said a quick prayer to St. Catherine of Alexandria,

who had known what it was to wonder about things, and she started down the stairs.

At the bottom she nearly fainted in terror as she stepped onto a pile of something soft that moved under her foot. She bent down and touched it.

It was clothing just like her own. A shift, a long tunic, a belt, and a pair of slippers. The discovery of something so familiar terrified Catherine even more.

What had happened to the woman who had worn these clothes?

Moonlight shone through the open door of the oratory. Catherine looked down at the floor. In her fear, she had almost forgotten to test her conclusion.

She was right. The floor was clean. So far, nothing had entered. Feeling a little more confident, she stepped out into midsummer night.

The herb garden lay tranquil under the moon. Catherine had been out once before at night, helping Sister Melisande pick the plants that were most potent when gathered at the new moon. This time she was here uninvited.

There was a break in the hedge on the other side of the garden. Catherine thought she saw a flicker of something white in the grove just beyond. Before she could consider the stupidity of her actions, she hurried toward it.

Within the grove there was a small hill that was empty of trees or undergrowth. Sheep grazed there by day, but tonight . . . *"Ecce! Mitto angelum!"*

Catherine stopped at the edge of the trees. There was someone on the hill, pale skin glowing silver in the moonlight, golden curls surrounding her face like a halo. It was Sister Felicitia, naked, dancing in the night, her feet covered with mud. Her arms were raised as she spun, her face to the sky, her back arched, moving to some music that Catherine couldn't hear.

A hand touched her shoulder. Catherine gasped and the hand moved to her mouth.

"Make no sound," Abbess Heloise warned. "You'll wake her."

Catherine nodded and Heloise removed her hand.

"How did you find out?" the abbess whispered.

"It was the footprints," Catherine whispered back, not taking her eyes from Felicitia. "We all thought they were from someone being let in. But it made much more sense if they were made by someone coming back. Then only one person was needed to open the door from the inside. What I didn't understand was the prints of bare feet."

"She always leaves her clothes at the bottom of the stairs and puts them on again before returning to bed," Heloise explained.

"But shouldn't we stop her?" Catherine asked. "She must be possessed to behave like this."

"She might be," Heloise said. "I worried about that, too. But Sister Bertrada convinced me that if she is, it's by nothing evil and we have no right to interfere."

"Sister Bertrada?" Catherine's voice rose in astonishment.

"Hush!" Heloise told her. "Yes, she's on the other side of the grove, watching to be sure no one interrupts. Brother Baldwin is farther on, guarding the gate to the road. Not everyone who saw her would understand. Do you?"

Catherine shook her head. She didn't understand, but it didn't matter. She was only grateful she had been allowed to watch. Felicitia, dancing in the moonlight, wasn't licentious, but sublime. She shone like Eve on the first morning, radiant with delight at the wonder of Eden, in blissful ignorance of sin. The joy of it made Catherine weep in her own knowledge that soon the serpent would come, and with it, sorrow.

Heloise guided Catherine gently away.

"She'll finish soon and go back to bed," the abbess explained. "Sister Bertrada will see that she gets there safely. Come with me. Astane has left some warmed cider for me. You have a cup also, before you go back."

When they were settled in Heloise's room, drinking the herbed cider, Catherine finally asked the question.

"I figured out who and how, Mother," she said. "But I don't understand why."

Heloise looked into her cider bowl for several minutes. Catherine thought that she might not answer. Perhaps she didn't know.

15

At last she seemed to come to a decision.

"Catherine," she asked, "have you ever believed that you were loved by no one? That you were completely alone?"

Catherine thought. "Well," she answered, "there was about a month when I was thirteen, but . . . no, no. Even then I always knew my family loved me. I know you love me. I know God loves me, unworthy though I am of all of you."

Heloise smiled. "That's right, on all points. But until she came here, Felicitia believed that no one loved her, that God had abandoned her, and she had good reason. That is not a story for you to hear. I only want you to understand that I am sure that Felicitia is not possessed by anything evil."

"I believe you," Catherine said. "But I still don't understand."

"I didn't, either," Heloise admitted. "Until Sister Bertrada explained it to me. Don't make such a face, child. Sister Bertrada sees further into your heart than you know."

"That doesn't comfort me, Mother."

Heloise smiled. "It should. Bertrada told me that Felicitia spent all her life being desired for her beauty, for her wealth, her family connections. In all that desire, there was no love. So she felt she wasn't worthy of love and consented to despair. She endured much to find her way to us. The scars on her face are mild compared to the ones on her soul. She struggles every day with worse demons that any Ursula can imagine. And until a week ago, she had nightmares almost every night."

"And then . . ." Catherine said.

"And then," Heloise smiled, "joy came to her one night, and she danced. It has only been in her sleep so far, but if she is left in peace, we are hoping that soon she will also have joy in the morning, all through the day, and at last be healed."

Catherine sat for a long while, until the cider went cold and the chantress rose to ring the bell for Vigils. Heloise waited patiently.

"Are you satisfied, Catherine?" she asked. "You assembled the evidence, arranged it properly, and solved the mystery. There is no need to tell the others."

"Oh, no, I wouldn't do that," Catherine promised. "I only wanted to know the truth."

"Then why do you look so sad?" Heloise prodded.

"It's only—" Catherine stopped, embarrassed. "I'm so clumsy, Mother. If only I could dance like Felicitia, even in my sleep."

Heloise laughed. "And how do you know that you don't?"

For once in her life, Catherine had no reply.

Exploring odd nocturnal activities behind convent walls in this story, Sharan Newman continues her twelfth-century series featuring the curious, muddy, and learned novice Catherine LeVendeur. Newman, an Agatha nominee for Best First Novel for *Death Comes as Epiphany* (1993), has published two additional Catherine novels, *The Devil's Door* (1994) and *The Wandering Arm* (1995), as well as an Arthurian series told from Guinevere's point of view. She is a doctoral candidate in history at the University of California, Santa Barbara.

Double Jeopardy

Eileen Dreyer

I swore on my mother's grave that I would never date a doctor. And that was before my mother had a grave. By the time she did, it was too late to admit that I'd made a mistake, much less make it up to her.

But that happened much later. The first sign of trouble I had was when my beloved first brought up the evil twin issue.

"An evil twin," I murmured, gazing rapturously into his eyes. Since he had great eyes, I could be forgiven.

Well, maybe not forgiven. Excused. Acquitted due to temporary insanity. After all, here I was an R.N. with more than ten years of experience under my proverbial belt, and I found myself sitting under a moonlit sky holding hands with, of all things, a surgeon.

He couldn't have been something nice, like a pediatrician. Even something boring like a urologist. No, he was the classic, mercurial, brilliant, demanding surgeon, who just happened to have spectacular blue eyes and a somewhat perplexing attraction to my much less impressive brown ones. But that doesn't address the evil twin problem.

"Yes," he admitted in those honeyed tones that sounded

so good over the phone—not to mention across a pillow. Reaching into his jacket, he produced an old color snap. Two gap-toothed, dark-haired boys, arm in arm by the shore. Identical smiles, identical, mesmerizing eyes. "His name is Rodney."

"With a name like Rodney, he didn't stand a chance," I said without thinking.

His handsome face darkened a little, even as he put away the snap and picked up my hand. "I'm serious," he said. "Rodney is . . . well, jealous of me. He never made much of a success of himself, and blames me."

"Your mother loved you more?"

That attempt at humor fell right among the others, like a dead animal.

Richard's—his name was Richard. Not Rick, not Rich, not R.C. Richard—anyway, Richard's eyes clouded over as he stroked his thumb across the palm of my hand, always a sure sign he was serious. A surer sign that I was about to get horny.

"Really," he insisted, his expression as intense as those times he broke bad news to families in front of camera crews. "If you notice anything . . . oh, out of place. You get any funny calls. Anything like that. Let me know. He can be a real pest sometimes."

I probably looked surprised. "You're serious."

"Deadly serious. He's usually no more than annoying, but sometimes . . . well, I've had problems before."

For the first time in our whirlwind three-week courtship, I felt a flutter of disquiet. Disquiet other than when my mother asked me whether I was nuts to date a surgeon, since so had she and look how well that turned out. But since my mother had been bitter ever since that unfortunate incident with my father and the slutty pharmaceutical salesman named Phil, in the mood I was in, I figured I could forgive her.

No, this disquiet revolved around lurking shadows with great eyes. Semi-sinister personalities checking me out who didn't belong to hospital administration or the IRS. I had finally found a man who thought I was more than just a beer and pizza stop, and he was telling me his brother wasn't going to be pleased.

His jealous brother.

His evil twin.

"You don't think he was serious, do you?" I asked my friend Claire two weeks later as we stood in front of my little yard and considered the waste that had been laid to my garden.

It wasn't much of a garden, a couple of tomato plants and a row or two of straggly annuals, but I had gone to a lot of trouble to plant them. I'd watered and nurtured and talked to them, and now they were all ripped up and shriveling in the sun as if a freak downburst had targeted the south wall of my condo.

My friend shrugged, as only friends do. "I haven't thought he was serious since he said you were the prettiest thing in the E.R."

"I was," I retorted evenly, bending to pick up some of the more pitiful victims from what seemed a random attack. "The only other people on duty that night were you and Zipperhead. And only Jacques Cousteau could consider Zipperhead pretty."

Zipperhead being a height-impaired, hair-deprived, semi-lucid medical resident with poor people skills and poorer hygiene who graced so many of our shifts.

"You don't think neighborhood kids could have done this?" Claire asked, ever the practical one.

I looked down at limp leaves and battered, vulnerable roots. "I haven't had any trouble with kids since I moved in here after the divorce."

All right, so my track record wasn't that good. It was a matter of self-esteem, and with my parents, I was lucky I had enough of that to apply for a job, much less be seen in public. I'd actually thought I'd been doing better since having the guts to file for that divorce. I'd thought I hit the jackpot with Richard. Since that first surprise dinner, I'd started dressing better, which for a woman raised in a uniform is no mean feat. Claire had given me the name of a great hairstylist, and another friend, her manicurist. I'd even been seen in slut pumps, which B.R. (Before Richard) would have been inconceivable.

So there were more reasons than simple hormones to wish the evil twin back to the realm of rumor.

"No," I admitted, still holding onto those flowers like a macabre bouquet. "I think Richard was telling the truth."

"So, not only is he blind, but he has a whacked-out twin who doesn't want him to date."

"Something like that."

"Sounds like the perfect man for the nineties." Claire could laugh, since she'd been happily married to the same engineer for almost fifteen years.

"Even so, what do you think it means?"

It meant, I found out within the week, a series of heavy-breathing phone calls that would have been a lot more fun if the breather involved hadn't added half-whispered threats. The "I know where you live" variety that sit so well with a woman who lives alone.

"I think it's time to get concerned," I told Richard the next night over dinner.

"I'll talk to him," Richard promised, his brilliant surgeon's hand covering mine. "Please don't do anything."

I didn't. Well, except for the caller ID I put on the phone and the call I made to a couple of police detectives I knew from the E.R. But I figured that really didn't count as far as Richard went. After all, it wasn't his flowers or his phone.

As for Richard, he was more attentive than ever. He called more. He accompanied me home from work and checked out the condo for intruders. And since more often than not he stayed, I found myself losing that self-protective edge. I was actually almost enjoying it. Danger was, after all, a great aphrodisiac. Especially if a blue-eyed man with great pecs and a jaw that could crush rock is involved.

"I won't let him hurt you," he promised as we lay in a tangled bed late in the night. "I promise."

"Hurt me?" I echoed. It was the first time hurting had ever been brought up.

Richard liked to use his hands to make points. This one

he made by stroking my cheek with the soft pad of his thumb. "I don't want you to worry."

"He followed you from Massachusetts just to act as a one-man judging panel on your love life. Why should I worry?"

"Your mother does the same thing," he reminded me, kissing the top of my head.

"She never once yanked out my flowers."

She'd thrown me out of her will seven or eight times, but the only member of the family who had never suffered that fate was the family poodle, an even surlier, shorter life-form named Amanda.

"I promise," he promised. "I'll talk to him."

I'm sure he meant that. Unfortunately, brilliant surgeons do, on occasion, have to do surgery. Richard was doing his a week later when I pulled into my driveway at two in the morning after a particularly hairy shift. I was tired, sore, and grimy with the accumulated detritus of a hundred-plus patients. My reflexes had been left back on the work lane, and my acuity dampened by about nine hours of screaming and yelling.

I didn't see the shadow. I didn't hear the rustle. I was already inside my house pulling my key back out of the front door when he rushed me.

I think my heart simply stopped beating. I know I stopped breathing, which would account for the fact that when I opened my mouth to scream, nothing came out but a rather pathetic croak.

Somehow I could still smell the cologne. Somehow I knew, even without seeing the face, that my attacker's eyes were spectacularly blue.

"Time to move on," he whispered in my ear as he lifted me completely off the ground with a set of well-muscled arms.

"Why?" I managed, even with his arm around my throat and my feet swinging about ten inches off the floor. At least I had a voice. I could reason with him.

"You're not his type."

"I don't suppose we could have this discussion over drinks at a nice restaurant. . . ."

Evidently, he didn't find me funny. He clobbered me on the head and almost ended the discussion right there. If I hadn't been a nurse, and hadn't developed the bad habit of carrying syringes home in my lab-coat pockets, that might have been the end of that story. Fortunately, I was trained to perform my duties in any circumstance, which meant he got an eighteen-gauge in the thigh, and I got out the door.

My house was trashed, but I, in the end, wasn't.

It would have been all right if I hadn't told my mother. I still think that. She might not have gotten personally involved. She might not have argued with Richard when he came to pick me up at her house the next morning to apologize and explain things. She might not have proved her point in such a graphic way.

"I don't trust you," she informed him, poking his considerable chest with her small, sharp finger. My mother was sharp all over—eyes, teeth, fingers, opinions. When she was in one of these moods, she reminded me of nothing more than a terrier on attack. I would say Amanda on attack, but Amanda was less relentless. "I think you're lying through your perfect teeth, just like *all* of them!"

All of them, of course, being doctors.

"Now, now, Mrs. Baker," Richard soothed with his patented voice. "It's all right."

"You do something about him," she retorted, impervious to soothing of any kind, "or I will."

Protectors all around me.

"It's my problem," Richard informed her, his arm across my shoulders in a classic position of possession. "I'll take care of it."

"You've done a great job of it so far," she snapped up at him.

I stepped out of his grasp as unobtrusively as possible, and stayed the hell away from her. All emergency room nurses know that the last place you want to get caught is in the middle of a catfight.

"The police didn't come up with any evidence," I said, gathering my stuff together. "For a nut, he's smart."

"That's why you should stay here, Mitzie," Mother snapped.

Mitzie. The poodle is named Amanda and I'm named Mitzie. That alone should have given me license to drool. It certainly made me a little more sympathetic about what forces drove Rodney to destroy.

"I'll stay with you," Richard promised. "Please."

"How 'bout I stay at your place?" I asked, even though I'd never been to his place before.

His smile would have broken the heart of any sane woman. "I think you'd just rather be with your own things, honey."

So I had the choice between my mother and a psycho killer. I chose the killer. Twenty minutes with my mother and you would have done the same thing.

It still doesn't do anything for my peace of mind when I think of the fact that if I'd stayed with her, she might not have died.

The reason I went over was because, for the first time in four days, she hadn't made any harassing calls. She hadn't threatened Richard and his brother, hadn't informed him that she knew all about him, that she was going to make sure everybody knew.

I still don't believe I expected the worst. A broken hip at the most, maybe a phone she forgot to hang up, a hot card game with the dog. I walked into the kitchen and found her dead on the floor.

Really dead. Pool of blood and staring eyes dead, the kind you carry with you for the rest of your life so that it flashes before you at the worst possible moments.

We hadn't gotten along so well, she and I. I'd even sided with my father once upon a time. But she'd fought for me. She'd protected me. She'd loved me. By the time I sat at the funeral home two nights later, I had been given a new mission in life.

"It was him," I said to Richard, who never moved from my side or let my hand wander from his.

"No," he protested. "He'd never do this."

"It was him," I told Claire as she perched on the seat on the other side, one eye on me and the other on the dull gleam of the closed casket.

"The police haven't come up with anything that would suggest that, Mansize. Let it go for a bit."

Mansize. My nickname at work, garnered for the fact that I so often found myself chin to chest with physicians of all ilk. It was a courage I kept for work, where I could displace all the snappy comebacks I'd been saving up for years for my mother.

My mother.

"He did it," I told the detective who stopped by to pay his respects and check out the mourners.

"It just looks like a burglary, Mansize," he commiserated. I'd stood up to him a time or two in the past. Funny how different people see you differently.

I shook my head. "No, it wasn't. And I'll prove it."

First, I thought, I had to find out about Rodney. Where he was, what he was, why Richard was protecting him.

"Talk to him," I begged my handsome surgeon a week later, when nothing more had happened but the newscast decrying violence in the suburbs. "Let me talk to him with you."

"I can't," he admitted woefully. "I don't know where he is. I never do."

I must have blinked like a head injury victim. "You don't know where he is."

Richard shrugged. "He was committed once. But with government cutbacks and all, they just let him out. I don't know where he stays. I've tried."

"If he's been living on the streets, how did he follow you from Massachusetts?"

Massachusetts, where my dearest heart said he'd grown up and trained. Where his parents, dead these many years, had raised him and his brother in middle-class splendor. Where he'd given up on the fast lane and moved to slower, sweeter, kinder Louisville.

Richard's smile was perplexed, yet sad. "I don't know, honey. I really don't know."

It was the first time I had seriously questioned any word that had issued from my beloved's mouth.

It led to others.

If he couldn't find him, I could. I had contacts. I had

people all over town who owed me for dumping their worst-case scenarios on me at the E.R. I simply plugged into the system and stood back waiting for results.

I waited until I knew Richard would be occupied with a hot transplant. While he was safely gowned and gloved, I made use of the social security number I got off Richard's license and my phone. I made use of my friends in the police department and the health department and the sanitation department and any other department who might in the course of their work have come across a homeless crazoid with a penchant for expensive cologne. I coordinated with the homicide team who hadn't been able to pull any evidence worth writing a report on from the crime scene. I preached the theory of the evil twin like creationism and watched them react like evolutionists.

I searched for him on my own before he found me again.

"Sorry," my friend from the local police said. "If he's touched the system anywhere, it ain't here. He doesn't show up in the NCIC computer, either. If this guy's nuts, he keeps a pretty low profile about it."

The same came from my friend in DMV, and my friend from the local homeless shelter coalition. The wraith that was Rodney Weatherspoon had not visited any of them.

And then I heard from my friend in the medical records division.

"Twins, huh?" she said. "Richard Lawrence and Rodney Allen Weatherspoon."

My adrenals were so used to going on fast alert that they were kicked in before she even gave me names. "That's them."

"Yeah, I tracked your friend's social security number back to Cambridge, Massachusetts. One of a set of live twins born to Peter and Gloria Jean Weatherspoon."

"Okay," I said, chewing on a pencil instead of the fingernail I really wanted to tear into, "this is what I'm hoping for. From the info, can we track Rodney? What I'm hoping eventually to find is somebody who might have been treating him recently. Say in the last five years or so."

"Rodney?" she countered. "I doubt it."

"You doubt it? Why?"

"He's dead."

Well, that kind of news'll make you sit down fast. "What do you mean he's dead?"

"I mean pushing up daisies, dust to dust. That kind of thing."

"When?"

"Well, ya know, it's funny. The guy I talked to actually remembers the incident. Says that somehow the death certificate doesn't show up, but he's sure Rodney died in a house fire that killed the parents."

"House fire?"

"When the boys were about twelve. The records were in the old coroner's files."

"House fire."

Sometimes repeating pertinent information helps. Funny thing, it didn't then.

"Yeah. Death was ruled an accident, a pile of flammables in the garage during renovation. The parents were both autopsied, but Rodney was nothing more than charcoal briquette. It's really sad."

"And Richard?"

"Beats me. Went to live with relatives, I guess. I checked, just 'cause I got curious after hearing about it. He went through Johns Hopkins. Pretty interesting success story, you ask me."

"Dead."

As in, couldn't break into my house. Couldn't leave messages on my answering machine and club my mother to death with her own skillet.

As in, we had a whole new problem here.

"Thanks," I said and hung up.

I'd known. Somehow I'd known. I'd taken care of a lot of guys who lived on the streets. A lot more guys who spent their waking hours wandering through an alternate time and space continuum. Not one of those guys had smelled like the guy who'd lifted me off the ground.

Not one had been so clean-shaven and had such soft hands.

Oh God, Richard.

27

It probably wasn't the smartest idea to call Richard next. More of a reflex. Hit a knee with a percussion hammer, it swings north. Hit a girlfriend with news of her honey's evil twin's early demise, her instincts prompt a phone call for explanation.

"Hello?" Only to find that her honey didn't answer his own phone.

"Who's this?"

"This is Amber. Who's this?"

There was a woman named after old sap in Richard's house. "Amber who?"

"Amber Sanders. Do you want to leave a message for Rickie?"

I think I just hung the phone up after that. Truth be told, I don't remember. I just remember walking out my door and down the block. I remember neighbors waving hello and kids skating out of the way. I remember that it grew darker, and that somebody's sprinkler soaked my shoes.

I remember somehow finding my way home and calling the hospital.

Yes, they said, Richard was there. Yes, they'd give him the message.

Okay, I thought, pacing the inside of my living room like a cage, from rocker to jukebox to sofa to bookcase and around again. There had to be some other explanation for this. Somebody out to make Richard nuts. Somebody working a scam to extort money or something.

It couldn't be Richard. Not brilliant, splendid Richard. Not the man who could tap dance around an aorta like Fred Astaire around a coatrack and then throw together a perfect pan of paella. Not Richard who told me I was beautiful.

Could that other twin still live in him, somewhere in the darkness? Could he really be going through his daily routine not knowing that a homicidal doppelganger lurked in his psyche?

And if he was subletting his subconscious, what the hell was I supposed to do about it?

He didn't call. I had a twelve-hour shift to get through at the hospital before I could do anything else. I made it through, somehow. Everybody excused my absent-mindedness due to my mother's recent demise. They made it a point not to comment on the fact that my nails were bitten again, or that my brand-new feathered, streaked, and shaped hair wasn't brushed. Instead they steered me toward the less demanding cases and patted my head and told me everything was going to be all right. And I spent all night wondering if I should talk to Richard first, the police, or one of the staff psychiatrists.

Emergency nurses are not notorious for their patience. It's not that we don't have stamina. We can't tolerate not knowing. That, finally, was what brought me to the front of Richard's house at dusk the next afternoon when I should have been on dinner break during my next shift.

I guess that means that if the lights were to go out in the house and noises were to come from the basement, I'd be the first one heading down the stairs. If Richard hadn't made me feel so good, I might have been a touch more logical in my approach.

His car wasn't in the driveway of the sleek cedar and glass home he'd bought on a back street that boasted more azaleas than dandelions. The lights were on, though. Lights I'd never seen go on or off, illuminating furniture I'd never sat on.

That Amber had sat on. God, could my head hurt worse? I'd passed critical mass on unanswered questions twenty-four hours ago and was still piling them up.

I parked my Jeep in front of the house and waited.

I practiced what I was going to say.

So, Richard, did you know your brother's dead?

Richard, having blackouts lately you can't attribute to Jack Daniel's?

Honey, what would you say to a double date with a real nice psychiatrist I know?

There was a very good reason I was an E.R. nurse and not a detective. It had to do with competent lurking. One does not need to lurk in E.R.'s. It is, in fact, actively frowned on. Evidently, one does on darkened streets in front of her lover's house.

I never knew he was there until he yanked open the door to the passenger seat of the Jeep.

"I've been trying to get in touch with you," he all but accused, sliding his handsome self into the seat as if he'd expected to find me there all along. "What are you doing here?"

My answer consisted of a couple of nods and a strangled little burble.

He leaned closer. "Mitz? You okay, hon?"

I shook my head. "It hasn't been a good day."

"Tell me about it." He sighed and rubbed his neck with one of those beautiful, talented hands. "I had back-to-back bypasses and a budget meeting with administration. What did you want?"

"Rodney."

That got me a whole new sigh. "I told you, honey. I can't."

"Can't because you can't find him?" I asked on a held breath. "Or can't because he doesn't exist?"

His hand stopped mid-rub and his gaze swung definitively my way. "You've been checking up on me."

Even then I thought he should have sounded more upset. More confused. Maybe even more surprised.

"Yes."

He turned to look out into the street and went back to rubbing away his worries. "We've had a pretty great few months, haven't we?"

In the end it would have been ridiculous to argue. "We have."

We had. Great and marvelous and exciting. All that and more.

"I've really looked forward to our time together."

It was my turn to sigh. "Are you about to sing the Mickey Mouse theme?"

He swung those big blues on me and all hope was lost. "You don't trust me anymore."

"Not when somebody named Amber answers your phone and calls you Rickie."

That wasn't supposed to come out. It's not very therapeutic, especially if we were talking multiple personality here.

Damn it if he didn't smile. "Well, there is that."

"Richard, you need to see someone," I tried, just as I'd seen people say in the movies.

His smile didn't so much as falter. "No, I don't, honey. But I'm afraid we can't see each other anymore. Ya know, I'm really gonna miss you."

"Richard, your brother—"

"Has been dead since I was twelve."

How's that for a stunner? And here I'd thought I was going to be the one with the big news.

"You know."

He chuckled. "Hard not to. I was there, ya know."

"But your story about evil twins . . ."

"Was exciting. Added a little spice to the relationship. Don't you think?"

I knew way back at the back of my head that my mouth was supposed to work about then. I was supposed to say something witty and deadly. All I could come up with was, "Are you nuts?"

He handled it with admirable aplomb. "Not at all. There's no death certificate, ya know. There was a mix-up at the state level. But by the time the fire crews could get to him, Rodney was a little pile of ashes. It was . . . something."

"And you just keep him around to terrify your dates?"

"Sure. Why not? Admit it, our sex life was never better. Maybe it's not politically correct, but you enjoyed having me around to protect you. And be honest. You'd love to have an evil twin to blame things on. Rodney has been my excuse through three states, four hospitals, and the end of a couple dozen relationships. Having an evil twin means never having to say you're guilty."

"And my mother?"

"Rodney. Bad Rodney. Evil Rodney. And nobody can prove otherwise."

This time his smile was scary. I was still struggling to form monosyllabic words. "You killed her?"

"No. Actually, Amber did."

"Amber."

"Sure. Amber and I go way back. *Way* back. How do you think I paid for medical school?"

"You scared your dates with an evil twin and Amber bumped them off?"

He held up a finger of objection. "Only the rich ones. After all, I had standards. If your mother hadn't been such a rag, she never would have qualified." He was really enjoying himself now. "I don't expect actual thanks, but when you begin to realize just how little you miss her nagging, think kindly of me."

He didn't say another word, just opened the car and walked off up toward the house. And me, the Mansize E.R. nurse who jumps into any emergency with forceps flying? I sat like a lump in my front seat wanting him dead.

Not just dead. Bad dead. Hurt dead. Bleeding and confused and helpless. I wanted him to pay for what he'd so callously done to me, to my mother, to whomever those other women were. I sat there shaking and knew damn well that, just as he'd said, he'd get away with it, because no one in their right mind would believe me.

"Oh, Mitz?" he said, leaning back in the window. "Nobody but you ever heard me mention Rodney. I'm sorry, honey. Really. Find yourself a nice accountant or something."

He was still chuckling when he turned to walk up the steps toward his front door.

So, I'd just kill him. Blow up the house with natural gas and take out that slimy life-form with him. I'd get past the fury that swelled like hot gas in my chest and lay a brilliant plan. I'd just walk in and bash his head until it was pulp. I didn't care.

"Be very quiet."

I jumped a foot and a half. I'd been so busy building up a head of steam, I'd completely missed the sound of someone tiptoeing to the side of my car. Suddenly, there was just this guy there, crouched by my window.

"Who the hell are you?" I demanded, turning his way. Stopping. Gaping like a landed fish.

He smiled. "I'm Rodney."

I tried very hard to say something appropriate, but what the hell's appropriate for something like this?

"I'd like to thank you for trying to find me," he said easily, those blue eyes devastating even in the dark. That handsome face marred at the edges by the wrinkle of old burns. "I've been trying to catch up with Rickie for a long time."

"How did you know?"

"I'm the guy at the Massachusetts records office. I've been there for the last three years waiting for something just like this to happen. I'd kinda hoped that now that he had his license he would have quit the extracurricular stuff, but I guess old Rick just can't pass up a messy situation. And no, Rickie doesn't know I'm alive. I've managed to hide from him ever since he set fire to the house. Now, though, I think I've had enough. It's time for it all to stop."

"What do you mean?"

He smiled, and I realized that he looked very little like his handsomer brother. "If you'll just wait a minute, I think you'll enjoy the show."

Sirens. I heard them treble in the distance. I heard Richard's front door close. I heard a terrible scream.

Rodney smiled. "She thought I was him," he admitted. "She even wrote his name in blood as she went."

"She died?"

"Oh yes. She wasn't a good person. Neither is my brother. I think it's a wonderful kind of poetic justice to finally blame him for something I did, instead of the other way around. Don't you?"

The sirens were drawing closer. "You killed her?"

"Uh-huh. Time to get going. If you don't say anything, you'll get a front row seat. You see, he'll say he got a call to meet you at your mother's house, and when he got back, found her when he walked in. But, of course, you never called him. He has no alibi, and the police will finger him first. And there's that blood in Amber's handwriting. Now, maybe you couldn't get him for murdering your mother, but you will for this."

And all I had to do was leave. Sneak back into one of the

call rooms at the hospital where my coworkers would find their exhausted, grieving friend asleep instead of at lunch.

All I had to do was let this man get away with murder. Help convict a technically innocent man. Go against everything I'd ever believed, ever been trained to do.

The sirens were getting close. I could see frantic movement through the half-open curtains, the kind that looked like CPR. I knew without looking that Rodney was gone.

I knew that there would be no evidence of mine in the house, because I'd never been there.

Is it too clichéd to say that when I started the car up, I looked back and smiled and said, "Blame it on your evil twin"?

Yeah, I guess it is.

———

Twin brothers mean double trouble for the heroine in this sly story from former trauma nurse Eileen Dreyer. A St. Louis resident, Dreyer has published over twenty books, including four suspense novels, *A Man to Die For* (1991), *If Looks Could Kill* (1992), *Nothing Personal* (1994), and *Bad Medicine* (1995).

Shelved

Barbara D'Amato

My name is Susanna Maria Figueroa. At ten-thirty on a cold
but sharply bright spring morning in Chicago, I was riding
alone in car 1–27, because my usual partner, Officer Norm
Bennis, was out with an injury. Not an IOD, injured on
duty. He claimed he had been trying to get out a *Terminator*
tape that was stuck in his VCR and Arnold Schwarzenegger
had attacked and mutilated his hand. Bennis's fingertips
were definitely mangled. But Bennis is so fickle in his
romantic life that I have learned not to inquire too closely
when bizarre accidents happen to him.

At any rate, I was on second watch, which is seven A.M. to
three P.M., and I called in on the radio.

"One-twenty-seven."

The dispatcher said, "Go ahead, twenty-seven."

"Could I get early lunch?"

"Sure. Where you gonna be?"

"Bookworm on Michigan."

"Bookworm? Doesn't sound like a lunch counter to
me."

"Trust me. To me it's lunch."

"Ten-four, twenty-seven."

I responded, "Ten ninety-nine." Ninety-nine means I'm a one-person unit. Two-person units say "Ten-four." Ten-four units are more likely to get sent to gang wars and men armed with Uzis holed up in alleys. Still, I'd rather have Bennis back and be a ten-four unit.

Bennis was the reason I was going to skip lunch and go to the Bookworm. Friday would be Bennis's anniversary. Ten years in the department. This was a very big deal, and I wanted to buy him something nice. But he's hard to shop for.

I'd racked my brains for a week—rhinestone handcuffs? A tweed wool deerstalker? A bottle of rye for his bottom drawer? A suede case with silver monogram for his walkie-talkie? And I finally thought of something. There was a history of the Peelers, the Irish constabulary founded in 1812 by Robert Peel. The Peelers are considered the first real police force.

So I parked and went into the Bookworm to shop.

The Bookworm contains three floors of floor-to-ceiling books. You can take a book down from a shelf and sit in one of the armchairs strategically scattered through the sales space, leaf through your book and see if you want to buy it. There are even shelves along the stairs, so as you walk up to the second and third floors, you run your eye along title after title. Yum!

And they have salespeople who *read!* When I asked for a book on Peelers, they wouldn't send me to cookbooks.

"I'm looking for a history of the Peelers," I said to a thirtyish man who stood next to a display of dictionaries—French/English, English/French, German, Polish, Dutch, Japanese, Hungarian, Navajo—

"Oh, yes. It's in History—in the back on the left, over there." He pointed. "If you'll just ask Sonia, she's our history specialist. I'm the reference specialist."

Sonia proved to be a thin woman of about twenty-five with long, lank black hair and a long, black, tubelike dress. She knew exactly what I wanted, even though I didn't know the author's name.

"That book's been doing pretty well," she said.

"I wouldn't think history would just jump off the shelves."

She laughed and waved an arm. "Look at these. This is our Kennedy section. Nine out of ten of those *do* jump off the shelves."

"How come the other ten percent don't?"

"Beats me. Some years the Civil War is hot. Some years it isn't. Some years it's the American Revolution. I wish you could tell me why."

From there I wandered into Reference.

The young man who had directed me to History said, "Can I help you?" His name tag told me he was Eric.

"Oh, just looking, thanks." I fingered a book on plant poisons. They had several copies. "Do a lot of people want to poison somebody?" I asked.

"Must be." He gave a shy smile. "We've sold quite a lot of them."

"That's unnerving. Well, thanks."

I browsed. What a nice word, browse. I picked up books and put them down, and somehow, two that I hadn't intended to buy managed to stick to me.

On my way toward the front I was waylaid by the mystery wing, which was in the right rear of the store, opposite the history area. A new novel by Carolyn Hart leaped into my hand, and I sat down in an armchair to read for just a minute. The Mystery salesperson, with a name tag that read "Jane," sailed near, pushing a wheeled cart with hundreds of paperbacks on it. She said cheerily to me, "Oh, that one's been very popular!" and passed by. Jane was pretty, big blue eyes, large hips, large bosom, small waist, bouncy blond hair.

Dimly, I was aware of some cheerful voices in the background, and my police radio stuttered and squawked now and then. But what was that to me? I was reading! Then I was aware of some irritable voices in the background. Not my problem. I was reading!

When I was a child, we lived in a house with an attic. There was something strange about the attic. It was all bare golden wood, and the sun came through a dusty, narrow little window. The light was amber, and it was warm and dry up there, with dust motes moving sleepily in the air. I could take a book up with me and start to read, and suddenly four or five hours had passed and I never noticed.

Bookstores affect me that way. I'll go in to buy exactly one item, and suddenly it's an hour later.

I jumped up at some really loud voices, and realized that I was going to run over my lunch period. That could be very bad! The CPD is like the Army: you're supposed to be where you're supposed to be when you're supposed to be there, and no yuppie-type arguments about lack of motivation.

I race-walked to the nearest cash register, which was in the mystery department. But there was no one there to check me out. I heard excited talking from farther to the front of the store and went there.

Six salespeople, including Sonia, Jane, and Eric, clustered around the front. Near them a man in a dark suit, labeled Gerald Johnstone, Manager, was just putting down the phone. Of the six salespeople, five were talking. The manager, Johnstone, said, "They're going to send somebody."

"I should've stayed there," one of the salespeople moaned. His name tag said "Mark."

"It's not your fault."

"This is just so—"

"Ohmigod!"

"In a bookstore! How could they take advantage—"

Sonia laughed wryly. "It's not any more *moral* to rob a shoe store! Or a drugstore!"

"What I meant—"

I said, "What's going on?"

Most of them looked at me as if it was no business of mine—and why should they think differently, since they didn't know I was a cop?—but Jane disgustedly said, "Teenagers!"

At that instant my radio spoke. "One thirty-three."

Another voice answered, "Thirty-three." It was my buddy, Stanley Mileski.

"Thirty-three, I have a robbery at 213 North Michigan."

I punched my radio. "Twenty-seven."

"Twenty-seven, go."

"Is that the Bookworm, squad? Because I'm there."

"Whoever called it in didn't give 911 the name of the store. They apparently hung up too soon." Behind Eric, Mr. Johnstone began to blush. So he was more flustered than he seemed.

"That's this address, isn't it, Mr. Johnstone?" I asked him.

"Yes, it is."

"I'm here, squad. I'll take care of it."

"Sure thing, one twenty-seven. Weren't you supposed to be back from lunch?"

"I was about to clear when I noticed the disturbance." Well, it was only half a lie. I'd been vaguely aware of the disturbance; but I'd been reading.

All right, I was more than a little annoyed with myself. Apparently I'd allowed a burglary to happen right under my nose. Susanna Maria Figueroa, fearless law enforcement person and noted screw-up.

I now had six salespeople plus Mr. Johnstone to deal with. The three I hadn't met were named Debbie, Mark, and Mike. All were under thirty-five. Debbie was a slight, attractive woman with chestnut hair cut short. Mark was solidly built, a hockey-player type with crinkly dark hair. Mike was tall and slender and blond. Don't any nice grandmotherly women with white hair ever get hired by bookstores anymore?

"Tell me what happened."

Johnstone, to make up for his dropping the stitch in talking with 911, was clear and unemotional. "About twenty minutes ago a big group of teenagers, well, twelve to fourteen years old, came into the store—"

"Seven teenagers altogether," Sonia said firmly. Johnstone slid his eyes at her sideways. I wondered how long Sonia would go on working here.

"Possibly seven, and they started running around the store, horsing around, picking up books, giggling at covers . . ." As he said this he was standing near a cover showing a naked woman standing on a giant pineapple. I looked at it, and he looked to where I was looking. We both turned our heads back. "They were distracting everybody."

"And . . ." I encouraged him.

"Ahh . . ." he sighed. "They were all over this floor, and I'm afraid the staff left their cash registers to try and round up the kids."

"They were wrinkling the dustcovers!" Jane said.

"And finger-marking them," Debbie said. "These matte-finish dustcovers, even if you wipe them with a soft cloth, you can't get the finger marks off."

Sonia added, "We weren't just leaving our *posts*. We were protecting stock!"

"Anyway, after they decided they didn't want to buy anything, and left, Mark here—Mark is Mainstream Fiction—Mark here went to his cash register to ring up a sale, and there was no cash in it."

"Some coins," Mark said. "No paper money."

"How much do you think you had?"

"About three hundred and fifty dollars. Could have been four hundred." He almost, but not quite, started to wring his hands. "I should have stayed at the register."

"Never mind that. Was it in small bills? Large bills?"

"Mostly ones, fives, and twenties."

"All right. Now, all of you tell me—where did they go and where did they *not* go?"

"Oh, I just don't know," Jane said. "Everyplace."

Sonia said, "Just this floor. They didn't go upstairs."

Sonia was emerging as a person of considerable alertness.

Johnstone said, "It's a known technique of thieves, isn't it? Create a diversion and empty a cash register?"

"Yes. It happens."

They stood about, gaping at me. I said, "Show me the register."

It was the one in Mainstream Fiction, of course. Sure enough, there was no paper money in it. "Don't touch it," I said. "I'll call the evidence techs."

Debbie said, "Fingerprints?"

Michael said, "Mmmm!"

"While this was going on, did any salespeople come down from upstairs?"

"No. They're not supposed to. There aren't as many of them upstairs and you can't leave the stock alone. We have a lot of shoplifting."

"Especially tapes and computer stuff from Three," Sonia said.

"Two is Music and Video," Debbie said helpfully.

Sonia added, "I think I would have noticed if any salespeople had come down the stairs."

I thought she would, too. "Good. So the upstairs people won't be able to tell me anything. Can you have one of them come down and run the front cash registers while we talk?"

Johnstone got on the intercom and called upstairs.

I went on, "Did all of you leave your posts?"

They squirmed, but the answer was that yes, they all did. They were running around shooing kids.

Mark said, "Nasty children."

Mike said, "And they had on these hideously bright clothes."

My niece favors lime-green worn with orange and electric-blue, but I wasn't here to argue.

"Did you see anything in their hands when they left?"

"I'm afraid we were just so glad that they *were* leaving . . ." Johnstone said. He let the sentence die there.

Sonia said, "No, I don't think they were carrying anything."

"But it could have been hidden under their clothes," Jane said.

"Did any customers come down from upstairs?"

"Not while the teenagers were here."

"It wasn't long," Mark added. "I mean, altogether they were in and out in less than five minutes."

Johnstone said, "And morning isn't our busiest time of day. It will be soon, though," he added nervously, looking at his watch, then at the front door. "Lots of people shop here on their lunch hour."

Sonia was more alert to the direction of my questions. "Why are you asking?"

"Well, obviously, the 'Gypsies' aren't the only people who could have taken the money."

"There weren't all that many other customers here," Johnstone said.

"But there were the seven of you."

"What? We didn't take it!"

"Has this ever happened before, Mr. Johnstone?"

"Cash register thefts? Maybe a couple of times. Shoplifting is more common, though—"

"I mean exactly this kind of thing. Cash registers rifled while there was a disturbance in the store."

"Ahhh . . ."

Sonia helped again. "About a month ago. There was a bunch of football player types in here with loud radios. And a few weeks before that we had a woman faint dead away in the store and the man with her totally freaked." There was something in Sonia's tone. Could it be suspicion? She added, "We don't get very many people making disturbances in here."

"Did you call the police both times?"

"Yes. But they never found the thieves. Or the money."

Mark said, "But it *is* a known theft technique?"

I said, "Yes, and it's a great opportunity for the staff, too. I'm sorry, but what I need to do is look in everybody's locker. Also, three hundred and fifty dollars in mostly smallish bills is too much to hide on your person very easily unless you're wearing outdoor clothes, but I want the women to pat each other down and the men to do the same, just to be sure."

"You can't make me do this," Debbie said.

Johnstone took this opportunity to get decisive, and I'm glad he did, because I'd have had a hard time carrying through. If people don't voluntarily agree, a police officer has to jump through hoops sometimes. Johnstone said, "I want everybody to be calm and cooperative about this. I'm sure we're all perfectly innocent, and this is the quickest way to prove it."

Nobody was wearing voluminous multilayered clothing, so they were done with the search in minutes. Then we trooped to the lockers in the back room. It looked like I was going to move around guided by a crowd of seven wherever I went in the store.

The lockers were in back, twenty-five of them. They were the metal kind like you have in high schools, and each employee had a combination lock.

"Which of you were here all three times the robberies happened?" I asked while I rummaged.

A chorus:

"I don't know . . ."

"Um, I was here . . ."

"All of us, I guess."

"I think I was . . ."

Sonia spoke up. "All of us salespeople were here. Mr. Johnstone was away at the ad agency the second time it happened."

There was a lot of stuff in the lockers. There were headache remedies: Anacin, aspirin, Tylenol. There were a couple of bottles of Pepto Bismol. Rubber bands, a Bible, paper clips, lots of knitted stocking caps and extra gloves, this being spring in Chicago. Several bottles of sunscreen in all ranges of "protection," also because of spring in Chicago. Scarves, boots, extra jackets, extra skirts, extra pants, a pressed shirt or two, dark glasses, candy bars, a pear, three apples, and several sandwiches, including a particularly revolting-looking banana and peanut butter on rye. There was one pack of cigarettes. It turned out Sonia smoked.

There was even money. Jane had a small plastic cup of coins. "For the bus," she said.

Mark had a twenty-dollar bill in a shoe. "Just in case."

"In case of what?" Sonia asked.

"In case of needing money."

But there was no stolen cash in any of the lockers.

"Where else could money be hidden?" I asked Johnstone.

"I don't know. Nowhere."

"The carpet's tacked down. The chairs don't have cushions."

"It wouldn't be—"

I said, "Wait. How about on a shelf? Behind some books?"

"Impossible!" he said.

"Why? Our crook could just stick the money behind some books and pick it up at the end of the shift, after the cops have left."

Jane said, "But this is the very beginning of the shift! The money would have to stay there all day. None of us gets to leave until five P.M. Any customer could come along any time all day and buy a book and find the money. It just wouldn't work."

"Except . . ." I said.

They all stared at me—Sonia, Johnstone, Jane, Eric, Mike, Mark, and Debbie.

"Except in their own department. Their own section. Every one of these specialists knows which books 'jump off the shelves' and which sit there month after month after month."

"And that means . . ." Johnstone said, an idea beginning to dawn on him.

"It means when you find the money, you'll also know who put it there."

"It'll take forever to look behind all the books," he started to say, but I didn't answer. I had turned to Jane, who was weeping.

"I needed it. I really, really *needed* it." Her big blue eyes were drowned in tears.

"So you decided to blame your thefts on people you figured would easily look guilty?"

"I didn't mean it that way. I just needed the money so *bad!*"

I called for the evidence tech. Backup prints wouldn't hurt in case Jane changed her mind and decided she'd been beaten into confessing.

Johnstone wanted to give me the books I was buying, but I couldn't let him do that.

By twelve the noon rush was starting and I was just about out of there. We found the money behind some Arsene Lupin reprints. I guess this shows Jane really knew her department—Lupin doesn't jump off the shelves the way Susan Dunlap and Margaret Maron do. Also Lupin is one of the few mystery heroes who doesn't solve murders. A thief turned detective, he solves thefts.

———————————

Barbara D'Amato's new sleuth, Officer Susanna Maria Figueroa, "throws the book" at a thief on her lunch hour. Her other two mystery series feature Chicago investigative reporter Cat Marsala and forensic pathologist Gerritt DeGraaf. D'Amato, winner of Agatha and Anthony awards for Best Nonfiction for *The Doctor, The Murder, The Mystery,* appeared on TV's *Unsolved Mysteries* about the case featured in the book. She was nominated for an Agatha for Best Short Story for 1994's "Soon to Be a Minor Motion Picture."

Takeout

Joyce Christmas

Lady Margaret Priam, in spite of a fine aristocratic upbringing in England at the hands of her mother, the Countess of Brayfield, and her father the earl, plus a select group of proper nannies, still harbored a dark secret that was allowed to surface now that she lived in Manhattan, rather than in London or at Priam's Priory, the family estate in England.

The secret—well, it was more of a shameful quirk—was that Margaret Priam, a woman of the upper classes, now in her mid-thirties and welcomed out and about in Manhattan society, possessed, indeed treasured, an extensive and wide-ranging collection of Chinese take-out menus for restaurants in her part of the fashionable Upper East Side of New York City.

Margaret was accustomed to being served, and she liked Chinese food, preferably eaten at home in the comfort of her well-appointed apartment on the twentieth floor of a fairly expensive high rise. Take-out food represented a workable solution, and the menus were the medium that made it possible.

She assumed, perhaps incorrectly, that deliverymen from New York City's Chinese restaurants received large bonuses based on the number of menus they were able to stuff under apartment doors when making deliveries. In any case, Margaret acquired every one she saw, and delighted in the grand names and flowery descriptions: "Three Kings of the Sea—shrimp, lobster meat and scallops fit only for the connoisseur" . . . "Crispy Whole Fish Hunan Style—fresh whole fish lightly battered and seared until golden brown, then smothered in a hot, pungent, homemade rice wine sauce. Delightful!" . . . "Special Garden—splendiferous array of vegetables enhanced by a bed of lotus stems, tasty wood-ear mushrooms, shredded dried bean curd, bamboo shoots, baby corn, snow pea pods, broccoli, and tomatoes in chef's special hot sauce." Tomatoes? Perhaps, although their wide distribution in China was somewhat doubtful.

She liked reading about the "delicious gentle sauces" and the creations "originally served to royal families, now brought to you." And of course, there were the many "Triple Delights," "Lover's Nests" and General Tso dishes, and finally "Happy Family," which she remembered dining on long ago on first meeting her gentleman friend, Sam De Vere of the New York police. De Vere especially liked the many variations of Happy Family.

Mr. Davidson, the strict concierge on the ground floor, who was one step up in the building's hierarchy from the pleasant young man who actually opened the door, had strictly forbidden deliverymen to leave piles of menus in the semi-ornate lobby. They were also discouraged from shoving menus under the doors on the upper floors as they made their deliveries. Mr. Davidson, at his discretion and with tenant permission, did allow deliverymen he recognized to ascend alone with their plastic shopping bags of take-out food up to the tenants' floors and doors. If, however, they were found scattering menus about (and sometimes they did), he banned them from the upper floors, causing them and those who ordered food no end of inconvenience. Those of whom Mr. Davidson disapproved were required to be accompanied by a member of the building's staff. Since such a person was not always readily available, food got cold, and the restaurant lost future business.

She wasn't sure the other tenants were as dedicated to the concept of dinner packed in cardboard containers and rushed on bicycles or in little vans through the streets of New York to fill empty stomachs.

For herself, she was never happier than when she was leafing through her pile of Chinese menus, pencil in hand, deciding which restaurant to call and devising just the right combination of dishes to order in. Who had the best pan-fried noodles, the best orange-flavored beef, the puffiest roast pork buns, the crispiest spring roll? Whose shrimp was not old and recently unfrozen? Whose fortune cookies not only gave fortunes but lucky numbers—enough to fill out one game of Lotto, surely leading to winnings in the millions of dollars?

She had many places to choose from, but she usually called Pearl of the Orient, only a couple of blocks away, and she never hesitated to call when a trip to the grocery store or deli was more than she could handle in the rain, snow, sleet, or simply the cold of a New York night.

Mr. Arrigo, whose apartment was two doors from hers, apparently had a taste for pizza, since she had several times seen a handsome youth with a large padded pizza delivery box standing at Mr. Arrigo's door and then be admitted.

Indeed, once or twice in the elevator she'd been engaged in conversation by Mr. Arrigo, who actually discussed the pleasures of a large pie with pepperoni, and a big order of hot mussels with good Italian bread to soak up the sauce. She did not admit that she was unfamiliar with hot mussels, nor did she comment that it seemed a great deal of food for one man to consume. Maybe Mr. Arrigo liked leftovers. It seemed that he rather liked her, but she had long ago learned that men of any age—Mr. Arrigo was perhaps in his fifties—found it hard to resist a well-put-together blonde with an English accent. Italian blood seemed to be especially stirred by blond hair and blue eyes. Her young friend Prince Paul Castrocani was similarly bowled over by blondes, although he preferred to have an idea of the woman's financial status before proceeding. Paul was undeniably nice, but he was also something of a gold digger. He had never, however, to the best of her knowledge, used hot mussels to open a conversation with a pretty wench.

As genial as Mr. Arrigo appeared to be in the close confines of the elevator, she was wary of him. He had cold eyes, and the aura of a man always keeping control of his temper. She remembered times when that control slipped. The elevator door did not close quickly enough to suit him, and he jabbed furiously at the buttons, purpling slightly, his mouth tight with anger. She'd heard angry shouts as she passed his apartment door; and she'd seen him become enraged when the doorman was not quick to open the door—and the door of his long black town car purring at the curb. She'd prefer not be the object of Mr. Arrigo's anger.

Tonight—rainy and blustery—was perfect for ordering takeout, and she had additional justification. Sam De Vere, when released from his duties as a police detective, had half promised to make his way later to her place. On that expectation, she'd turned down an invitation to dine at the showplace apartment of a prominent woman realtor to the well-known and well-heeled. Her legendary dinner parties drew the celebrated and the social from both coasts, as well as Washington's seats of power. Margaret preferred a quiet evening at home with De Vere, and she'd have something for him to eat when he arrived.

Margaret phoned Pearl of the Orient with her order, with the total cost precalculated from the menu prices, including the tax and, of course, the tip for Mr. Feng, the regular deliveryman.

Within fifteen minutes Mr. Davidson rang her intercom to announce the arrival of Mr. Feng, who was already on his way up. The concierge knew him well, and Mr. Feng knew his way around the corner from the elevators, along the corridor to her apartment.

The doorbell buzzed. Mr. Feng was outside the door, grinning and offering with a polite bob of his head a shopping bag crammed with brown paper bags holding white cardboard containers and aluminum foil dishes with cardboard covers which were invariably splashed with soy and sweet and sour sauce from someone else's order.

No matter how horrid the weather, Mr. Feng was always cheerful, as though he had personally cooked Margaret's meal (perhaps he had) prior to delivering it on his beat-up bicycle through the inclemencies outside. He worked long hours. Margaret had seen him from time to time during the day careening through traffic on his rounds to deliver lunches to offices in the area, the bag of take-out food hooked over the handlebars. He did not seem to take particular heed of the traffic, but then, not many people did.

"Bad night," Mr. Feng said as he handed her a double order of wonton soup, stir-fried spinach with garlic, and prawns with black bean sauce.

A large drop of water made its way slowly down his nose. After a moment's suspension at the tip, it dropped to the carpet outside her apartment door. "You always calling on a bad night." He spoke it not as a complaint, but as a simple truth.

"Yes," Margaret said, "I do." She really didn't mind a bit that it was Mr. Feng rather than she out on a night like this.

She handed Mr. Feng the exact amount she'd calculated, a modest enough sum for her evening meal, with leftovers for De Vere or even breakfast. She stepped into the hall to take the bag from Mr. Feng, and saw from the corner of her eye that the pizza delivery boy was entering Mr. Arrigo's apartment, laden with bags and a big white pizza box.

Mr. Feng looked at the money she'd handed him. "Ah, miss," he said, "is not enough. Look . . . lobster . . . eleven dollar fifty cents . . ." He showed her the bill, with three items neatly printed in Chinese characters. "Lobster very expensive."

"Lobster! Then there's been a mistake! I ordered shrimp. I cannot eat lobster. I am allergic. It makes me very ill."

Mr. Feng looked concerned, and then suddenly alarmed, as though she might topple over from her doorway into his arms.

"You'll have to go back and bring me the right thing," Margaret said. "I simply can't eat lobster. I'll call the Pearl right away and have them fix the shrimp, so it will be waiting when you get there. You can bring it right back to me." The aroma of the dishes in the white bag seeped into the hall. She was hungry, but she handed the bag back to him.

"Ah," Mr. Feng said again, and brushed away another enormous drop of rain from the end of his nose. He looked so disconcerted that she felt sorry for him, since it couldn't have been his fault, but rather that of the abrupt woman who took telephone orders. Mr. Feng was a nice, gentle man, shorter than she by several inches, with smooth tannish skin and floppy black hair, very badly cut. Tonight it was plastered down damply because of the rain. The poor man was wearing nothing in the way of rain gear, and he had a large white bandage affixed to the side of his head.

"Did you have an accident?" Margaret indicated the bandage with her chin.

Mr. Feng thought for a moment. "Car hit bicycle," he said. "Happens all the time. Is nothing."

"I'm so sorry," she said. "You must be more careful. Now let me just call the restaurant and tell them about the mistake."

She left him at the door and called the Pearl of the Orient. She had the number on speed dial. The explanation took some time, and then she agreed to examine the dish to be sure it was lobster. She fetched the bag from Mr. Feng, who was lounging against the wall in the hallway. He seemed distracted as he peered down the corridor. She looked at the food he'd brought her. It was definitely lobster and not shrimp.

As she spoke to the restaurant again, she could hear the rain lashing the window that overlooked Third Avenue. The woman at the Pearl of the Orient sounded quite put out, but finally agreed to correct the error. In the competitive take-out business, it paid to humor a good customer.

"All right," she said to Mr. Feng. "If you go back to the restaurant, they'll have the shrimp ready for you to bring back to me. I'll just keep the other things, so you don't have to carry them back and forth."

Mr. Feng appeared to be thinking hard, and seemed not even to be listening to her. She wondered if he understood, since she wasn't sure how strong his English was.

"Have to hurry, miss," he said. "Very bad night." He

seemed anxious to depart. Then she wondered if she ought to tip him again when he returned. She probably should, since he was the one braving the bad weather, when it could so easily have been her.

"I'll be seeing you in just a few minutes," she said. As she closed the door, she remembered that De Vere loved fried dumplings. Mr. Feng could bring some back with the shrimp. She opened the door again. "Mr. Feng—"

She stopped abruptly. Mr. Feng was edging along the corridor, close to the wall, and was now opposite Mr. Arrigo's apartment door. He stopped and stared, with that look of alarm she recognized. The door was certainly open, because she heard it being slammed shut. Mr. Feng hesitated, and suddenly he ran—toward the branching hallway that led to the bank of elevators.

Mr. Arrigo, an impressive figure in a finely tailored charcoal business suit, stepped from his apartment and shouted after Mr. Feng, "Hey, you!"

Mr. Feng had disappeared around the corner. Mr. Arrigo sighed heavily and muttered to himself. Then he noticed Margaret. "Well, Lady Margaret . . ." He took a step in her direction. She was surprised to note that he was wearing a witty Nicole Miller necktie. "Who was that fellow? Know him? I saw him hanging around outside your door."

"Oh, it's only Mr. Feng, the deliveryman."

"Delivery?" Mr. Arrigo's tone was not warm.

"You know, Chinese takeout. Like your pizza boy."

Mr. Arrigo looked quickly back at his apartment door. "Izzat right? Like Tony? I don't think so. Tony knows to mind his own business. Where's your guy from?"

"I don't think . . ." She didn't like the look on Mr. Arrigo's face. "Pearl of the Orient," she said quickly. "The restaurant just up the avenue a few blocks. They made a mistake with my order, so he's gone off to bring back the right thing."

"Yeah, well, you can't get reliable service nowadays," Mr. Arrigo said. "Say, I'd have you over tonight for some of those hot mussels Tony just brought, but I got business associates in. You know how it is. We'll do it sometime, though, one of these days. Tony'll deliver 'em to us right off the stove, practically right out of the ocean."

"Lovely," Margaret said. "I'd like that. Sometime." She wasn't terribly keen on a tête-à-tête with Mr. Arrigo, since as far as she knew, there was no Mrs. Arrigo, although any number of times she'd noticed sexy, well-dressed women coming and going from his place. Professionals, perhaps, who for a fee would agree to enjoy hot mussels and pizza with pepperoni.

"It's a deal," he said, and in an instant he had disappeared back into his apartment, calling, "Hey, Tony! On your feet!"

Margaret pondered Mr. Feng's hasty departure as she took from a cabinet a beautiful antique Chinese bowl of considerable value that her former employer, Bedros Kasparian, the Oriental art dealer, had given her when he closed his shop. He would be horrified—or maybe not—to know that she used it for the purpose for which it had been created. She dumped the wonton soup into the bowl and delicately placed some spinach on top, using her prized ebony chopsticks with tops of Baccarat crystal banded in gold.

She ate a little, but slowly, watching the news and the weather on television. The bad weather was due to continue all week.

It was quite a long time after Mr. Feng had left that Mr. Davidson rang to announce, "Delivery."

Poor Mr. Feng, she thought, wet through again. She found a few more dollars for a bigger tip.

"Oh!" She was startled when she opened the door at the doorbell's ring. It wasn't Mr. Feng at all but a different Chinese man she didn't recognize. He held out the white plastic bag to her.

"Shrimp, black bean sauce," he said. "No charge."

"Where is Mr. Feng?"

The deliveryman looked serious, shook his head. "Gone home," he said quickly. "Sick."

"Well, yes. He was soaked." She gave him a couple of dollars, not the whole amount she'd planned to tip Mr. Feng for his second trip.

"Bad sick," the man said. "Hit by car on Third Avenue." He started back in the direction of the elevators.

"Wait!" He stopped. "Tell me what happened. Please."

The deliveryman shrugged. "Little van from . . ." He gestured, making a wide circle with his arms.

"Pizza!"

The man smiled and nodded agreement. "Mr. Feng coming back with your order, van goes right at him. Don't worry, chef cooks more shrimp for you." He hurried back toward the elevator.

She found she was no longer very hungry.

Margaret put the shrimp aside in the kitchen, along with the spinach and the remains of the wonton soup. She was restless, remembering Mr. Feng's widened eyes as he looked into Mr. Arrigo's apartment, Mr. Arrigo's questions about Feng and the restaurant, and his shout for Tony.

Then Mr. Feng had been hit by a pizza delivery van as he bicycled back to her.

Ridiculous. There could be no possible connection, but she couldn't stop imagining things. What could Mr. Feng have seen through the open door or while he stood in the corridor? Something that would have caused him to be silenced on Mr. Arrigo's orders?

Which pizza restaurant did Tony deliver for? She couldn't, under the circumstances, ask Mr. Arrigo, even if she confessed an irresistible longing for her own order of hot mussels.

She remained as uncertain as ever as to the exact nature of hot mussels. She glanced at her shelf of cookbooks, but instead of leafing through an index or two, she suddenly remembered *moules marinere,* mussels cooked in white wine, vegetables, and herbs. That was a French dish, of course, but then she realized that it was an easy step linguistically from French *marinere* to Italian *marinara.* Aha! Hot mussels were certainly mussels cooked in marinara sauce, spiced with red pepper. She was rather proud of herself for figuring it out.

Again she thought how difficult it would be for one man to eat a large pizza and a large order of hot mussels—with bread to dip up the spicy red sauce—but Mr. Arrigo had said he had business associates visiting. No doubt all hearty eaters.

She didn't enjoy harboring suspicions about Mr. Arrigo. True, he was invariably polite, well-dressed, quite distinguished-looking, but she had no idea what he did for a living, and certainly no idea what he might have been doing in his apartment—with the door open—that had alarmed Mr. Feng, and perhaps had led to his "accident." Or maybe it was something his "business associates" were doing. What was the worst thing she could imagine seeing? She made a mental list:

. . . The expression on Princess Margaret's face when she was told that she was not allowed to smoke.

. . . Getting off a subway train late at night at an empty station and seeing that the exit was at the far end.

She also imagined the look on people's faces if she showed up at the Metropolitan Museum of Art's Costume Institute Winter Gala in old jeans and a plaid man's shirt— without having had her hair or nails done.

. . . Finding a dead body, possibly murdered. A terrible sight.

The choice was easy. She'd found bodies, and the sight had been quite unnerving.

Now she was convinced that Mr. Feng must have seen something awful, like a body. What could be worse? Well, she'd once cautioned Princess Margaret about smoking, and that had been pretty awful, too.

She pushed the speed dial button for Pearl of the Orient.

"I . . . this is Lady Margaret Priam," she said to the woman who answered. It sounded like the woman who usually took phone orders.

"Boy is on the way," the woman said with some irritation. "No more trouble. Food is right this time."

"Yes, yes, it is," Margaret said hastily. "The deliveryman has been here. I wanted to ask about Mr. Feng."

The silence was so long she eventually said, "Hello? Are you there?"

"You want to order?"

"No. I mean, I wanted to know how Mr. Feng is. The deliveryman said he was hit by a car."

"No," the woman said firmly. "Everything is good. Mr. Feng fall off bicycle. Gone home. No car."

"But the deliveryman said—"

"No car," the woman said even more firmly, and hung up. Surely, if the substitute deliveryman saw what happened, someone else must have. The temptation to call De Vere was very strong. If a man had been hit by a car, even a lowly deliveryman who paid little heed to traffic, the police would know about it. But then she would have to explain why she wanted to know, and she had repeatedly promised De Vere that she wouldn't involve herself with mysterious deaths. She had encountered murders once or twice too often for De Vere's taste. Maybe Mr. Feng wasn't dead, but she was now certain that someone was, in Mr. Arrigo's apartment.

There were always the hospital emergency rooms, but she suspected that if Mr. Feng were able to make his way from such an accident, he would indeed have gone home.

By the time the local ten o'clock television news came on, De Vere had not yet appeared at her apartment. Margaret was still wondering what to do about Mr. Feng, when she heard a brief report of a hit-and-run accident on a street corner on the east side of Third Avenue. A victim, dead at the scene. A small van seen by witnesses speeding from the accident. The name was not given, but Margaret felt a sudden pang of sorrow for Mr. Feng, whose smiling face and punctilious courtesy had often softened the harsh realities of New York life. He was a kind of friend, the way the old servants at Priam's Priory were her friends. And her responsibility. She had to know the truth.

But what could she do tonight? Advancing on Mr. Arrigo to demand an explanation was considered. Very briefly. Affable, distinguished Mr. Arrigo might chat easily about trivialities in the elevator, he might find her attractive, but he did not appear to be a man who could be manipulated by a proper Brit lady into confessing a crime against his will. Given what she now suspected, crime could very well be his business, and murder—either of a "business associate" or a harmless deliveryman—only a minor blip on his screen of life.

She remembered with sadness the huge raindrops plopping from Mr. Feng's nose.

Then she remembered Tony. She got out the classified pages of the phone book and turned to the section on restaurants. On the page listing restaurants by type and location, there were lots of Italian restaurants, lots of pizzerias. And lots of them were in her general neighborhood. She picked up the phone.

"Hello? Do you have hot mussels and a delivery boy named Tony?"

"Lady, everybody's got a delivery boy named Tony." This was the fifth place she'd called. "Yeah, we got mussels . . ." The man sounded wary.

"Aren't you the place that delivers to Mr. Arrigo at . . . ?" She gave the building's address.

"Hey, yeah. Enzo Arrigo. You know him?" The man sounded impressed, and wavered between truculence and a desire to ingratiate himself with someone who was a friend of Enzo Arrigo's.

"My neighbor," Margaret said brightly. "He's so terribly enthusiastic about your food."

"Arrigo said that? Hey, it's only pizza and calzone, some pretty good lasagne, the usual stuff . . ."

"And Tony."

"Lady, Tony's only a kid, you know? Give him a break."

"I have no . . . no designs on Tony," Margaret said primly. "I just want . . ."

"So, what *do* you want?"

"Mussels. Hot mussels. Umm . . . Do you have a car for deliveries? I'll need them fast, I have a guest coming."

"Tony's just gone off," the man said quickly. "You'll like Sal just as good. He's a little older, you know? More of a man of the world. Yeah, we got a delivery truck for bad nights like this. I'll put your order in now. Fifteen, twenty, maybe twenty-five minutes at the outside, it'll be there. Apartment?"

Margaret was too impatient to wait quietly for Sal's arrival. If she took a stroll down the hall, past Mr. Arrigo's apartment, she might get an idea. . . .

Outside Mr. Arrigo's door, she looked down and froze.

On the deep pile hall carpet was a splotch of red. Several splotches.

It can't be blood, she thought. It can't. Things involving blood don't happen in my apartment building.

Hesitantly she touched one of the splotches with her finger, and retreated rapidly to her apartment. Inside, she looked at her finger, then sniffed it, but refused to taste it. It didn't look like blood, but still . . . There was a very faint scent of garlic and fennel, Italian herbs and spices.

Margaret relaxed with a sigh. Marinara sauce. It had to be. Not that it explained anything, unless some of the other splotches were not marinara, but something else.

Where was De Vere? He'd know what to do. She wiped the red substance from her finger, then wondered if she should collect more samples, just in case.

What if Mr. Feng had seen a body covered in blood in Mr. Arrigo's apartment? Or even one covered in marinara sauce? Something must have happened in or just outside of Mr. Arrigo's apartment that put Mr. Feng in danger. Someone had taken note of Mr. Feng.

The sharp ring of her doorbell startled her. Mr. Davidson rarely failed to advise her from downstairs of a delivery.

She took a deep breath and prepared to meet Sal, the man with the hot mussels.

Sal was outside her door, all right, but so was Mr. Arrigo, looking as grim as she'd ever seen him. He entered her apartment without waiting to be asked. "Come on in, kid," he said to Sal. "This here's a real lady, even if no lady I know pokes her nose into other people's private business."

Margaret heard herself babbling, "How nice of you to drop by. I kept thinking of how good those mussels you like sounded, so I ordered some. Have you eaten? Well, you must have, since Tony brought in all that food. What do I owe you, Sal?"

Mr. Arrigo cut her off. "It's been taken care of. So, you didn't like the Chinese takeout you got before?"

"I . . . I rather lost my appetite for it," Margaret said, and took a deep breath, "after what happened to the delivery-man."

"Yeah? So what did happen? Put that stuff down, Sal, and

get lost." Sal obeyed promptly, closing the apartment door behind him.

"He was killed in a hit-and-run accident. Silly man, he paid no attention to traffic. I liked him."

"Did you, now? He's another one who poked his nose into things he shouldn't. It can be dangerous."

"Look, Mr. Arrigo . . . Enzo . . ." Margaret attempted wide-eyed winsomeness, but it didn't seem to work with Mr. Arrigo.

"No problem," Mr. Arrigo said. "He's dead." He stood in front of Margaret. "Now, what do I do about you?"

"Me?" Margaret said. "Whatever do you mean?"

"Hey, if that little Chinese guy saw my . . . associate, who was . . . seriously indisposed, he mighta told you, since you're such big pals." Arrigo ignored her vigorous denying headshake. "Anyhow, next I hear you're calling around about Tony and then I see you prowling around outside my door. . . ."

"Someone was terribly careless," Margaret said. "The building people will be very cross about the marinara stains on the carpeting."

Mr. Arrigo stared at her. Then he laughed a loud, rumbling laugh. "Marinara! Geez! I bet you thought it was, like, blood. Well, so did I. We took this guy away. I was going to clean it up later. Hey, the joke's on me."

"Mr. Feng is dead," Margaret said. "That's no joke."

Mr. Arrigo grinned. "He was taken out by Tony, with his dinky delivery van." He rumbled again. "Taken out by the take-out guy! Now *that's* a joke. Get it?"

Margaret looked away. Yes, she got it, but she was rather more worried about herself, now that Mr. Arrigo had confirmed her suspicions.

"Sweetheart, you know a little too much." Mr. Arrigo frowned.

"I don't know anything," Margaret said firmly, "except that you spilled sauce from the hot mussels on the carpet when you were taking the trash to the trash room."

Mr. Arrigo chuckled. He seemed to be in high spirits. "Yeah, the trash. Right. Still . . ."

The buzzer from the concierge in the lobby sounded. "What's that?"

"More takeout," Margaret said, and hoped he would believe her. "I've got to answer, or Mr. Davidson will send someone up to check."

"Okay, then. Just say, 'Yes.' No yelling for somebody. I mean it."

Margaret was sure he did. She said into the intercom phone, "Yes?"

Mr. Davidson said, "Your boyfriend's here. He's on his way up."

"That's good," Margaret said evenly. "Thank you." She hated the idea of being rescued by De Vere, but consider the alternative. She faced Mr. Arrigo. "Could I put the mussels away? I'll heat them up later." Was she being optimistic about there being a "later" for her?

"Go ahead." Arrigo followed her into the kitchen and watched her remove the aluminum container from the bag. The metal was very hot. Sal must have raced to the apartment.

The doorbell rang. De Vere at last.

"Could you get the door, please? My hands are full." She was busy dumping the container of mussels and sauce into the big cast-iron pot she always used for simmering pasta sauce.

Surprisingly, Mr. Arrigo went obediently to the door. He opened it to reveal Sam De Vere, who was definitely startled to be facing Mr. Arrigo and not Lady Margaret Priam. Margaret edged out of the kitchen, carrying the heavy pot full of mussels. Raising it to her shoulder, she hurled it at Mr. Arrigo's back.

Her aim was perfect. A spray of shiny blue-black mussels and bright red sauce exploded over Mr. Arrigo's handsome charcoal jacket, the iron pot striking the back of his head. He staggered, and was perhaps too stunned by the blow to think to reach for the gun she imagined he carried.

Nevertheless, she shouted, "He has a gun!"

De Vere merely endured the surprise of his life and a few splashes of marinara sauce on his sport jacket and jeans.

But then, he was not what one would call a cutting edge dresser. As Mr. Arrigo, awash in red marinara, lurched against the doorjamb, De Vere managed to gain control of him. No gun was drawn, although there was in fact a gun, which De Vere managed to liberate from Mr. Arrigo's person.

"Margaret," De Vere said sternly, "exactly what is the meaning of this?"

"It's about ordering takeout," Margaret said. "Come on in, and I'll explain."

"Yes," De Vere said, "you will." Mussel shells crunched under the men's shoes as De Vere prodded Mr. Arrigo into the apartment.

"For heaven's sake, put him in the leather chair, I don't need marinara all over my chintz cushions," Margaret said.

De Vere said, "Now, how did you know that this gentleman would have a gun?" Mr. Arrigo looked a little the worse for wear as he sat heavily in the leather chair and rubbed the back of his head.

Margaret shrugged. "The thought just occurred to me. Because he arranged to have a friend of mine killed tonight. He's my neighbor, Enzo Arrigo. He might have had someone else killed, too." She gestured at the sauce and mussels on her floor. "He likes Italian stuff, like hot mussels, so I called for takeout. Not that I was planning on entertaining him . . . Sam, I'm so glad you came in time, even if the mussels are gone."

"Margaret." De Vere was stern again, but he reached out and squeezed her shoulder. "You know I prefer Chinese."

With Murder You Get Egg Roll . . . In this outing, Joyce Christmas's elegant British expatriate Lady Margaret Priam finds more than moo shu pork with her take-out order. Priam is featured in *Suddenly in Her Sorbet* (1988), *Simply to Die For* (1989), *A Fete Worse Than Death* (1990), *A Stunning Way to Die* (1991), *Friend or Faux* (1991), *It's Her Funeral* (1992), and *A Perfect Day for Dying* (1994). Christmas, a New York editor, also writes a series featuring retired secretary Betty Trenka, who appears in *This Business Is Murder* (1993) and *Death at Face Value* (1995).

Crossed Keys

Patricia Moyes

"Late again, Edward." Herbert Burnside glared at me through his thick horn-rimmed spectacles. He was a tall, florid man in his fifties, but still handsome. He always called me Edward, while to the rest of the hotel staff I was Ted.

I tried to be reasonable. "Only ten minutes, Mr. Burnside. There was some flooding on the waterfront road, and I had to get off my bicycle and—"

"I don't want any excuses, Edward. You are paid to be here at nine, and now it's ten past." He cleared his throat, changing gears. "Now, is everything ready for this evening?"

"I think so, Mr. Burnside."

"What do you mean—you think? You should know. It's the job of the assistant manager—"

I felt my face reddening. Conversations with Herbert Burnside, the manager of the Green Turtle, often had this effect on me. As gently as I could, I said, "Surely it's also the job of the manager—"

"Don't take that tone with me, young man." He broke off

to give a quick smirk to a couple of guests who were passing through the lobby on their way to the beach. "Now, come into my office and we'll go over the arrangements."

The Green Turtle, I should explain, was a medium-size hotel, restaurant, and bar on a small American Caribbean island. It was some miles out of the main town—if you could really describe it as a town—along the coast. It had an attractive white sandy beach, a lot of palm trees, fourteen bedrooms, and enviable seclusion, for which our clients were willing to pay rather more than the accommodation was worth. In my view, that is. Mr. Burnside thought they should be paying a lot more. He didn't own the place, of course—it was part of a chain of small inns—but he had an obsession with money, whether it was his own or not.

The event due to take place that evening was something rather special—the annual district meeting of the Tigers Club—that most worthy charitable institution—which was being held for the first time on our island. Delegates were coming from all over the Caribbean and parts of South America. They were staying at the island's one big hotel in town, but they had booked the Green Turtle for their dinner and dance that night. It was September, and therefore low season, and we had only a handful of guests, who had been asked to take their dinner on the terrace that evening. Nevertheless, it was going to strain our resources to the limit to fit all the Tigers and Tigresses into the dining room. Dancing afterward would be in the bar and on the terrace, and possibly on the beach as well. We had hired a local steel band to provide music.

Our small kitchen couldn't possibly cope with so many meals, so we had to arrange for the dinner to be catered by a firm in town that specialized in weddings and official government parties.

I explained to Herbert Burnside what I had done. He was unimpressed.

"What about the bar stocks?" he demanded.

"I have to check them today," I said. "I was leaving that to Gina, but now—"

"Please don't start that again, Edward. I did what I thought best."

"You fired the best office manager we ever had."

"I did not trust Gina Lopez." He sniffed. "Besides, she was from Puerto Rico. The guests didn't like her."

"That could be called racism," I pointed out.

"You can call it whatever you like. I am the manager here, and I hire and fire whom I wish."

"Well, Sally Martin may be a true-blue WASP English girl," I said, "but I don't think she's up to the job. She may work out all right in the end, with some training and experience, but to land her with tonight's complications in her first week just isn't fair."

"That's for me to decide."

"Anyhow, Sally and I will go through the bar stocks together, Mr. Burnside, and I think you'll find that everything is in order."

"Parking?"

"Most of the delegates will come in the bus that they've hired, and the rest by taxi."

"Flowers?"

"From our own gardens. There will be a centerpiece on each table, and a single hibiscus flower at each place setting."

Herbert Burnside grunted. "Sounds satisfactory," he admitted grudgingly. "Well, now for the important part."

"I thought we'd covered everything."

"I mean the money. You realize that we'll be taking in a lot of cash this evening?"

"Yes, I do."

"The dinner guests have been asked to pay in cash at the door, and then with the bar takings—well, we should have in the region of ten thousand dollars in the till by the end of the evening."

"I'll make sure it's all locked away in the safe, Mr. Burnside."

"*I* will make sure of that," he said nastily.

"If you like, I'll take it into town and put it in the bank's night safe after everybody has gone home."

I thought Burnside was going to explode. "You? Twelve miles on your miserable bicycle on a lonely road with all that money?"

"Well, it's true I had to sell my car," I said. I didn't add that because he decided that my staff cottage could be rented out, I had to move to an apartment in town, and trade my old Jeep for a bicycle. "I thought I might borrow one of the hotel's cars just for the evening—"

"You certainly may not. The money will stay here in the safe, and I will take it to the bank tomorrow."

"I can take it, Mr. Burnside."

"You? I wouldn't trust you with it."

This, I felt, was going too far. Of course, I knew exactly what he was referring to. A few months earlier there had been a small scandal at the hotel, when a guest complained about losing an expensive watch and some cash. We never got to the bottom of it, but he had left his valuables and money on the dressing table in his cottage—a thing we always warned people not to do—and I don't consider it fair to put such temptation in the way of people who may be less fortunate than yourself.

Nevertheless, I very much resented Burnside's implication that I might be in some way responsible, and I said so.

"It's impossible for me to do my job if you don't trust me. After all, I have the key to the safe where the money will be tonight—"

"I've been thinking about that," Burnside said, with an unpleasant sniff. "And I have decided to ask you to turn the key over to me."

This time, I felt myself going white with anger. "In that case, you might just as well fire me and have done with it."

"Very well, Edward. If that's your attitude, you can take a month's notice. And now I'll have that key, if you please."

I always wore the precious key to the safe on a chain around my neck, unless I was actually swimming, when I left it in the office with Gina Lopez—or, since last week, the decorative but inexperienced Sally. Remembering Gina, I became even angrier. She had been, as I said to Burnside, the best office manager we ever had, as well as being extremely attractive, with her coffee-colored skin and fine bone structure. Herbert Burnside had dismissed her a week ago with no explanation, and, of course, without consulting me. It had occurred to me at the time that he wanted to create a job opening for Sally, in whom, I suspected, he took rather more than a paternal interest.

I fumbled in my shirt and brought out the key on its chain, which I slipped over my head. "Here you are. Take it and welcome. But I'd like a receipt."

We glared at each other. "Very well," Burnside said stiffly. He marched over to his desk and scribbled on a piece of paper, which he handed me. It read, "Received from Edward Taylor, one key to the office safe of the Green Turtle," and the date.

"Sign it, please," I said.

He took the paper back, scrawled his signature at the bottom, and handed it to me again. I folded it and put it in my shirt pocket.

"You will kindly keep to yourself the fact that you are leaving the hotel until after this evening's party," Herbert Burnside remarked. "It might unsettle the staff, and I am determined that everything shall go without a hitch."

So the day started, in such a flurry of activity that I hardly had time to think of my predicament. I wasn't unduly upset about losing my job—I couldn't have gone on working with Burnside much longer, anyway—but I didn't want to leave the island, and I would have to find a source of income. I knew I could get a job of sorts at one of the bigger hotels, but I doubted it would be anything as grand as assistant manager. Well, like Scarlett O'Hara, I decided to think about it tomorrow. There was far too much to do today.

First, I had the staff arranging the dining room, dragging the tables together and bringing in reinforcements in the shape of dressing tables from vacant cottages. When all the tables were in place, the maids covered them with white sheets, tacked together to make tablecloths. Meanwhile, the gardeners were combing the grounds for flowers—mostly the lovely red, pink, and yellow hibiscus, because these blooms live only for a day and require no water. I commissioned Sally to arrange a floral centerpiece for each table—but she made such a mess of it that I shooed her back into her office and did the job myself.

I also found that she had failed to order nearly enough stock for the bar, so I spent a frantic hour on the telephone to our suppliers, arranging for more to be delivered. As I did so, I mentally cursed Burnside yet again for sacking Gina. She would never have messed things up like this. I hated to think of her wasting her talents, serving in a local shop.

During the afternoon, the caterers arrived with the food, which had to be refrigerated until it was time either to warm it up or serve it cold. They seemed to have done a good job, and I reckoned that the Tigers would be pleased. When a small island hosts a big meeting, we are all put on our mettle. For this reason, I had also arranged to hire extra china, glass, and cutlery from the catering firm. I was damned if the Green Turtle was going to insult its distinguished guests with cardboard plates and plastic glasses.

The steel band arrived about five o'clock and set up their instruments—if you can call an oil drum, however finely tuned, an instrument—on the terrace. Soon, the sound of their rehearsing raised all our spirits, and the staff were fairly dancing to the infectious rhythms as they went about their duties.

At half-past five I knocked briefly on Herbert Burnside's door and went into his office. I was not really surprised to find him sound asleep, his head on his desk. He woke with a start as I came in, shaking his head and grunting a little.

"Sorry, Edward. Must have dropped off. Not feeling too good."

I had heard it all before. He claimed that he had a dicky heart and needed to rest, especially after lunch. Everybody knew that the reason he needed to rest after lunch was that he consumed too many rum punches before, during, and after his meal.

Formally, I said, "I think you'll find that everything is ready, Mr. Burnside. Perhaps you would like to come and look it over."

"What? Oh, yes . . . yes, indeed . . ." He was still fuddled with sleep, but he got to his feet and lumbered out of the office after me.

Though he did his best, even Herbert Burnside could find very little to complain about. He thought he had caught me out when he inquired gloatingly if I had considered that some of the guests might be vegetarians, but his face dropped when I showed him the excellent vegetable pasta dish I had ordered. He had a final try with decaffeinated coffee, but failed there, too. At last he was forced to admit that all was well.

"Now, Edward, about the money."

"What about it?"

"Sally will be on the till, taking the cash for dinners and drinks. She will not leave her post all evening."

"Suppose she wants to go to the bathroom?"

He shot me a nasty look. "In that case, I will take over for a few minutes."

"I could—"

"Oh, no, you couldn't. You will be needed for other duties."

It was extremely unpleasant not to be trusted with a few thousand dollars, and I told myself that I probably wouldn't work out my full month's notice. However, all I said was, "Very well, Mr. Burnside. Just as you wish."

"When the last guest has gone, Sally and I will put the cash into the safe."

I couldn't help remarking, "You'll have to, since I now have no key."

He smirked. "As you say, you now have no key. Well, I think that's about all, Edward."

Our guests began arriving soon after seven o'clock. The band was already tapping away merrily on their tuned oil drums, there was a general atmosphere of jollity which promised a good party, and the bar started to do brisk business. The Tigers and Tigresses in their green and gold jackets made a colorful sight, while the non-Tigress wives ran to brilliant cotton caftans and swirling printed skirts and blouses. Candles glowed on the tables, the light glinting off silver and crystal, and, despite Burnside and his grouchiness, I felt proud of the Green Turtle.

At half-past seven dinner was announced, but it was eight before everybody was seated and tucking into their hors d'oeuvres. Soon after nine the inevitable speeches set in with the coffee and liqueurs, but before ten dancing was in full swing.

I had been keeping an eye on Sally, sitting demurely at the cash till, and noticed that she had not needed Mr. Burnside to pinch-hit for her while she went to the ladies' room. In fact, our manager was nowhere to be seen, which added considerably to the festivity of the occasion. I went over to Sally.

"How's it going?" I asked.

"Very well, Ted. I haven't counted, of course, but there must be well over five thousand dollars in there, and they're still buying plenty of drinks."

"Good." I smiled at her. She wasn't a bad kid, really. Just not very bright. "No sign of Burnside?"

"Haven't seen him all evening."

"You will," I promised her. "He's going to put the cash in the safe himself."

"He is?" Sally's eyebrows went up. "I thought that you—"

"Not anymore. Old Burnside has confiscated my key."

"Whatever for?"

"You'd better ask him. You're on good terms with him, aren't you?"

Sally blushed. She had that very white skin that goes with reddish-blond hair, and it colored easily. "I wish," she said, "that people wouldn't go 'round saying—"

"This is a small island," I reminded her, "and an even smaller hotel. People are bound to go around saying."

"Well, it's all nonsense." She had a prim English voice, like the head girl of a posh school.

"I wouldn't worry," I said, and went off to supervise the clearing of the tables.

At midnight the band played their final number—"Island in the Sun," of course—and started to pack up their gear. The reveling Tigers began drifting off to their waiting bus, but some had come by taxi, and this hard core stayed at the bar after the others had left. However, by one o'clock the place was empty, and I went in search of Herbert Burnside.

I knocked respectfully on his office door, and was rewarded by a ripe snore from within. I had seen him socializing with some of the prominent local Tigers before dinner, and it wasn't difficult to reconstruct what had happened. I pushed the door open and went in.

Burnside was sitting in his chair, his head and arms on his desk, sleeping the sleep of the unjust and inebriated. I shook his shoulder.

"Mr. Burnside. Wake up. The party's over."

"Whassat?"

"I said, the party's over. They've all gone home."

"Good." He put his head down on the desk again.

"Mr. Burnside," I said patiently, "it's time for you to put the cash in the safe."

This remark had the effect of waking him up. "Oh. Oh, yes. You're quite right. Where's Sally?"

"Still guarding the till," I said. "You'd better get the key and come along."

It wasn't easy, but I got him to his feet and propelled him to the bar, while he fumbled for the safe key, which he had decided to wear on a chain around his neck, as I had. Sally was waiting by the till, and together we counted the cash, which amounted to just over ten thousand dollars.

Sally sorted it into bundles of different denominations, which were secured by rubber bands and put into envelopes. Then the three of us went into Sally's office, where the safe was kept. Burnside seemed somewhat recovered, and produced the key with a flourish. He opened the safe and took the envelopes one by one from Sally. When they were all in the safe, he announced his intention of having a nightcap in the bar while I told him details of how the evening had gone. This was a palpable excuse. He always had a nightcap before going off to his cottage for a good night's sleep.

Sally announced that she was dead beat and was going to drive straight back to her little apartment in town. She had bought an old beat-up car, which was barely roadworthy but did enable her to get to and from work. So Burnside and I repaired to the bar, where I poured him his favorite drink— a rum and cola—and assured him that the evening had been a great success.

He was hardly complimentary. "Good planning, Edward. If you plan carefully ahead, as I did, you can't go wrong."

I nearly choked on my 7UP, but managed to say, "I do so agree with you, Mr. Burnside."

"Young people," he added, with an owlish sort of wisdom, "tend to give all the credit to the executives—the people who rush around doing things. They don't realize that the success is due to the planners."

"Absolutely right, Mr. Burnside."

He drained his drink. "Well, I'll be off to bed. Good night, Edward."

I walked with him to his staff cottage, which was at the far side of the hotel gardens, well away from the guest cottages. I was afraid he might not make it on his own. When I was sure that he was inside and on the way to dreamland, I went back to the main building and collected my bicycle. I did not, however, ride back into town on it. It was understood that if my duties kept me at the hotel until after midnight, I might sleep in an unoccupied guest cottage, if there was one available. As I have indicated, it was low season and we had very few guests, so I had my pick of several cottages that night.

I was still in the garden when I heard the wail of a siren approaching rapidly from the direction of town. Police or ambulance? I wondered which. In any case, it couldn't have anything to do with us. There was nobody at the hotel but Burnside and myself, plus half a dozen guests. Must be an accident on the road, I thought. Then I saw the blazing headlights turning into the hotel entrance, illuminating as they did so Sally's car, which was parked outside Burnside's cottage. I set off toward it at a run, and almost collided with Sally as she came out of the building.

"What on earth—" I began, but she cut me short.

"Oh, Ted," she wailed. "It's too awful! Poor Herbert—I hope to God they're in time!"

"Where is he, miss?" The ambulance driver and his team were out of the vehicle. Mutely, Sally gestured toward the cottage, and the men went in, carrying a stretcher.

"Now," I said, "for heaven's sake, explain. What has happened and what are you doing here?"

"I . . . I don't know what to say. . . ."

"Don't bother," I remarked. "It's clear enough. You and Burnside are lovers. That's why he fired Gina and gave you her job. I don't know how he wangled a green card for you—"

She turned on me, suddenly angry. "All right. Make it sound as terrible as you like. It's true I've been coming back here after everyone else left. But when I got here tonight, Herbert was just lying there on the bed. I thought he was asleep, but I couldn't wake him. He must have had a heart attack—you know he had a bad heart. So I called the hospital and—"

"Excuse me, miss." The ambulance team was back, carrying the stretcher on which Burnside now lay. He was breathing stertorously, which at least showed that he was still alive. The paramedics maneuvered him into the ambulance and began connecting up bottles and cylinders.

"Can I go with him?" Sally asked.

"Are you a relative?"

A little pause, then Sally said, "Not exactly. I'm his fiancée."

"Then I'm afraid not, miss. He'll be taken straight into intensive care, with no visitors. What you can do is pack up some of his things—dressing gown, shaving kit, and so on—and bring it along to the hospital, for when he gets better."

"He will get better, won't he?" Sally sounded concerned.

"We hope so, miss. But there's no time to lose. The sooner we're off, the better."

And with a screaming siren, the ambulance sped away toward the town.

"Can I help you with his things?" I asked.

"No, thanks, Ted. I can manage." Sally disappeared into the cottage, and came out a few minutes later with a small zip-up suitcase. "You'll be staying here, won't you, Ted? We can't leave the place alone with all that money in the safe." She jumped into her car and set off after the ambulance.

Suddenly, I felt very uneasy. I turned away from Burnside's cottage and made my way through the gardens to the main office. I switched on the light and went in. The door of the safe was hanging open, and it was empty. It only took a quick look to see that there was no sign of forcible entry. It had been opened with the key.

I went straight to the telephone and called the local police.

Three of them turned up in a very short time. A plain-clothes detective, our inspector—a jolly black man called Barnaby Wilkins, who was an old friend—and a uniformed constable.

While the plainclothes man got busy with technicalities such as fingerprints and photography, Inspector Wilkins got out his notebook.

"Now, Mr. Taylor, let's go over this carefully. How much money do you say is missing?"

"Ten thousand, one hundred and four dollars."

Wilkins's eyebrows went up. "As much as that? Isn't that rather unusual?"

"Very," I told him. I explained about the Tigers' dinner and dance.

"Unusual again," the inspector remarked. "I can understand about the drinks, but surely members pay for their dinner in advance, by credit card or check."

"I quite agree," I said, "but our manager, Mr. Burnside, insisted on it being done this way."

"Who had the key to the safe?"

"Until this morning, I did," I said, a little bitterly. "But Mr. Burnside took it from me. Apparently he didn't trust me." I felt in my pocket and brought out the receipt. "I'm glad I made sure I got this."

"Hmm." Wilkins studied the paper. "Seems to me I should talk to Mr. Burnside."

"I'm afraid that isn't possible. He's in the hospital, in intensive care."

"Good heavens, man. When did that happen?"

"Late tonight." I hesitated. "He'd had a bad heart for some time."

"And you say he was the only person with a key?"

"To the best of my knowledge."

"Can you think of any possible reason why he should want to rob his own hotel?"

I shrugged. "I suppose he needed the money."

"Well, we'd best go and look at his cottage."

"Prints all over the desk and typewriter." The plain-clothes man sounded smug.

"And the safe and key?"

"None, sir. Wiped clean."

"You'd best come along with me to Mr. Burnside's cottage, and bring your bag of tricks." The inspector was getting impatient. "Constable, you stay here and keep an eye on things."

"Right, sir," the man in uniform said.

Burnside's cottage looked just as we had left it—the bed rumpled, everything else neat and tidy. The two police officers worked systematically, taking prints and searching. Not surprisingly, there were plenty of prints.

There was, however, no sign of the money. The inspector left no stone unturned, as the saying goes. The mattress was ripped apart, the lavatory cistern investigated, all drawers and closets ransacked. All appeared perfectly innocent.

"Two sets of prints, sir," the detective remarked. "One looks like the same as on the typewriter in the office."

I suddenly remembered Sally and the packed suitcase.

"I think I can explain that," I said. "Mr. Burnside's, em . . . fiancée was here last night. It was she who found him and called the ambulance."

"Very interesting," Wilkins remarked. "You know her?"

"Yes, indeed. She's our office manager, which is why her prints were on the typewriter. Her name is Sally Martin—an English girl."

"And where does she live?"

"She has a small apartment in town, when she's not—that is, she has a small apartment in town."

"Address?"

"Somewhere on Main Street, as far as I know. I don't know the exact house number, but it'll be in our records."

"Well, Mr. Taylor, I don't think there's anything more we can do here for the moment. Thank you for your cooperation. Will you come back to the office and find that address for us?"

"Of course, Inspector."

As we walked through the gardens, Wilkins said, "Just one thing, Mr. Taylor. What made you go back to the office and look at the safe?"

"Well, I felt uneasy. I knew there was a lot of money in the safe, and that I was the only staff member in the hotel. I thought I'd just check."

"But you had no key?"

"No, but if everything had been securely locked up, I'd have slept easy."

Wilkins frowned. "That's what I mean." But he didn't elaborate. "You have a cottage here in the grounds, do you?"

"I used to." I tried to say it lightly, but I could not keep a certain amount of edge out of my voice. "A few months ago, during the high season, Mr. Burnside decided that he could let the staff cottages to paying guests. Except for his own, of course."

"So tonight . . . ?"

"If the hotel isn't full, and I have to work late, I'm allowed to use a guest cottage."

"I see. Well, here we are."

I quickly found the details of Sally's address and bade the inspector good night—what was left of it. The unfortunate constable was still dozing in a chair in the office.

Next morning—which was only a few hours after the inspector had gone—I took one of the hotel's cars and drove to the hospital.

The receptionist was polite, but firm. "I'm sorry, sir. Mr. Burnside is in intensive care and can receive no visitors."

"Is he conscious?" I demanded.

"I really can't tell you, sir." She flashed me a smile, brilliant white teeth in a satiny black face.

"Look here," I said, "he's my boss and I have to see him."

The smile was not repeated. "If it's anything to do with work, then it's quite out of the question."

"Well . . . it's just something that he may need when he—when he's better."

"You can leave anything with me, sir."

"His fiancée packed a small suitcase for him last night. If I could just put this envelope into it . . ."

The receptionist was still stony, but relented a little. "I have the suitcase here," she said. "I don't think it's locked."

"Then if I may—"

I couldn't believe my luck. A moment later I had the case in my hands. I unzipped it and pulled the envelope out of my pocket.

As I did so, I heard a familiar voice behind me.

"Excuse me, Mr. Taylor." Inspector Wilkins sounded as affable as ever. "May I just take a look at what you are putting into Mr. Burnside's suitcase?"

Well, there was nothing to be done. All I could think to say was, "How did you find out?"

"It was Miss Sally who got suspicious," he said. "So I visited Miss Gina Lopez early this morning. She admitted everything. How she had brought you a strong sleeping draught from the pharmacy where she now works. How you had arranged to provoke a row with Mr. Burnside, so that he would demand your key back. If he hadn't, you'd have given it to him in a huff. You never believed in his bad heart, but it was real, all right, and the drug you gave him, on top of the alcohol he'd drunk, was too much for him. When you took the key and opened the safe, you thought he was just sleeping, and you were going to replace the key and accuse him of taking the money. It would have made a nice little nest egg for you and Miss Lopez—but I suspect it was spite against Mr. Burnside that was your real motive.

"It must have come as a shock to you when you discovered that he really had had a heart attack. You were stuck with the key and the money. It didn't take a lot of figuring out that your only hope was to get them both into that suitcase. I'll take the envelope now, please, sir. And you'd better come along with me."

In this mystery, Patricia Moyes sticks close to home in exploring skulduggery at an island resort. Moyes, a resident of the British Virgin Islands and Guest of Honor at *Malice Domestic* II, has authored over twenty books featuring Scotland Yard Inspector Henry Tibbett and his easygoing wife, Emmy.

Ham Grease Jimmy
and the No Shirt Kid

Sue Henry

Ham Grease Jimmy and the No Shirt Kid were partners who, late in the summer of 1897, made the long trip from Seattle to Skagway and on to Dawson to *make their fortunes* in the Klondike Gold Rush. Ham Grease, a *Canuck* from Saskatchewan, had gone to Seattle to find a berth on a boat headed for Alaska Territory. He met up with No Shirt, a younger, but more experienced California miner, on the docks and they agreed to join forces and grub stakes for the long journey, for they had heard of the fantastic labor that was required to move outfits over the Chilkoot Trail and down the Yukon River to the goldfields.

The trip was conducive to the formation of partnerships, for two men could accomplish what one man had less chance of doing alone, but it was also such an enormous trial and undertaking that partnerships often split up as quickly as they had formed. The enforced association of traveling partners, unable to escape each other's company and compelled to work together, bred familiarity and its companion, contempt, which in their case soon deepened into a bitter and stubborn hatred of each other.

At Lake Bennett, where they not only had to build a boat in which to run the Yukon, but also cut the lumber for it, the first serious conflict occurred. Two sawyers were essential to pull a long whipsaw up and down through the length of each log; one man atop the log on its scaffold and one under it, where, on each downward stroke, he got a shower of sawdust that sifted into eyes, ears, and shirt collar, a constant and infuriating irritation. Most of the planks for the boat were cut and the craft's shell roughly completed when a dispute arose as No Shirt accused Ham Grease of shirking his shift under the strong-arm mill.

The argument grew heated and a punch or two was thrown before they settled into an icy silence after agreeing to sever their partnership. With utmost care, practically counting the beans, they divided all the grub and gear. For the single tent and stove, they flipped a coin; Ham Grease claimed the tent, No Shirt the stove. The problem of the half-finished boat they solved by employing the whipsaw to slice it neatly and evenly in half from bow to stern.

With a line drawn precisely through the camp, and their goods piled on either side, they were settling down for the night when it commenced to rain. They spent the hours of drizzly darkness wide-awake in misery; Ham Grease freezing in the unheated tent, and No Shirt trying his best to dry out his wet clothes by the unprotected and sizzling stove. By morning they had patched up their differences and were busy fitting the boat back together. But the seed of individual indignation and anger was sown. From that point on, neither trusted the other, nor was willing to give an inch toward reducing the friction.

By the time they reached Dawson, staked a claim fifteen miles outside of town, and constructed a small log cabin in which to spend the winter, they had not only ceased speaking to each other and split what was left of their grubstake, but had once again drawn a line that divided their rude domicile down the middle. Unwilling to share anything but the door, they even went to the trouble of hauling a second cast-iron stove over the miles of ragged trail and, in silence, installing it on Ham Grease's side of the one-room cabin.

Through the long winter they worked the claim in mute obstinacy, communicating, only when absolutely necessary, through a mythical third partner they called Oddy.

"Oddy, tell No Shirt to toss some a *his* wood on the fire in the shaft, or we won't have no ore to shovel come daylight."

Or: "I ain't got but two hands, Oddy. Tell Ham Grease to stop yanking the dern rope on the windlass and dump them buckets some speedier."

Or: "We got sixteen nuggets today, Oddy. Tell Ham his eight are on the line, where he can get 'em hisself."

When it began to show sure signs that spring must be on its way, two things had transpired that aimed them both irrevocably toward the events that finally terminated the partnership. One, the food was running dangerously low, and two, they had both come to the inescapable conclusion that the other would be better off dead, and were individually plotting how best to bring this about.

The winter of '97 was a horror for most of those in the Klondike. A large number of the stampeders who had slipped through the passes and arrived before freeze-up traveled light, with little more than they could carry on their backs. They had money, expected to make more, and figured they would purchase goods and gear in Dawson. With hundreds of hungry people on the streets, however, the price of consumables soared to unbelievable heights, when they could be found at all. There was no *grub* in Dawson, and would not be. The steamboats, on their way upriver from St. Michael on the Alaskan coast, froze solid in the ice. Winter had held off long enough to allow many would-be miners to complete the trip to the goldfields, then clamped down harder, faster and colder than usual that year.

Poverty, illness, and famine were the lot of the unlucky ones. But there was gold—incredible amounts of gold for those on whom fortune had smiled. Two hundred thousand dollars worth piled up from the famous Eldorado claim alone, waiting to be shipped out in the spring. One Dawson saloon had a whole row of old-fashioned glasses on display, one after another in a line, full of gold dust; a hundred thousand dollars each. Dust, however, could not be eaten.

A meal with beans as the main course cost five dollars that winter. A damp and rancid pound of flour went for three. Eggs and onions sold for a dollar apiece. A dance-hall girl auctioned herself off for five thousand dollars for the duration; willing to live for the winter as the wife of the miner who purchased her, and also do his cooking and housekeeping. No one actually starved to death *in* Dawson that strange winter, but many came uncomfortably close, and scurvy was rampant. In the wilderness between it and civilization, others were not so lucky. When two miners were found in their cabin on the Porcupine River, they were frozen solid beside a kettle hanging over a long-dead fire. In the kettle was a pair of boiled moccasins in a cake of ice.

Out on the claim of Ham Grease Jimmy and the No Shirt Kid, there was still some flour and beans, but they had both run out of salt pork and bacon. Deciding, through Oddy, that a hunting trip was in order to replenish their supply of meat, they agreed it would have to be done together, as neither was willing to leave the other at the cabin alone and unobserved.

No Shirt was taking care to keep close guard over his remaining supply of grub, and mashed his eats with a fork, after finding glass fragments in his mess of beans. Ham Grease slept with one eye open, the result of waking to find the Kid creeping away from his coffeepot in the dark. Discarding the pot with grave suspicions of poison, he proceeded to boil his brew in a skillet.

When the bottle of quicksilver they had set outside as a thermometer froze solid, they knew it was colder than forty below zero, the temperature at which mercury freezes. One morning No Shirt found that his mittens had *mysteriously* grown damp overnight, a condition that could have caused serious frostbite to his hands if he hadn't noticed. A day or two later Ham Grease was limping slightly from an *accident* with a large rock that had *fallen* into the shaft and hit his leg, barely missing his head. Everything heavy had then been moved away from the hole, and the pair worked the claim tied together by a long cord, so that each could know when and how far the other moved.

Watching his partner limp around, the idea of the hunting trip inspired No Shirt to what he was convinced was his best plan yet for getting rid of Ham Grease, in a way that would keep anyone from guessing that he was responsible for murder. This was crucial, for the Northwest Mounted Police from Dawson would investigate any suspicious death with a jaundiced eye.

Alone, on an earlier hunting trip, before the snow had deeply covered the hills, he had spotted a fat mother grizzly a couple of miles above the claim, digging out a den in which to spend the winter with her two not-yet-year-old cubs. Now he recollected this, and knew that it was just about time for that same *elder sister* to emerge, hungry and bad-tempered, from hibernation. If he timed it right, he might make sure they ran into that *old woman in a furred cloak* on their way to hunt.

For several cold days No Shirt made one excuse or another, through Oddy, to keep from going out. When a sunny morning dawned that would undoubtedly warm the half-melted southern slopes and encourage the bears to search for new vegetation, he finally agreed that this was the day he and Ham Grease would go looking for fresh meat. Banking the fires in their separate stoves and closing up the cabin, they started up the cut, heading for higher ground on a game trail slick with mud and melting snow.

The Kid was dismayed to see that Ham Grease's limp was decidedly improved and he could swing along almost normally in his snowshoes. He had hoped simply to run his partner into the bear without warning, while Ham Grease was still unable to move quickly away from the dangerous and ill-minded beast that would be instinctively inclined to protect her cubs from any threat. Now it would be touch-and-go whether that would be good enough, especially as Ham Grease had a twelve-gauge shotgun over his arm, ready to raise into firing position at the slightest opportunity for game. This state of affairs required some revisions to his plan.

They had tramped for less than an hour and he was

concentrating hard on the complication when, Ham Grease in the lead, they neared the top of a ridge and ran smackity dab into the *b'ars* heading downhill. The first awareness No Shirt had of the encounter was the deep rumble of an angry growl ahead, beyond his partner, who had stopped dead in the snow and raised his gun to shoulder level. He peered past Ham Grease to see the mother bear approximately seventy-five feet farther up the cut, facing the man with the shotgun.

A winter of nursing her cubs and living off her body fat had thinned her down some from what she had weighed in the fall, but she was mighty impressive all the same at around five hundred hostile pounds. Nearsighted from peering at ground level for food, she swung her massive head from side to side, trying to identify what it was that confronted her. Unable to distinguish details from that distance with the piggy eyes in her dished face, she snorted for scent, then proceeded to raise herself up on hind legs to tower over the two men that surprise had frozen where they stood farther on down the slope.

She was indeed a terrifying sight to behold. Claws, four or five inches long and sharp from disuse in the den, dangled on huge paws in front of her belly. Opening and closing her mouth over the rumble of her growl, she exposed fearsome, pointed canine teeth and incisors specialized for grasping and ripping. Once more she snorted the air, hackles up, jowls peeled back, and roared—a sound to shake loose just about any man's courage. *The beast that walks like a man.*

The No Shirt Kid shifted his feet slightly, adrenaline widening his eyes and sending tingles down his arms.

"Stand still, for God sakes," Ham Grease hissed over his shoulder, not taking his eyes, or his aim, from the bear.

Ten feet back, his younger partner had no intention of going anywhere—anticipating his chance.

At that moment the sound of a small avalanche of soft snow falling off the bank to his left drew his attention, and glancing in that direction, he saw one of the cubs slide down to land between himself and Ham Grease. More curious than frightened of the men, the cub sat still, sniffing at the human scent and blinking. Then it whined.

The Kid had learned from past hunting experience that there was positively nothing more dangerous than a mama grizzly separated from her cub, and though they were always unpredictable at best, in this kind of standoff there was no doubt in his mind what would happen next. He gloated as Ham Grease, glimpsing the cub, looked around wildly for some sort of protection, knowing there wasn't a tree for miles and the lay of the land wouldn't have encouraged an attempt if there had been one. At high speed, *grizzled* bears could travel thirty-five miles an hour, easily outrunning a human, and, with its downhill advantage, this one would be on top of snowmelt-hindered Ham in a half-dozen rolling strides.

No Shirt couldn't have been more pleased with the situation. Now, he thought, I for sure have him fixed all right. And he knew immediately and exactly what he would do next to ensure that Ham Grease would soon be only a memory, and *all* the winter's gold nuggets and the *whole* cabin his alone. Ham Grease stood there between the giant grizzly and her cub, and if he couldn't run, she would be on him in seconds with her ferocious jaws, teeth, and terrible tearing claws. She would rend him limb from limb—only if he couldn't run.

It happened just as anticipated—almost. The cub whined again, and with another earth-shaking roar, the grizzly charged, huckety-buck, straight at Ham Grease. At the same time, No Shirt, who had raised his rifle, shot his partner's bad leg out from under him. Almost simultaneously, Ham Grease's shotgun blasted away, but he was already falling and completely missed the bear coming at him like a freight train, covering fifty feet a second.

The Kid lowered his rifle in order to fully and gleefully appreciate watching the great bear savage his doomed partner, who was lying, totally vulnerable and unmoving, directly in its path. It all seemed to happen in slow motion, as the bear gained speed and came on, her paws splashing mud and snow like waves from the trail. He could see her eyes, red with rage and the intense desire to destroy what threatened her family.

Then he heard the cub whine for the third time, and, as

the bear passed over Ham Grease without slowing its charge, a horrified realization swept over him—before he could bring the gun back up to his shoulder—before the bear reached him with its lethal claws and knocked him somersaulting backward away from her child. He recalled what the crippled and scarred survivor of such an encounter with *Old Ephraim* had once told him:

"Best thing you kin do is jes lay down and play dead."

Ham Grease had had no trouble playing dead at all . . . thanks to him. The last thing he saw, as the grizzly closed its jaws around his skull and he heard and felt his scalp rip, was a glimpse of the satisfied grin on his partner's face as he sat up to watch and reload the shotgun.

=====

A real-life historical incident is turned into fictional fodder in this story from Alaskan author Sue Henry. Henry's *Murder on the Iditarod Trail* (1991) won both the Anthony and Macavity awards. Her second book, *Termination Dust* (1995), features Alaska State Trooper Alex Jensen.

The Death of
Erik the Redneck

Toni L.P. Kelner

I'd known Erik Husey ever since we were in grammar school, but when I looked at the smoking mess that had been Erik and his dog Lucky, all I could think of was that I never thought he'd be that *dumb*. To go out in a rowboat and set yourself on fire with a cigarette when you're so drunk that you don't even *think* to jump into the water, is just out-and-out stupid.

"Who found him?" I asked Mark Pope, my deputy. We were both standing on the floating platform that served as a dock for Walters Lake, looking down at Erik's body in his boat.

"Wade Spivey. You want to talk to him, or shall I give you the high points?"

"I may as well talk to him myself." I didn't doubt that Mark had all the facts, but sometimes it helps to get the story from the horse's mouth. Before I went over there, I asked, "Did you call the medical examiner?"

"Right after I called you."

"How about Erik's wife?"

He shook his head.

Mark just can't stand breaking the news to the next of kin. It's a good thing it doesn't bother me so much. As the chief of police of Byerly, North Carolina, I can't avoid it. "I'll talk to her later."

I walked down the dock to where Wade was staying out of our way. "Hey, Wade. How're your folks doing?"

"They're fine, Junior."

"Glad to hear it."

"And your folks? How's your daddy liking retirement?"

My daddy was police chief before me, like his daddy had been before him. Which is why I'm named Junior, instead of the kind of name you'd expect for a woman. "He likes it pretty well." With manners attended to, I said, "Mark tells me it was you who found Erik Husey."

"That's right."

"Why don't you tell me about it?"

"Well, I saw his boat on the lake with smoke coming from it this morning."

"What time was that?"

He thought about it. "I slept late this morning so it must have been after ten before I came outside to get the paper."

Knowing Wade, that meant he had been out drinking the night before, but unlike Erik, he had had enough sense to stay off the lake. "And then you saw the smoke?"

"Well, it wasn't much smoke. Just a little curl coming up, like he was smoking a cigarette. Only I couldn't see him over there. I called out a couple of times, and when nobody answered, I got to thinking that something might be wrong, so I went to take a look."

"Was your boat handy?"

"Tied up at the dock like always. It didn't take me no time to go over there, and that's when I saw him."

"Not a pretty sight."

"It sure wasn't," he said, shaking his head. "Anyway, I tied a line to the bow and towed it in. Then I called you folks."

"Any idea of how long he'd been out there?"

"He wasn't there when I left for town yesterday evening, but I don't know about when I got back. It was dark last night, and I don't think I even looked in that direction."

"Didn't hear anything?"

Wade shook his head.

"Good enough. I appreciate you letting us know right away."

"No problem. Y'all want some coffee? I put a pot on right after I called."

"I sure would. Thank you."

Wade went into his trailer, and I went back over to Mark.

"Good thing his boat's aluminum," Mark said. "If it was wood, it would have burnt right through and sunk. There's no telling when we'd have found him."

I nodded, looking inside the boat again. Like I had said to Wade, it wasn't a pretty sight, and it didn't smell too good, either. Erik was lying flat on his back, with a bottle in his right hand. The label had been burned off, but the bottle looked like Rebel Yell whiskey, the cheapest brand I knew of. On his left side was what was left of Lucky, a brown and white mutt who had wagged his tail at everybody he met.

"Lucky must have passed out first," I said, "or he'd have tried to wake up Erik."

"Lucky was probably drunk, too," Mark said.

"Erik gave whiskey to his dog?"

Mark nodded.

"That man was dumber than—" A station wagon drove up before I could finish the insult. "Dr. Connelly's here. Why don't you get the Polaroid from my trunk and take a few pictures before he gets started?" I handed him the keys.

While he left, I took another look at Erik and Lucky. I've seen people dead from gunshots, blunt instruments, and way too many car wrecks. I was pretty sure that this was the first man I had seen die from stupidity.

Which is how I ended the story when I was telling it to my parents that afternoon over Sunday dinner. I suppose most people wouldn't have thought it a fit subject to speak about at the dinner table, but after all the years Daddy was a cop, he and Mama had heard it all.

"That must have been awful for you," Mama said.

"I've seen worse." Smelled worse, too, but not many times.

"But this time it was somebody you knew."

"Mama, I know most of the people who end up dead in Byerly." Byerly isn't that big.

"But Erik was your age. In your grade at school, wasn't he?"

I nodded.

"Doesn't that bother you?"

"It always bothers me when somebody dies in my town."

"That's not what I mean. Andy, you know what I mean, don't you?"

"What your mama means, Junior, is that she's surprised that you're not taking it more personal this time."

I took one last bite of pecan pie. "Can't say as I am, Daddy. I didn't know Erik that well, and I didn't like him much. About the only time he ever spoke to me was to make fun of my name or to complain about speeding tickets."

Mama just sighed and tapped the maple dining room table. "Junior, I swear you haven't got a bit more feeling than this table here. What about Rinda? How did she take it?"

Rinda was Erik's wife. "About as well as you'd expect. She cried a little at first, but then wanted to know what happened. She hadn't been up long enough to worry about where Erik was. Said he'd gone out drinking the night before, and she figured he'd fallen asleep at somebody's house."

"Erik always did drink too much," Daddy said. Despite retirement, he kept up with most people in Byerly. "But I thought he drank at home. Cheaper that way."

"Rinda said he usually did, but they had had a fight."

Mama said, "That's terrible! The last words they spoke were in anger."

"Kind of suspicious, too," I said.

"Junior! It was an accident."

"Probably," I agreed. "She said they weren't fighting about anything important anyway, just about him not taking care of the house when she was out of town last week.

She just got back from going to her father's funeral in Tennessee."

Mama said, "I heard about that. She hopped right onto a bus when she heard how bad off he was, but missed being able to say good-bye to him by an hour. It really hit her hard." She shook her head. "First her daddy, and now her husband. Junior, I've got a big dish of chicken and dumplings that I was going to freeze for later this week, but I want you to take it over to Rinda."

"Mama, I'm the police chief. I can't be taking food over every time somebody gets killed in an accident."

"I don't see why not. Especially when it's somebody you've known your whole life."

I looked at Daddy, hoping he'd be on my side, but he said, "I don't think it would hurt anything, Junior." Then he winked. "Besides, she might confess."

"Andy!"

So on Sunday afternoon, when I should have been cleaning up my apartment or doing nothing at all, I drove back to the lake and Rinda Husey's house. There were extra cars in the driveway, meaning that Rinda had company, so I wouldn't have to stay any longer than it would take to drop off the chicken and dumplings. At least, that's what I thought.

It wasn't Rinda who came to the door, it was Erik's aunt Mavis.

"Afternoon, Miz Dermott. My mama wanted me to bring this over for Rinda." I held out the dish, but she didn't take it from me.

Instead she called out, "Mary Maude, did you call Junior?"

My mama tells me that Mavis Dermott and Mary Maude Foy had always had dark hair, but now they dye it solid black, without the first highlight to make it look real. Both wear face makeup so thick that it could be a mask, especially the way it ends right under their chins. Mavis is a widow, and since Mary Maude's husband is an invalid who never leaves the house, she might as well be one, too.

"No, I didn't call her, but I'm glad she's here," Mary

Maude said. "Junior, I want you to tell Rinda that it's not legal for her keep things that Erik inherited from his mama. Those things ought to come to me and Mavis."

Now I had to go inside. "Hello, Rinda," I said, ignoring Mary Maude for the time being. "My mama sent this for you."

Rinda looked a lot more tired than she had before, but with Mary Maude and Mavis pestering her, I wasn't surprised. She had been blond and vaguely pretty when she and Erik started dating in high school, but between the marriage, a few extra pounds, and what she had been through, she didn't look pretty anymore. Even her blond hair had grown out so that the dark roots were showing.

"Thank you, Junior." She took the dish from me and went out into the kitchen.

"Miz Foy, did Erik have a will?" I said.

"Of course not, him being so young. But I know he'd have wanted those things to come to me and Mavis."

"With no will, his property belongs to Rinda, and she can do with it as she sees fit."

"But it's not right," Mary Maude insisted.

"That's the law."

She muttered under her breath about law and police.

Mavis said, "Didn't I tell you that, sister?" To me, she added, "She didn't pay a bit more mind than the man in the moon. It's just a shame, that's all. Those things have been in our family for three generations."

I wanted to ask what things they were so worried about, but it didn't really matter and Rinda came back in then.

"Junior, do you know when I'll be able to claim Erik's body?" she asked.

"Dr. Connelly said he'd get to it just as quick as he could."

Mary Maude said, "That's another thing. Why can't we bring Erik home now? You've got no business cutting into him."

I guess Rinda had heard it before, because she didn't even wince. I said, "I'm sorry, Miz Foy, but when a man is found dead under—" I started to say "suspicious," but changed it to keep from riling her up further. "Under unusual circumstances, there has to be an autopsy."

This gave Mary Maude a chance to mutter some more, and Mavis a chance to say, "Didn't I tell you that, sister? They'll fix him up for the funeral. Isn't that right, Junior?"

I hesitated on this one. Usually Connelly does keep an autopsy as neat as he can, but in this case, the body had been pretty messy to start with.

Rinda came to my rescue. "He was burned to death. There's nothing an undertaker can do with that."

Just for a second, the aunts were struck silent. Then Mavis said, "Lord almighty, Rinda, I didn't know you were so hard. Don't you have any feelings?"

That sounded darned close to what my mother had said to me, so I felt like I should defend Rinda. "She's right, ma'am. You wouldn't want to see him the way he is."

Both Mary Maude and Mavis started bawling then, and I was impressed by the way their makeup repelled the tears. Rinda tossed a box of tissues at them, then walked me to the door. "Thank your mama for me, Junior."

"I will. Are you going to be all right with them two?"

"They'll quit as soon as they realize they don't have an audience." She didn't sound hard to me, just realistic.

I was just getting into the car when Mark called me on the radio. So much for the rest of my day off. "This is Junior."

"Junior, Dr. Connelly wants you to call him."

"Let me get to a phone." Mark gave me the number, and I started up the car. I could have gone back inside to use Rinda's phone, but I wanted to stay as far away from that house as I could. Besides, the only case Connelly was looking at was Erik's, and I wasn't about to discuss it in front of his family.

There was a filling station with a pay phone a mile down the road, so I pulled in there to call. "Dr. Connelly? This is Junior."

"Junior, I found something that might interest you."

"What's that?"

"When I examined Lucky's body—"

"Don't you mean Erik's body?"

"No, I mean Lucky's."

"You autopsied the dog?"

"I thought it would be interesting. I dissected cats and pigs in school, but never performed a postmortem on a dog. That was all right, wasn't it?"

Different strokes for different folks, as Daddy says. "I don't see why not. What did you find?"

"A couple of things. First off, that dog's lungs were clear as a bell."

"Meaning what?" I asked, though I thought I knew the answer.

"Meaning that that dog never inhaled smoke from any fire."

"Which means that Lucky was dead before the fire started?"

"That would be my opinion."

"Then what killed him?"

"There's some fluid in the stomach, and it looks like antifreeze. You know dogs love the taste of antifreeze, even if it is toxic."

I ran through a few possibilities in my head. First, maybe Erik accidentally left antifreeze out where Lucky could get it, and burned himself to death in a fit of remorse. Or maybe it was some sort of dog murder/suicide pact. Or maybe it was just plain old everyday murder. It seemed to me that the last idea was the most likely.

"You said a couple of things?"

"This may not be important, but Lucky had been operated on in the past few weeks. He had a scar in the stomach area, healing nicely. Clearly done by a professional."

I didn't see how that mattered, but you never know. "What about Erik? How did he die?"

"I was just getting ready to start on his autopsy, but I thought you'd want to hear about the dog immediately."

"You thought right. Let me know what you find out about Erik." I hung up the phone and got back in the car to radio Mark and tell him what Dr. Connelly had told me. "I guess you know what I want you to do."

He's not got much imagination, so he had to think about

it. "Go talk to everybody living near the lake and see if they saw anything?"

"That's right."

"I'm on the way. How about you?"

"I'm going to see Wade Spivey again."

Actually, it wasn't Wade I wanted to see so much as it was his boat, but I thought I better check with him before I went sniffing around. He was watching a football game when I knocked, but invited me in anyway.

"Hey, Junior. Anything wrong?"

"A couple of odd things have shown up in the Husey case. You mind if I ask a couple more questions?"

"Not at all. You want a Coca-Cola?"

"No, thank you." Drinking coffee with someone who found an accident victim was one thing. Drinking a Coke with the first man on the scene of a murder was something else. "Did you know Erik well?"

"Just enough to speak to."

"But he docked his boat right next to yours."

"Only because he bought the boat from Ralph Stewart. Ralph had always kept it there, so I said Erik could just keep on leaving it there."

"So y'all never went fishing together?"

"Erik wasn't a real fisherman. He'd throw out a few lines, but mainly he just went out there to be by himself."

"Did you ever know anybody to go out on the lake with him?"

"Just his dog. I shouldn't say this after what happened to him, but I used to think Erik would only bring Lucky because of him being so tight-fisted. He'd have had to share his Rebel Yell with a human being."

"He was a careful man with his money," I said, but knowing how Wade drank, I couldn't blame Erik for not wanting to share. "But didn't he give whiskey to Lucky?"

"He used to," Wade said, "but the vet put a stop to it. She told him that Lucky was going to die from cirrhosis of the liver if he didn't stop. And Erik thought the world of that dog."

I was glad to hear that Erik had had some sense after all.

Though Lucky would have been better off with the whiskey than the antifreeze. "Now you leave your boat out there at the dock so anybody could come use it if they wanted to."

"I suppose so. Do you think somebody did?"

"I don't know. Do you mind if I have a look at it?"

"Not at all. You want me to come with you?"

"No, you watch your football game. I've messed up enough of your day."

I knew darned well he was going to be watching me through the window instead of the game, but I wanted to look around on my own.

Wade's boat wasn't much of a much. It had a motor, and enough room in it for two or three people. Maybe more, if one of them was dead. I squatted on the dock, looking down into the boat. No blood, but there was some light-colored hair or fur caught on the bench. Wade's hair was brown, but Erik's had been dirty blond and Lucky's brown and white.

I had some evidence bags in my pocket, so I put the hair into one of them. I thought about dusting for prints, but decided it wasn't worth the effort. Wade's boat was made of wood, not the best surface for prints, and everybody knows to wear gloves these days.

I gave the boat another look, this time getting in and looking under things, but didn't find anything more incriminating than a package of fish hooks, so I went back to my car. Wade was trying to hide behind a curtain, so I pretended not to see him.

I radioed Mark, getting him as he was driving to the next person on his circuit of the lake. I told him I'd start on the other direction, and we'd meet in the middle.

Neither of us got anything. Walters Lake isn't that big or that scenic, and not many people live right on the water. Wade's place was the closest, and Erik's own house the next after that. Nobody saw or heard anything.

There was another dock on the other side, but the only boat there was leaky and I don't think even a murderer would take a chance on taking it out at night.

"So what have we got?" Mark asked when we met.

It seemed right obvious to me, but Mark likes to have things spelled out. "It looks like somebody brought the bodies out here, arranged them in Erik's boat, used Wade's boat to tow Erik's boat out to the middle of the lake, set it on fire, then left Wade's boat where he found it."

"Had to be a local to know where the boat was, and that Wade wouldn't be home."

"I don't think Erik had many enemies from out of town. Or Lucky either." I looked at him sidewise to see if he had noticed he was being made fun of. He hadn't. "But I want to talk to Dr. Connelly before I do anything else. Why don't you head back to the station, and I'll call and see if he's finished with Erik's autopsy." I found another pay phone, reminding myself to ask the city council for a couple of cellular phones in the next year's budget.

I guess he wasn't done yet, because it took a while for him to answer the phone, and when he did, he said, "Dr. Connelly," in a tone of voice that meant I had interrupted him.

I decided not to ask about the autopsy right off. "Dr. Connelly, this is Junior. I've got a sample of hair or fur I found in Wade Spivey's boat. Can you tell me if it matches either Erik or his dog?"

This must have interested him, because he sounded less cranky when he spoke again. "I'm not sure. I can tell if it's human or canine, and if it's human, I can tell you if it matches Husey. But I don't know if I can get a positive identification on a dog. I'd have to do some research."

"Should I run the sample up to you?" Byerly didn't have its own coroner. Connelly served the whole county, and he was a good thirty minutes away.

"It's getting late. Why don't you call the vet in town. He can tell you if it's dog or not, and maybe he knows if you can ID canine hair."

"I'll do that." Now to butter him up. "Do you think you'll have the autopsy on Husey done by the first part of the week?"

"First part of the week?" he said, sounding pleased with himself. "I should have preliminary results this evening."

I whistled in appreciation, some of it sincere. "That's fast work." If I had asked him to have it done that night, he'd have fussed. "Will you call the station when you're done?"

"Of course."

I hung up the phone, grinning a little. And Mama said I didn't have feelings. Of course, I had to admit, I hadn't treated Dr. Connelly like that to make him feel better so much as to get what I wanted.

I was out of quarters, so I drove on over to the veterinarian's place. Josie Gilpin, who insisted everybody call her Dr. Josie, was an older woman with no family who spent most of her weekends tending to animals who were too sick to go home. I didn't think she'd mind a little company, and from her smile when she opened her door, I was right.

"What can I do for you, Junior? You didn't find another dog hit by a car, did you?"

"Not this time. I was wondering if you could take a look at a sample of hair I've got and tell me what it came from."

"I'll take a look. Come on in." She led me through a room where the floor was strewn with dog toys and the furniture covered with dogs. They were well-trained and didn't even bark as we walked through and down a hall to where Dr. Josie had a lab set up, complete with microscope, test tubes, and such.

"What animal do you think it came from?" she asked.

"Either human or dog," I said, handing her the evidence bag. "I want to see if it came from Erik Husey or his dog Lucky."

"I heard about them two," she said, which didn't surprise me. News travels fast in Byerly. "Erik should have had more sense, risking Lucky's life like that."

Dr. Josie is partial to animals, and I guess that's why she lives alone. She used tweezers to pull part of the fur out and put it on a slide. Then she turned on the microscope, put in the slide, and peered at it.

"Lucky had been operated on recently," I said. "Was that your work?"

"Sure was. Erik brought Lucky in a few weeks ago, said he was acting puny, not eating."

"Was it from the drinking?"

"Did you know about that? You know, Junior, there are laws about mistreating animals."

I held up both hands in surrender. "I only heard about it this morning, or I'd have said something to him. Anyway, I hear you did a good job of laying down the law to Erik yourself."

"You bet I did. But it wasn't the whiskey that made Lucky sick. He had a blockage in his intestines. I had to operate."

"Is that how you found out about the drinking, when you had him cut open?"

She was still peering, so I couldn't see her grin, but I could tell that she was. "As a matter of fact, I didn't see the first sign of it. It's just that I had heard that Erik was giving that dog whiskey, and knew if I scared him, he'd stop."

For an animal doctor, she was pretty smart about people. Then I said, "I'm surprised Erik paid for an operation like that, him being so close with his money."

"He didn't even argue with me. Paid half up front, and the rest in payments. He may have been cheap, but not when it came to Lucky." She pulled the slide out of the microscope. "Well, it's not dog, cat, horse, or squirrel."

"Human?"

Dr. Josie shrugged, no longer caring, and handed me the evidence bag. "Probably."

"I appreciate your looking at it for me." She showed me out past the dogs, and I went to the station to see if Dr. Connelly had called.

He had, and what he had told Mark caught me by surprise. Erik really *had* died in the fire. Only thing was, he had been hit in the head beforehand, hard enough to knock him out. Dr. Connelly said that he might not have lived even without the fire.

"What do you think?" Mark said after he made his report, letting me draw any conclusions there were to be drawn.

"I might convince myself that Erik got so drunk that he fell and hit himself on an oar or something. The fire could have wiped out any trace of that. But there's two things that bother me."

"What two things?"

"One, Lucky already being dead. And two, the hair I found in Wade's boat."

"So how do you make it out?"

I sighed, wishing he could put one and one together without my help. "Somebody killed him."

He nodded like I had confirmed something rather than giving him the whole idea. "Who do you think it was?"

"We'll start with the obvious suspects. Rinda, of course." The spouse is always the first one you look at. "She said they had a fight Saturday night."

"Would she have told you that if she killed him?"

"Maybe she thought the neighbors heard yelling. And I want to look at those aunts of his. They were fussing about something they wanted and how Rinda wasn't going to let them have it. Maybe it's valuable. And I guess I have to consider Wade Spivey. It wouldn't be the first time that the killer was the one to 'find' a body."

The only other person I could think of was Dr. Josie, and I didn't think even she'd burn a man alive for giving whiskey to a dog. And she'd never have hurt Lucky.

I looked at the clock. "It's too late to start anything now. I'll see you tomorrow." Mark frequently slept at the station, one ear listening for the phone. I did it too, when I had to, but preferred my own apartment.

I guess Mama would have been put out if she had known how I slept, knowing a man had been murdered in Byerly, but I slept like a baby. Not even a bad dream.

Dr. Connelly had told Mark he had a couple of early appointments and I should wait until eleven or so before calling. So I spent the morning making phone calls.

First I called Erik's insurance agent. There's only two agents in town, and I guessed the right one the first time. He was the cheaper of the two, and of course, Erik's life insurance had been the cheapest available. There was just enough money to bury Erik if Rinda didn't mind a pine box.

Then I called Mary Maude Foy to find out just what it was that Rinda was keeping from her and Mavis. I made it sound like I was seriously investigating their claim, and she was mad enough at Rinda to believe it. The thing was, it turned out to be nothing more than a double bed, a dresser, and a chest of drawers. Mary Maude and Mavis were strange, but I didn't think they'd kill their own nephew for a bedroom set. I did make a note to ask Rinda if that's all they were asking for, and to call Maggie Burnette, a dealer at the local flea market who could tell me if the pieces were worth anything.

Then I headed for Dr. Connelly's with the sample of hair. Other than the drive, the visit didn't take long. Dr. Josie had already told me that it wasn't Lucky's fur; it turned out that it wasn't Erik's hair either. Which I should have known, since Erik and the dog had been in Erik's boat, not Wade's. Dr. Connelly showed me something that told me who it was in that boat.

Now I knew who, but I spent the drive back to Byerly trying to figure out why. Mama had said that I didn't have any feelings, but the person who killed Erik must have had feelings, strong ones. To burn a man to death would take an awful lot of feeling. Not to mention killing his dog. It took me most of the drive to figure out just why the killer had hated Erik that much.

I radioed Mark as I got into Byerly so he could make a phone call for me, and had just got out to the circle of houses around the lake when he called me with the answer I needed. Then I told him to come out there and meet me, just in case there was trouble.

There was only one car in the driveway at Rinda's house this time, and she answered the door herself. "Hey, Junior," she said. "What can I do for you?"

"I wanted to let you know that the doctor's finished Erik's autopsy," I said. "He'll be able to release the body today."

"I'll be glad to get the funeral taken care of."

"I know you will be," I said. "One thing I wanted to ask you. How did you find out about the vet bill?"

Her face turned white as a sheet, much whiter than her hair. "The vet bill?"

Her reaction was enough for me. "Rinda, I have to arrest you for the murder of Erik Husey. Before I go any further, let me read you your rights." I did so, put the cuffs on her, and walked her out to my squad car just as Mark showed up to escort us to the station.

"She killed him over a vet bill?" Mama asked that night

over dinner. We don't eat together every night, but I knew Daddy would want to hear the whole story. Mama, too, even if she wouldn't admit it.

I said, "It wasn't just the money. Rinda said she had always known that Erik was cheap, and she accepted that. So when her daddy was dying and he said they couldn't afford for her to fly to Tennessee, she didn't argue. You know she only missed being able to say good-bye to him by an hour—she'd have made it if she had taken a plane. Then when she got back, she found the last vet bill, and it showed how much Erik had paid for Lucky's operation."

"So she killed the dog to keep him from barking while she killed Erik for revenge," Daddy said.

"Nope. Rinda said she never intended to kill Erik, and I believe her. She just wanted to kill Lucky. She left a bowl of antifreeze out for him that morning. Only he didn't die right away like she thought he would. Dr. Josie says that it takes twelve to twenty-four hours for a dog to die from antifreeze poisoning. Rinda watched that dog all day long, waiting for him to die."

Mama shivered a little, and I didn't blame her.

I went on. "The later it got, the more desperate Rinda got, so she finally gave him some more and that did it. She was meaning to put the bowl away before Erik got home, but he left work early. When he found Lucky dead next to the bowl, he knew Rinda had done it on purpose."

"So he came after her and she was only defending herself," Daddy said.

"Yes and no. He was carrying on pretty bad, and said he was going to kill her. When he took a swing at her, she picked up a skillet and hit him."

"Cast iron?" Mama asked.

I nodded.

"So she thought he was dead when she burned him," Mama said.

"No, she knew he was still breathing. She wanted him dead."

Daddy said, "Did she think he'd come after her again when he woke up?"

"I asked her that, but she said she wasn't a bit scared. She was mad. Mad about not being able to say good-bye to her daddy, and mad about him spending money on a dog, and maddest of all about him wanting to kill her over that dog. She was determined to kill him. Now she thought that if she burned him, we wouldn't be able to tell he'd been hit in the head. First she was going to put him in the car and run it off the road, but she wasn't sure it would catch fire. Besides, she said, it was the only car they had. The boat she didn't care about, so she put Erik and Lucky in a wheelbarrow and pushed them over to the lake. She knew Wade would be out drinking, so she borrowed his boat to tow with. She wasn't sure how she caught her hair on the boat." I had known it was hers as soon as Dr. Connelly told me the sample was bleached blond. "She used whiskey to start the fire, actually stayed and watched. Said she had to make sure he didn't wake up." It made me right sick to my stomach to think about it. "And you said *I* don't have any feelings."

"I didn't mean that, Junior, and you know it," Mama said. "I just don't want you to forget that it's people you're working with, not cases."

I nodded. She just might have a point.

"What happens now?" Mama asked.

"I think Rinda will plead guilty, but even if she doesn't, it should be open and shut," I said.

"What about Erik's funeral?"

"His aunts are going to take care of it. Spending their own money to do it, too, because Rinda won't let them have the insurance money. Maybe they aren't so bad after all. And they'll get that bedroom set."

"All over but the paperwork," Daddy said. "Nice work, Junior."

"One other thing," Mama said. "You said Rinda didn't resist arrest. So how did you get that dirt on your uniform?"

I looked down at the dark patches on my knees. "Well, Dr. Connelly called and said the funeral home had come after Erik, but he didn't know what to do with Lucky. Rinda said we could throw him on the trash heap for all she cared, but I just couldn't see it. So I took him over to Dr. Josie's place and buried him there. She's got a little cemetery for dogs and cats."

Darned if Mama didn't tear up. "That's the sweetest thing I've ever heard. And I said you didn't have any feelings."

With her crying, I knew I had feelings all right, but what I felt most was embarrassed.

———

Temporary Yankee Toni L.P. Kelner returns to her southern roots in this story which involves an incinerated dog and series protagonist Laura Fleming, chief of police in Byerly, North Carolina. Fleming appears in *Down Home Murder*, *Dead Ringer*, and *Trouble Looking for a Place to Happen*.

The Bun Also Rises

Jill Churchill

"Violet Fasbinder is dead? Oh, no. I'm so sorry to hear that," Jane Jeffry exclaimed. "I just visited her a week ago and she was doing so well."

Jane and her next door neighbor and best friend, Shelley Nowack, were in Jane's kitchen. Shelley had just arrived and was divesting herself of packages, purse, coat, and gloves while Jane unloaded the dishwasher. Once finished, she poured them each a cup of coffee and sat down.

"You've cut your own hair again, haven't you?" Shelley said.

"Just a little trim. Why? Does it look like the dog's been chewing on it?"

"The dog—or a madman with hedge clippers."

"Shelley, what happened to Violet? I thought her broken hip was healing so nicely."

"It was, but it was a stroke that killed her. Or rather, a couple of strokes. One last evening that was pretty severe. She went to the hospital, but had another overnight that killed her."

"What about her daughter Marie? She couldn't have

suspected Violet's health was so poor or she wouldn't have left her. They were very close."

"I keep forgetting that you don't know Marie well. She knew Violet was in very fragile health, but she had to leave because her daughter—Marie's daughter, that is—was at the end of a dangerous pregnancy. Twins. Toxemia. And something else. Breech maybe. Anyway, Marie got that second cousin, that Betsy person, to come stay with Violet so Marie could go see the daughter through the last week of the pregnancy."

Jane shuddered. "Betsy Ballantine, her name is. Loathsome woman."

"Oh? What's wrong with her?"

"She's a smarmy bitch, that's what," Jane said.

"Is this another of your irrational dislikes?"

"Shelley, you make me sound like a curmudgeon. I don't have irrational dislikes, only insightful ones."

"Yes, like that man you thought was stalking you in the grocery store."

"All that twit had to do was say I'd accidentally taken his cart!" Jane objected.

"What is it you dislike about the Ballantine woman?"

"She's a nurse, you know, one of those nurses who talks about how 'We' are feeling today in the most patronizing way. As if Violet was some kind of idiot child. When I visited, the Ballantine woman hung around monopolizing the conversation. Going on about how We were getting our appetite back a wee bit and wasn't it nice that We were using our time to be so kind to neighbors and We couldn't visit long because We tired so easily."

Shelley cringed. "That *is* pretty hard to take."

"Poor Violet just kept looking at her with a look of dumb misery, but what could she do? The woman was a relative and was helping out in a crisis. It couldn't have been easy caring for Violet in that cast and the traction setup. Violet's bed looked like a homemade helicopter. Violet probably should have been in a nursing home while her daughter Marie was gone, except that it meant so much to her to be at her own house."

Shelley nodded. "Violet could certainly have afforded the

best. Her husband once owned most of the land around here, and made a killing when he sold it off."

"Speaking of Marie, is she back yet? Does she know about her mother yet?" Jane asked.

"That's why I came by. I offered to pick her up at the airport, and wondered if you'd ride along."

Jane was surprised at what a cold reception she got from Marie. They didn't know each other well, but had always gotten along pleasantly enough.

"You remember my friend Jane Jeffry, don't you, Marie," Shelley said as she put Marie's suitcase into the back of her van. "She worked with your mother when the church put together that membership roster with all the family pictures."

"Yes, of course," Marie said, not meeting Jane's gaze as she climbed into the van.

Shelley gave Jane a questioning look, which Jane answered with a shrug. She got into the backseat behind Shelley and said, "Marie, I'm terribly sorry about your mother's death. If there's anything I can do—"

"I think you've done quite enough, thank you," Marie said.

They were silent while Shelley maneuvered them out of the parking lot and onto the highway. Jane was stunned by the chill in Marie's tone, but told herself the woman must be in shock. She had, after all, lost her mother only hours earlier. As Jane recalled, Marie had been widowed at a young age, left with a small daughter and no means of support. An only child herself, she had moved in with her mother, who had also been recently widowed. It was a rare thing for three women to share a home with such unusual accord. Everyone who knew them commented on it, some with envy, others with shades of disbelief.

As they drove toward the Chicago suburb where they all lived, Shelley said, "We'll have you home in a few minutes. We'll see then what needs to be done first. I'd be glad to do any shopping or—"

"Shelley, I'm not going to Mother's house. I'm staying in a hotel," Marie said.

"Why is that?" Jane asked.

Marie turned and finally looked straight at her. "As if you don't know!" she exclaimed angrily.

Shelley, normally the most polite of people, regarded driving as personal combat. At these words, she suddenly crossed three lanes, leaving half a dozen motorists gasping, honking, and swearing, as she nipped onto an exit ramp with the speed and agility of a motorized chipmunk. Her passengers were transfixed with horror as she took a sharp left at the bottom of the ramp and wheeled the van into a parking space at a fast food restaurant. She turned off the engine and said, "Marie, we're not leaving here until you tell us exactly what's wrong. I know you're upset about your mother, and I understand, but there's no reason to be rude to Jane. First, why aren't you going home?"

Abruptly, Marie put her face in her hands and sobbed silently. Only a few little mouselike squeaks escaped. Shelley reached across, opened the glove box and handed Marie a small packet of tissues. Marie finally pulled herself together, blew her nose, took a deep breath and said, "I have no home. Mother has left everything to Betsy Ballantine."

"What? No! I can't believe it!" Shelley exclaimed.

"Neither could I, but I spoke to our lawyer, Fred Stonecipher, this morning. Mother wrote a new will last week. She left everything, including the house, to Betsy."

Shelley shook her head, still not willing to believe what she was hearing. "But why are you angry with Jane about it?"

"Because she knew."

"I knew?" Jane exclaimed. "How in the world would *I* know such a thing?"

"You witnessed the will."

"I what? I never—oh. Oh! Was it a will? I had no idea. I just thought it was some kind of business thing—"

"I can't make sense out of what either of you are saying," Shelley said. "Let's go in and sit down over some coffee and sort this out."

They were barely seated when Shelley fixed Jane with a prosecuting attorney glare and said, "Okay, start from the beginning."

Jane stirred some sugar into her coffee and said, "Violet and I worked on that roster thing together. It involved a lot of phoning, which we did at the church because they had three lines and we could consult with each other and update our lists as we went along."

"Jane, I didn't mean to start *that* far back! Is this relevant?"

"Yes! Every time we met, Violet would bring along a box of those raisin rolls of hers. It was a bribe to get us to work. I guess I carried on with disgusting greed about the rolls because last week I got a phone call from Betsy Ballantine. She said she was calling for Violet, who couldn't reach the phone, what with being in traction. She said Violet wanted me to stop by because she'd written up her recipe for the raisin rolls for me."

"Mother gave you her recipe?" Marie said. "She never even gave *me* that recipe. She used to joke that it would be part of my inheritance." She got teary again, and this time Shelley produced a little box of tissues from her purse. Jane wondered how many more of them Shelley had secreted about her person, but felt this wasn't the time to ask.

"Go on, Jane," Shelley said briskly.

Jane had been surprised, too, at the offer of the recipe. When she had asked for it months before, Violet had been coy, but firm. It was an old family recipe, she said, brought over from Bavaria when they came to this country at the end of World War I. Violet herself had been a little girl at the time, and the raisin rolls, she told Jane, were the first thing her mother had ever let her make all by herself. And it was quite an honor to be trusted with the precious ingredients. All during the war there had been no raisins; sometimes even flour had been a luxury.

When Jane got to Violet's house, she met Betsy Ballantine for the first time. "You must be Mrs. Jeffry," Betsy said. "It's so good of you to call on Aunt Violet. We'd gotten ourselves into quite a little fuss about the recipe."

It took Jane a moment to realize Betsy meant Violet, not both of them. She cringed mentally. Nurses who called patients "we" were such a stereotype, and Jane hated to see anyone live up to unpleasant images. She followed Betsy up the stairs, wondering vaguely why the woman was togged out in full nurse regalia for home care of a relative. Betsy was a big woman and her crisp, white uniform spoke of lots of ironing and starch. Her shoes were white and sturdy, but Jane noticed they were much worn, had been resoled, and there was even a darn in her stocking. Having come of age about the time panty hose were invented, Jane had only the dimmest recollection of hose that were worth darning.

"Auntie Violet, our guest is here," Betsy trilled as she tapped on the master bedroom door before flinging it open.

"Oh, do come in, Jane dear," Violet responded weakly. Though she had spent nearly three quarters of a century in this country, Violet still had a trace of her German accent. Just a little blurring of *v* and *w* and a slight shifting of vowels. Jane had always felt Violet's voice was perfect for the telling of fairy tales.

But Jane had been shocked when she saw Violet. She was strung up in a hospital bed that looked like a torture device. There were weights, pulley, ropes, and a huge plaster leg cast. Poor, elderly Violet, small and fragile at best, looked like a wounded bird. "Violet, I'd give you a hug and a kiss except I'm afraid I'd fall in there and hurt you trying to thrash my way back out," Jane said, trying to make a joke of it.

Before Violet could answer, Betsy said, "We wouldn't want that. We need to keep perfectly still so our bones will knit properly." As she spoke, she pushed an armchair up to one side of the bed for Jane and moved a straight chair close to the other side for herself.

"Betsy, you don't have to stay," Violet said. "I'm sure Jane could get me anything I need."

"How sweet of you, Auntie Violet, but we mustn't ask visitors to fetch and carry for us." She sat down in the straight chair, folded her substantial arms and smiled at Jane.

Violet stared at her for a moment, then said, "Jane, it's good of you to come see me. I do miss being out."

"Oh, we wouldn't want to be out in weather like this, would we?" Betsy said.

"Some of *us* might," Jane said tartly.

Betsy only smiled in a bland and vaguely superior way at this.

"Violet, I got a call from a new member of the church just yesterday. She'd gotten a copy of the photo roster when she joined and called to tell me what a wonderful thing it was. She commented especially on the quality of the photographs. I told her the photographer was your choice, and she asked me to tell you that you chose well."

She had guessed right that even Betsy, as practiced as she was at butting into conversations, would have nothing to contribute to this. Violet talked about the roster project, the relative merits of the photographers who'd been considered, and the printers who'd submitted bids. Jane wasn't interested in rehashing it all, but listened politely because Violet was enjoying herself, and wonder of wonders, Betsy had become so bored she picked up a magazine and started reading without any pretense of taking part in the conversation.

As Violet talked, Jane became aware of the sound of a vacuum cleaner elsewhere in the house. The humming came closer and finally there was a tap on the door. "Could I do in here now? Oh, I'm sorry. I didn't know you had company," a thin young woman in jeans and a T-shirt said.

"That's quite all right, Sarah," Betsy said. "In fact, since you and Mrs. Jeffry are both here, you might do us a little favor. We have a document we need to sign, and you could be witnesses." She took a folder from the dressing table and removed some papers. She rolled a wheeled hospital table to the bed, set it at a slight tilt, and handed Violet a ballpoint pen. "Here we are. On the line with the X, Auntie."

Violet signed, then Betsy whisked the table and document away. "Now, if you two would just sign below as witnesses to the signature . . ."

It was done and the document was tucked back into its folder in a matter of seconds. "Now, Sarah, if you'd like to take your lunch break, I'm sure Mrs. Jeffry won't be staying much longer and tiring us. Then you can do this room."

Jane was annoyed at Betsy's rudeness, not to mention her

precious speech pattern, but as she glanced back at Violet, she decided perhaps Betsy was right. Violet was looking pale and a little frazzled. She was feeling around in the bed for something she had lost. Though she couldn't reach the bedside table, she did have a few things laid about on the covers: some crossword puzzle magazines, a couple mechanical pencils, a pad of notepaper, and, of course, her Bible.

Jane smiled. She'd literally never seen Violet without her Bible. It was a fine old Bible with tissue-thin pages and a soft purple leather cover. It was, as always, bristling with scraps of paper, religious tracts and newspaper clippings. Even a few stems of flowers she'd pressed into it stuck out from between the pages. It was like a traveling scrapbook. Jane had once taken Violet shopping, and Violet had removed from the ubiquitous Bible a sample of yarn she was trying to match. Violet opened the Bible carefully so that none of the yellowed obituaries, dried ferns, or lace scraps fell out, and removed a thin, pink sheet of paper. "Here's that recipe you wanted, Jane dear."

Jane reached, but Betsy got it first. She all but snatched it out of Violet's hand. "Let's put this in a nice envelope, shall we?" she said, glancing at the paper. "Oh, my. Such pretty handwriting we have."

". . . and that was it," Jane concluded. "She put it in an envelope, I told Violet good-bye and left. That was the last time I saw or spoke to your mother, Marie. I had no idea that was a will. I just thought it was one of the dozens of documents we all have to sort through all the time. Renewing a CD or something."

"But Jane, you don't have to have witnesses to your signature to renew a CD," Shelley said.

"No, but then I sign things like that right at the bank. I suppose if I thought about it at all, I assumed it needed witnesses because it was being done at home."

Marie finally spoke. "So you didn't read it?"

"No, of course not!"

"I'm sorry. I'm just so stunned by the whole thing."

"Marie, tell us what Fred Stonecipher said about all this. Did he draw up the will? Why didn't he do something about this absurd change?"

Marie sighed. "He caught me as I was literally running out the door to catch my plane, so I don't know much. He drew up the previous will, and this one, he says, is exactly the same except that Betsy's name is substituted for mine. He said that Betsy called his office practically at dawn this morning saying she had something important to discuss. So important it couldn't wait. So he ran over to the house on his way to the office and she showed him this new will. She said Mother had insisted that she type it up. Betsy claimed to be very upset about it, said she didn't feel she deserved it, that she was only doing what any loving relative would have done under the circumstances, but that Mother was so grateful for her help that she insisted on changing her will."

Shelley mumbled something that Jane translated as, "What a load of crap!"

Marie nodded. "I don't know what to do."

"Well, the first thing to do is to have a serious talk with Fred Stonecipher. I'll take you straight to his office," Shelley said. "And we'll wait for you."

There was an elaborate atrium in the lobby of the professional building where the attorney had his office. Jane and Shelley sat on a bench in a corner where they couldn't be overheard and considered the situation.

"Violet must have lost her mind," Shelley said.

"I wish that were true, but she was as sharp as a tack," Jane said. "She remembered every tedious detail about that roster. Who the printers and photographers were that she consulted. What weight paper she'd decided on. Her memory certainly hadn't gone."

"But she simply wouldn't have done such a thing. I still can't believe it. I'll bet Violet had no idea what she was signing. It had to have been a trick."

Jane shook her head again. "Afraid not. I didn't look at the document I signed, but Violet did. At least, she flipped through the pages. How could I have been so stupid and not realized what it was!"

"Jane, it wouldn't have mattered if you'd known it was a will. You couldn't have demanded to read it to pass approval. And if you'd refused to witness it, Betsy would've found someone else to do it. The man who mows the lawn or the mail carrier or someone. It's not your fault."

"I know. But I'm sure Violet didn't want to leave everything to that patronizing bitch. She had to have been tricked or coerced."

"I agree, but how would you ever prove it?"

When Marie returned from the attorney's office a few minutes later, she echoed much of what they'd discussed. "Fred says he's certain this was not Mother's intention."

"So what's he going to do about it?"

Marie started sniffling again. "He said there's almost nothing we can do. He knows Mother was of sound mind. We all know that. We'll file a protest, of course. But without any grounds except that it wasn't like her, he doesn't hold out much hope. It's not the money," she said, her voice cracking. "Although the money is important. It's that I *know* this isn't what Mother wanted. It's just wrong! Mother loved me. And my daughter."

"You're coming home with me, Marie," Shelley said. "I'm not leaving you at some hotel. You need some rest."

Marie made a token protest, which Shelley squelched. When they were back in the van, heading for Shelley's house, Marie said, "Jane, you said Mother gave you her raisin roll recipe? Could I have a copy? It would mean so much to me."

"Of course. In fact, I have it in my purse."

Shelley stopped at a grocery store and Jane ran in to make a photocopy. She came out and gave the original to Marie. "You should have this."

"Oh, look! It's so—so 'Mother,'" Marie said.

The recipe, in Violet's delicate, frilly handwriting was typical of her. Jane could almost hear the faint German accent in the old-fashioned phrasing:

Find a good heavy cookie sheet
(or a large iron skillet) and heat in
real hot oven. Then turn oven to medium.

Combine 4 cups flour, 1 sugar, one fist-size butter
   lump.
(Even more, if you want.)
Don't mix too much. Leave some lumps.
Take three brown eggs and mix in copper bowl.
Over cold water, beat until fluffy. Add cup milk.
Stir into flour and sugar mixture.
(If too thick, do not worry.)
Grind a cup of raisins and skin of one ripe navel
   orange.
Whip into mix, one spoon at a time.
In buttered hands, make rolls and put on hot cookie
   sheet.
Let sit one hour, then cook in medium oven until
   brown.
Let get half cooled, then drizzle orange icing.

                                        Isaiah 59:17

"I never could make her understand that you need to lay
out a recipe with all the ingredients first, in actual measure-
ments," Marie said. "She always wrote them down this way,
the way she talked. And the Bible verse, too! How typical!
Thank you, Jane. No matter what happens, I'll treasure
this."

"We'll come up with something," Shelley said. "That
Betsy person won't get away with this. We promise you that.
Don't we, Jane?"

Jane had no idea how Shelley proposed to make sure
justice prevailed, but it didn't seem politic at the moment to
question her fervor. "Of course we promise," she said.

By the next day, they had talked it to death. And if there
was a solution, it hadn't appeared to them. They couldn't
even find straws to clutch at. Fred Stonecipher, Violet's
lawyer and the father of one of the boys in Jane's oldest
son's high school class, even came by Shelley's house after
dinner the second day to discuss it and commiserate.

"If there was the slightest proof—even a suggestion of
proof—that Violet had been coerced, there might be a
case," he said.

"But we know she must have been coerced," Jane said. "She loved Marie and 'she didn't even seem to like Betsy Ballantine."

"Did she seem afraid of her?" Fred asked.

Jane shook her head. "I don't know. I don't think Violet would have shown fear if she was scared out of her wits. She took pride in being both tough and proper. Sniveling wasn't proper."

When Marie excused herself to take a phone call, Jane said quietly to Fred, "Do you think Violet might have been abused by this woman? You hear such awful things about people mistreating the elderly."

"I thought of that, too," Fred admitted. "I asked her doctor about the possibility, in fact. He said she had some bruises, but frail old ladies on blood-thinners tend to have bruises. I wish there was something else I could do. Just don't encourage Marie in thinking she can win a suit against the Ballantine woman. She's good."

"What do you mean?"

"I mean if you didn't know Violet well, you'd be convinced by this Ballantine person. She says she doesn't want this inheritance, that she'll probably give it away to some worthwhile charity, and that she's really saddened by Violet's cutting her own child out of her will."

"But she's not refusing the money," Jane said wryly.

"No. She's claiming that's what dear Auntie Violet wanted and she has to respect those wishes. She's even making a great show of staying out of the way of the funeral plans. Said Marie could plan any kind of funeral for her mother that she wanted and it would be paid for without any questions."

"Generous of her to let Violet's money pay for Violet's funeral. When is it to be?"

Marie came in the room and overheard this. "Tomorrow afternoon. That was the funeral director on the phone. Fred, I have to go over to the house and pick out the clothes for Mother to wear. Would you come with me?"

The next morning, Shelley came over to Jane's house and found her elbow deep in flour. "What in the world are you doing? It looks like a band of Cossacks have been raping and pillaging in your kitchen!"

"I'm trying to make Violet's raisin rolls. I thought it might cheer Marie up to have some of them around. But I've really botched it. The dough came out all gummy and revolting. And look at the rolls now."

The ill-fated rolls, sitting in sticky wads on two cookie sheets, had bubbled nastily on the bottom where they'd been placed on the already hot cookie sheets. "Jane, you must have misread the recipe," Shelley said. "Or maybe when they rise they'll look all right."

"But they're not rising. They've been sitting out for almost the whole hour the recipe says," she lamented.

"Let me see the recipe," Shelley said. She studied it for a minute and said, "But Jane, they can't rise. There's no leavening agent. No yeast. No baking powder. Nothing."

June took the sheet from her and reread it. "My gosh. You're right." She stared at Shelley for a long minute, her mind racing. "This can't be the real recipe. Why would Violet have given me an impossible recipe? Look, there's no mention of nutmeg either, and I'm positive they had a nutmeg flavor. Shelley . . . ?"

"Maybe she really was slipping, mentally."

"No. She was as sharp as I am." Shelley raised an eyebrow meaningfully. "Well, sharper," Jane amended. "Shelley, I think this recipe was meant to be a message."

"What message?"

"That something was wrong! Don't you see? Violet couldn't use the phone because it was out of her reach. It didn't need to be out of her reach, but Betsy Ballantine arranged things so it was. And the Ballantine woman never left us alone for a second. Violet probably knew she wouldn't. So she wanted to tell me something, and giving me this seemingly legitimate recipe was the only way she could do it! Shelley, this recipe might be the way we could help Marie."

"I don't think anybody's going to negate a will just because Violet gave you a badly written recipe. But what about the Bible verse cited at the end? Maybe there's something there."

They raced for the family room and pulled down a Bible, flipping through until they found Isaiah 59:17. Jane read it: " 'For he put on righteousness as a breastplate, and an helmet of salvation upon his head; and he put on the garments of vengeance for clothing, and was clad with zeal as a cloak.' "

They stared at each other.

"Hmmm. If there's a message in that, I don't get it," Shelley admitted.

"Vengeance? Zeal? Righteousness?" Jane muttered. "This is the King James version. A more modern one might say something slightly different, but Violet wouldn't have tolerated a more modern version. Rats! If she was trying to say something to me with this, she vastly overestimated my powers of deduction." Jane folded up her copy of the recipe and stuck it in her purse. "Poor Violet. I know she was trying to tell me something, but what?"

"Well, I don't know Violet's message, but mine is get rid of those disgusting lumps of dough in your kitchen."

In spite of her distress, Marie had planned a lovely funeral for her mother, and there was a large turnout. Violet had been active in the church for years and had made a lot of friends with her hard work and practical, down-to-earth attitude—and her famous raisin rolls, the recipe for which now seemed to be lost for all time.

The burial was to be private, so after the funeral service, Marie stood in the vestibule, accepting the condolences of her mother's friends. She had asked Shelley and Jane to attend the burial with her, so they stood to one side, waiting patiently. Jane was relieved that Betsy Ballantine was keeping a very low profile as well. She sat in the back pew during the service and had disappeared for this awkward interlude.

Jane slipped the little memorial pamphlet into her purse and drew out the photocopy of the raisin roll recipe. She'd already looked at it a dozen times since discovering that it was wrong, but she kept hoping if she studied it once more, something would leap out at her. But no. Fidgeting aimlessly, she accordion-folded it from top to bottom and, pinching it together at the bottom, fanned it out. Violet's pretty, old-fashioned handwriting with the frilly capital letters made such a graceful pattern, she thought. The letters lining up along the left side looked almost like a floral design.

Suddenly she gasped.

Shelley tried to shush her.

"Shelley, look at this!" Jane hissed. "Here's the message!"

The first letters of each line spelled out F-O-R-C-E-D-T-O-S-I-G-N-W-I-L-L.

"You see? Forced to sign will!"

Shelley grabbed Jane's arm and hustled her back into the sanctuary, where they wouldn't be overheard. "Let me see that again! My God! You're right!"

"Don't you see? Violet knew Betsy had done a new will and was going to make her sign it next time two people were around at the same time to be witnesses! So Violet invented a reason for one of them to be me and gave me this recipe."

"Ladies, if you will join us please," the minister said from the doorway.

There were three funeral limos waiting in front. One had Violet's casket. The second was to take the minister and Marie and three of Violet's best friends who'd been invited to the graveside service. The third was designated for Jane, Shelley, Fred Stonecipher, and Betsy Ballantine. Given the composition of this group, there was no way Jane could share her discovery with the lawyer. Betsy, wearing what looked very much like a nurse's uniform that had been dyed black for the occasion, got into the limo awkwardly and the other three followed.

Fortunately, the cemetery was only a few short blocks away and they only had to endure her company for a little while. "Lovely service, wasn't it?" Jane ventured. Nobody replied. The limos pulled through the cemetery gates, down a winding drive, and stopped where a green canvas tent had been set up. The sad little group reassembled in the tent and sat patiently on folding chairs while the funeral home pallbearers brought the casket along. When it was in place, the minister said a few comforting words, then read a verse from Psalms.

"Excuse me," Jane said when he had completed the final prayer.

There was a horrified silence at this breach of funeral etiquette. Even a cardinal, warbling in a nearby tree, shut up as if appalled by Jane's lapse of manners.

"Excuse me," Jane repeated, "but I think it would be lovely if Marie would read a verse from Violet's own Bible. That is your mother's Bible you're carrying, isn't it, Marie?"

"I—uh, yes," Marie said, looking at Jane as if she had lost her mind. Betsy Ballantine, standing behind the others, had an expression of wary distaste. Fred Stonecipher and the minister were looking shocked as well, and Violet's three old friends were whispering among themselves so frantically that they sounded like a nest of baby rattle-snakes. But Shelley was smiling complacently.

"If you would read Isaiah 59:17?" Jane suggested.

Marie fumbled carefully through the delicate, overstuffed purple Bible. A piece of pink embroidery thread, tied around its little paper label, fluttered out. She turned to the page and removed a folded sheet of paper.

"Wait," Jane said before Marie could begin to read. "Perhaps you should read the paper stuck in that page first."

Marie read silently for a moment, then looked up at Jane with astonishment. "It's a will."

"What is the date?" Fred Stonecipher asked sharply.

"The day after the one leaving everything to that woman!"

Everyone turned and looked at Betsy. All the starch had gone out of her. She slumped for a moment, looking as doughy and miserable as the failed raisin rolls, then she turned and ran.

Shelley and Jane went to Violet's house that evening. Marie came to the door wearing an apron. "I'm glad you could come by. Fred Stonecipher just called. They caught up with cousin Betsy at the airport. She had Mother's jewelry in her handbag."

"No! Does Fred think a handwritten will in pencil will hold up in court?" Jane asked.

"Oh, yes. Betsy has signed a statement saying she bullied Mother into signing the other will. In return, she's asking that I not prosecute her for attempted theft of the jewelry. The handwritten will coupled with the original, which also left everything to me and my daughter, makes clear her intent."

Marie motioned for them to sit down. "You gave me a lovely surprise and I have one for you in return."

She came back a minute later with a crystal platter piled high with raisin rolls. "You found the real recipe!" Jane exclaimed.

Marie smiled. "Yes, and I made copies for you two. It was tucked into the Songs of Solomon. Where else would Mother have hidden something so sensuous?"

Jill Churchill's housewife sleuth, Jane Jeffry, whips up the answer to this recipe for mystery. Jeffry appears in *Grime and Punishment* (winner of the Agatha and Macavity awards for Best First Novel in 1990), *A Farewell to Yarns* (1991), *A Quiche Before Dying* (1993), *The Class Menagerie* (1994), *A Knife to Remember* (1994), *From Here to Paternity* (1995), and *The Silence of the Hams* (1996). Besides specializing in punny titles, Churchill is the alter ego of Kansas resident Janice Young Brooks, who has published numerous historical novels under her own name and seen one adapted for television.

Hill People

Dean Feldmeyer

We found Mort Clay on the third day of the search. Tom Coozy didn't actually say that Mort was dead, but we could tell by the way he spoke over the walkie-talkie that the news wasn't good. There was a click and a scratch and Tom's voice, "Ray, it's Tom."

Ray Hall was leading the search on Sassafras Ridge with me, Naomi Taylor, the Carmack twins, and several folks from the church. Ray pulled off his mittens, whistled for us to stop, and keyed his radio. "Go ahead, Tom."

"We found 'im, Ray. He's in an old Rambler down in Shadow Gorge. Looks like he crawled in there to get warm."

"On our way," Ray said, and replaced the radio on his belt.

Ray looked at me, frowned, and shook his head. He blew on his hands, pulled his mittens back on, motioned for the group to gather around him, and told them the news. He thanked the folks from the church for their help and told them to go on home. "Me and the reverend will take it from here." He turned to Gilbert and Gaylord Carmack, the cocaptains of the volunteer fire department. "Gil, you an' Gay go back and get the unit. Bring it around the Gorge

Road." They nodded seriously and tromped off through the woods to get their old Cadillac ambulance.

Naomi took my gloved hand in hers. "I'll go with you and Dan, Ray."

Ray nodded and looked through the woods. "It's about a mile," he said. "We'll cut across the ridge and come up to the gorge from the south end. Take about thirty minutes, I guess."

We walked mostly on deer paths and creek beds. The creeks were either dried or frozen, and the lack of leaves made the deer tracks passable. In summer it would have been stiflingly hot and close in these woods. In January it was brisk and invigorating, dry and sunny with temperatures hovering in the high twenties in the day, teens at night. They said the weather was about average for that time of year, but I was new to Appalachia. What did I know?

Two and a half years earlier my career had been on the fast track. A big church in the city. A big salary to go with it. A wife and two kids and a dog, a station wagon, and a split-level parsonage in the suburbs. Now, after a stupid, embarrassing affair, a messy divorce, and two years of teaching in the inner city, the bishop had decided to give me a second chance—Baird Methodist Church in Baird, Kentucky, a small, isolated village buried in the foothills of the Appalachian mountains.

Ray Hall, the constable, and his wife, May June, had taken me under their wings and made me feel welcome, teaching me the ways of "hill people." Naomi Taylor, young, beautiful, college educated, and Appalachian to the core, had taught me how to love again and reintroduced me to passion and excitement and joy. Every time she took my hand, I felt an electric thrill that ran up through my arm and into my chest to settle in my heart.

There had been thirty people in the search parties, and most of them went home when they learned that Mort Clay had been found. About a dozen men were gathered around the rusted, old Rambler when we got there. Most of them were smoking or chewing tobacco, waiting to see the thing through to its end. Someone had brought a flask, and it was being passed around, but it disappeared as soon as they saw me coming.

They made way for Ray and me as we approached, and I could hear the words "Ray" and "Reverend" being mumbled back and forth. The driver side door of the Rambler had been pulled open and Ray leaned in. I let go of Naomi's hand, took a deep breath and leaned in through the passenger side window for my introduction to Mortimer Clay.

"Looks like he froze," Ray said, his left hand on the steering wheel, his right on the back of the seat. Mort was lying on his right side on the rotted car seat facing the dashboard, his head toward me and his arms wrapped across his chest. He looked to be in his early sixties, balding, with a shaggy apron of gray hair hanging down his neck. His eyes were closed and he looked for all the world like he was sleeping, except his lips and fingers were blue. He was wearing a dirty, sleeveless undershirt, patched knit trousers with suspenders, and worn house slippers.

Ray pointed to some abrasions on the dead man's hands and forearms. "Looks like he ran into some trouble in the woods. Probably stumbled into a tree or fell over a stump." He looked around the interior of the nasty old Rambler. "Car probably kept the animals away from him. See anything from your end?"

A relatively clean, pint Mason jar poked out from under the seat of the car. "It looks like he probably wasn't cold when he went to sleep."

Ray reached across the corpse and picked up the jar, sniffed it and nodded. "Corn squeezin's," he said. "That it?"

I nodded.

"Okay, you do your thing and then I'll do mine."

I pulled my head out of the car and announced that we would now say a prayer for the soul of our departed brother Mortimer Clay. Everyone took off their caps and bowed their heads and I prayed one of the traditional prayers for the dead.

Ray cleared his throat. "Y'all can go on home, now. Me and the reverend and Naomi'll talk to the family. Funeral will probably be at Whiteker's in Perry. You can call the church or my office to find out when." The Carmack twins arrived a few minutes later, and we helped them get the body up the side of the gorge and into the unit. They headed off to Perry so Doc Pritchard could do the autopsy. LeRoy Whiteker would take the body from there.

Tom Coozy took Ray, Naomi, and me to the end of Sassafras Ridge, where Ray's old Willys Jeep was parked. From there we drove over Mt. Devoux to Coons Gap, where Mort Clay's wife and daughters were awaiting the outcome of our search. As usual, Ray drove as though he was in hot pursuit of John Dillinger, banging at the gear shift and taking the corners and cutbacks wide.

There wasn't much to say, and even if there had been, the ragged state of Ray's muffler and the wind screaming through the Jeep would have made normal conversation impossible. I tucked my hands under my arms and tried to imagine what I would say to Mort Clay's family. They weren't members of my church or any other in the township that Ray knew of. All I knew was that Mort had wandered out of the house sometime on the night of the sixteenth or morning of the seventeenth. When his wife and daughters had not been able to locate him the next morning, they called Ray. Ray called Gil and Gay Carmack, and they put out word on the VFD network that searchers were needed. When he called me, I called the two ladies on the top of our prayer chain at the church and set our own church women's network in motion.

By noon on Sunday, the seventeenth, there were thirty people combing the hills and gullies around Coons Gap shouting Mort's name. When he hadn't turned up by dark, the mood had turned sour and everyone was getting worried. When, after a second day of searching, we still hadn't found Mort, everyone seemed to realize that we weren't going to find him alive.

No one was surprised when we found him frozen in the old Rambler on the morning of the nineteenth. Neither did they seem shocked or even sad. Several of the men had shaken their heads and tsk'd through their teeth, but none seemed very broken up about the death of their neighbor. I decided to use my preacher's voice against the noise and ask Ray about it.

Hearing me trying to shout over the noise, Ray slowed the Jeep. "Mort was a hard-drinkin' man most of his life," he said. "'Bout ten years ago his brain finally surrendered and went into hibernation. Since then he's been like a man in the final stages of that Alzheimer's disease. Didn't hardly know his own name."

Naomi leaned forward from the back of the Jeep, laying her chin on my shoulder. "Remembered how to drink, though," she shouted. I could just hear her.

Ray nodded. "Drinkin', cussin', and beatin' up on Ophelia was the onliest things he did remember. The way I hear it, she took care o' him like he was a toddler child, and he'd take a swing at her whenever the notion entered his empty head."

"Why didn't she leave him?" I shouted.

Ray and Naomi looked at each other and shrugged. "Hill people," they both shouted simultaneously. "She was probably livin' off his pension from the mine," Naomi said. "Besides, she has them two girls to feed."

"This wanderin' off of his was gettin' to be a regular thing," Ray said. "Last time was right before you got here, back in July. We found him walkin' down Barton's Hollow Road in his underpants and a Stetson hat. I guess we all figured it would finally come to this."

Naomi nodded against my shoulder and her cheek brushed mine. "It's kind of a blessin' really."

Ophelia received the mixed blessing of her husband's death with the flinty stoicism I'd learned to expect from hill people. She was a small, thin, but strong woman with long, gray hair done up in a bun. She nodded once at me and Naomi when Ray introduced us and again after he delivered the news. Then she looked at me and said, "You'll do the funeral, I reckon."

"If you want," I said.

"I want." She wrung her hands and looked around the living room of her mobile home. The furniture was worn but clean, factory seconds except for the nineteen-inch RCA color television in the corner. Like most poor hill families, the home was old and in need of repair, but the satellite dish in the yard, the deep freezer on the front porch, and the pickup truck in the driveway were all in good repair. Home-canned fruits and vegetables lined the walls on shelves that had been put up in the living room, dining area, and kitchen. "I got coffee if you like," she said. "The girls'll be back directly. They went over to Melrose for some things."

We accepted the coffee, which was hot and strong and heavily laced with chicory. Ophelia and I talked about the funeral arrangements but it was hard to keep her on the subject. Her mind seemed to wander away. The girls arrived just as we were finishing our coffee.

Misty Dawn Clay and Amber Sunrise Clay. That's how their mother introduced them. The names, I suppose, were her idea, and she was proud of them. They were both of a type: late teens, plump, overly made up with their bangs sprayed stiff and standing straight up from their foreheads. Their blue jeans were tight and their blouses were frilly and low-cut. They were each carrying a brown grocery bag full of junk food. They unpacked Twinkies, Ho-Ho's, R.C. Cola, Fritos, and other goodies as their mother told them the news of their father's death.

When the information finally sunk in, they stopped unpacking and stood uncomfortably in the kitchen for a few seconds. Finally, Misty hugged her mother stiffly and said, "I'm sorry, Mama." Then she and her sister popped open a bag of Fritos and a couple of sodas and turned on the television. "Our stories are startin'," Amber said to her mother.

Ophelia settled herself on the couch with another cup of coffee and tried to be a good hostess, but her interest was really in the television and we took the opportunity to leave. Not only did life go on, it didn't even hiccup at the passing of Mortimer Clay.

Being the township constable doesn't pay a living wage in Durel County, so Ray supplemented his income by being the postmaster as well. His wife, May June, ran a store and diner in the same building as the post office and constabulary office in Baird. Across the road was the VFD and the Mountain Baptist Children's Home. Down the road was my church and attached parsonage. Six little houses made up the rest of the village.

Ray greeted me the next morning when I came into the diner for breakfast. He was sitting at the counter smoking a cigarette, drinking coffee, dressed in his usual, Sears gray work clothes, reading some papers over a large manila envelope. "Got Doc's autopsy report on Mort Clay," he said, waving the papers. "Wanna hear?"

"I thought those things took weeks to get," I said, reaching for the mug of coffee May June placed before me.

"Nah. You're used to the city. We don't have that many accidental or suspicious deaths out here. Doc probably doesn't do more'n a handful of autopsies a month. 'Sides, this is the preliminary. Doc said he probably wouldn't do any more on accounta death was obviously caused by hypo-whatchacallit."

"Thermia?"

"Yeah. Wanna hear the rest?"

"I was going to have some breakfast. Could it wait?"

"Sure," Ray said, stubbing out his cigarette. "Anyway, the only thing it tells us is that his hands and arms was all skinned up and he had rabbit stew for dinner the night before he died."

"So he died not long after he wandered away," I said.

Ray nodded. "Yep. Doc says that since we found him nearly three mile from his trailer, the exercise would have slowed down digestion but he still probably froze on the first night. Took a jar o' shine with him, went off to drink it, got lost in the woods, crawled in that old car and froze."

"Simple," I said. May June slid my breakfast in front of me. Three eggs, over easy, bacon, homemade bread, and grits. I never ate grits, but she always put them on my plate.

Ray took a piece of my bacon and nibbled at it. "I reckon."

"You reckon? Why? What's wrong?"

He sighed. "Well, it's just that three mile is a long way for a drunk man to walk. And he's only got them skinned up places on his hands and arms, along the outside edges."

"So?"

"So, if he fell down in the woods, there'd be places on his chest or knees or chin or somethin'. Even if it was from saplings and thorns, you'd think they would have torn his clothes or cut his face. But there ain't a thing other than his hands and arms." He took a bite of bacon and chased it with some coffee.

"Well, the walking is easy to explain," I said. "A man who's been drinking as long as Mort drank has a tolerance for alcohol. One pint probably just gave him a glow. It warmed him and invigorated him but it didn't make him drunk."

Ray nodded. "Maybe. What about all them abrasions?"

"Who knows?" I said, dragging some bread through my egg yolk. "He's tight as a drum head, stumbling lost through the woods in below-freezing weather in the dark. Maybe he started to fall and grabbed a tree or something. Did Doc find any wood splinters in the skin?"

Ray examined the papers again. "Doesn't say."

"It's a possibility," I said.

"I guess," Ray said. Then he changed the subject. "You and Naomi want to come over and play cards tonight? Nothin' much on the tube."

"Poker?" I asked. Winking at Ray. We both watched May June's shoulders rise at my question.

"Pinochle," he said. "May June don't take with gamblin' in her house."

"That's right," May June said without turning from the griddle.

"I'll call Naomi," I said.

I spent the rest of Wednesday working on Sunday's sermon, hanging out at the diner, reading, and preparing for Mort Clay's funeral. LeRoy Whiteker called around noon to tell me the funeral would be the next day, Thursday.

"Kinda fast, isn't it?" I asked.

"That's the way they want it," LeRoy said. He was about my age and handsome as the Baldwin brothers. His wife was a former Miss Eastern Kentucky, and he was the third or fourth richest man in the county. "Ophelia didn't even come in, just spoke on the phone. No viewing. Just a quick service and then in the ground he goes. Might as well get him buried before a big freeze comes up and we have to warehouse him till spring."

"There's a pleasant thought," I said.

"Been done before," he said. I could hear him smiling over the phone. LeRoy always smiled unless a funeral was in progress. "You and Naomi want to come into town and try that new Chinese restaurant with me and Andrea this weekend?"

"I didn't know there was one," I said.

"Just opened up. The family that owns it is Vietnamese, I think. Real nice folks. Joined the Episcopal church first thing they got here even though they're Buddhists."

"I'll talk to Naomi," I said. "She's crazy about Vietnamese Chinese Episcopalian Buddhist food."

"Okay, see you tomorrow, little 'fore ten."

Thursday morning Naomi, Ray, May June, and I rode to Perry in Naomi's big old Ford LTD for Mort Clay's funeral. We arrived a few minutes early and I met with LeRoy to go over last-minute details. Mort would be buried in Crestview Cemetery just outside of town. I told him I would ride with Naomi, as we were all going back to the Clay home for the wake immediately after the interment.

LeRoy reminded me that Ophelia and the girls had made it clear that there was to be no eulogy and no long service bemoaning Mort's passing. I was to render his soul to God and his body to the ground and be done with it. "No love lost between them and the old man, I guess."

He left me in his office to go over my notes while he started the recorded organ music. A few minutes later he came back and said there would be a small delay. He started out the door and then stopped and came back in. "Maybe you oughta come out and see this," he said.

I entered the little chapel just as Ray was coming in from outside, where he had gone for a cigarette. At the front of the chapel, Ophelia was draped over the closed coffin, wailing and weeping like a banshee. Dawn and Amber were standing on either side of her crying and moaning, smearing mascara over their plump faces with wet tissues.

"What the hell," Ray said to no one in particular.

"They came in, hung up their coats, and went up front to sit," LeRoy said. "Then, all of a sudden they start in like that. Whataya wanna do?"

"Let them cry for about three more minutes, then try to get them back to their seats," I said. "I'll start and see if we can't get things under control."

They cried through the whole service. Most of it was gulps and sniffles and sobs, but there was the occasional gasp and even a moan or two. The girls kept Ophelia squished between them, so she wouldn't go charging up to the casket, I suppose. They put her in the middle in the pickup truck for the ride to the cemetery, where they sat on either side of her under the funeral tent. They looked a little embarrassed by the time we lowered Mort to his final resting place. Ophelia had not stopped crying for even a moment.

Some hill people still call the ritual that takes place after a funeral a wake. Most, however, just call it "after." As in, "You comin' over to the house after?" It's a long-established custom, and even the most bereaved of survivors are not spared it.

Those few folks from the church who came to the funeral brought covered dishes with them and took them on to the Clay trailer after the graveside service. May June and Ray stopped by the store/diner/constabulary/post office on the way back from the funeral. Darnell Kody, the town handyman, was watching the store and stirring the beef stew May June would serve that night for supper. May June ran in and came back out to the car with two two-liter bottles of soda and a huge platter of fried chicken. "Darnell's doin' fine," she announced. She plopped the platter of chicken on my lap. "I fixed enough chicken for the four of us to take." Ray grumbled about trying to feed the entire county for free, and Naomi headed the LTD toward Mt. Devoux and the Clay home.

All the way up the mountain, May June and Naomi talked, mostly about the Clay girls. The dresses the sisters had worn to the funeral were so short and tight as to be nearly indecent, not to mention inappropriate. And that hair!

Ray looked out the window and smoked three cigarettes, holding them so the smoke escaped out the small crack he had opened in the window. As we rounded the bend about a mile from the trailer, he said something about three women living out this far by themselves with no neighbors to look after them.

"You mean men?" Naomi said, smacking me on the leg as she drove. She was smiling. "You mean three women can't take care of themselves without a man up here in the hills?"

Ray snorted. "Them three been takin' care of themselves and a brain cripple for ten years," he said. "I guess they'll do all right. That's what makes it so curious."

"Makes what curious, Dad?" May June asked.

"The way they carried on at the funeral. Sure was different than the way they acted when we told them he was dead." He opened the window and flipped his cigarette butt into the wind and rolled the window quickly up.

"Grief has a lot of faces," I offered. "Maybe it just took seeing the casket to make it real for them. Maybe they weren't mourning the man he was when he died as much as the man he was when he was young."

"Maybe," Ray said, but he wasn't convinced. "I don't recall how he was ever much of a husband and father."

"Still," I said. Sometimes people can't be figured out and you are butting your head into a wall to try. Ray loosened his tie, lit another cigarette and looked out the window some more.

Ophelia Clay was sitting in the corner next to the television when we arrived. She was wringing a tissue in her hands and staring into space. About twenty people were there, mingling shoulder-to-shoulder in the trailer, eating food and drinking beer and R.C. Cola from cans and moonshine from jelly glasses.

The girls were in the kitchen, smiling stiffly and trying to hide their exasperation at having to miss their stories. The tears were gone now, replaced by an adolescent desire to get on with life.

I mingled with the folks and said pastorly things, went out on the porch and smoked my pipe with some of the men, and ate fried chicken and drank coffee. After a while the women all seemed to claim the kitchen and dining room and the men took the porch and living room. Someone turned on the television and found a basketball game on ESPN.

While we watched the game, Ray wandered around the room with a jelly glass in one hand and a cigarette in the other. Occasionally he would take a jar of home-canned something off a shelf, examine it, and put it back. He walked around the room and did this several times before he finally brought one over to me. On the lid was a little sticker, and on the sticker was written, in a woman's flowing script, *Raspberry Preserves* and the date it had been put up.

"Meticulous," Ray said, showing me the lid.

"Don't they always do that?" I asked. "So they can use the older stuff first."

He nodded and reached into his pocket. He came out with another Mason jar lid. On it was a sticker with the date and no name. "Got this off one of the white lightnin' jars. I guess they knew what was in the jar."

I nodded, not knowing what he was getting at. After a few seconds he said, "I think I'll see if the women need anything," and wandered off toward the kitchen.

He came out almost immediately and went out the front door to the porch. He was gone several minutes and came back in again, carrying four one-gallon freezer bags full of ice cubes. He was smiling when he went back into the kitchen, and he winked at me just as the swinging saloon doors closed below his chin.

A few minutes later Naomi came out of the kitchen, kissed me on the cheek and said, "What's up?"

"Notre Dame's winning," I said, nodding toward the television.

"No, with Ray," she said. "He just told me to tell you that we'd be the last ones to leave."

I shrugged my shoulders in my best imitation of a says-everything-and-nothing Appalachian shrug, and Naomi laughed. "You're gettin' pretty good at that."

It took two hours for everyone to drift out and head home, with most of the wives driving. Watching basketball can be thirsty work.

The seven of us—Ray, May June, Naomi, Ophelia and the girls, and I—were puttering around the trailer, cleaning up. As we would bring platters of leftover food into the kitchen, Ophelia put everything in freezer bags and labeled each one with the name of the contents and the date, and set them aside to go into the deep freezer on the porch.

Ray leaned back against the counter and lit a cigarette. "Ophelia, do you do that with all your leftovers?"

"I do," she said stiffly. "Waste not, want not."

"What about rabbit stew?" Ray asked. "If you was to have some rabbit stew left over, would you do that? Put it up in the freezer for later?"

She didn't even look up. "I reckon," she said.

"You usually have leftovers when you have rabbit stew?"

Now she looked up. "Why you so interested in rabbit stew? What's rabbit stew got to do with anything?"

Ray shrugged. "Just wonderin'. When was the last time y'all had rabbit stew, anyway?"

"I don't remember," Ophelia snapped. Now the girls had stopped puttering and were watching Ray and their mother, as were Naomi and I. Only May June continued with her clean-up chores.

"Could it have been last Wednesday? Say the thirteenth?" Ray took a drag on his cigarette and stubbed it out in one of the clean ashtrays.

"Mighta been," Ophelia said. "Mighta been since then. I don't make a habit of committin' all my meals to memory."

Ray took three steps to the refrigerator and opened the freezer. He rummaged around behind two bags of ice cubes and brought out a freezer bag with a ball of gray matter about the size of two grapefruits frozen in the bottom of it. He looked at the label. "No, Ophelia. I don't think you've had rabbit stew since the thirteenth, because if you did, you would have used this here leftover. You wouldn't have made fresh, would you?"

"I mighta. I don't know what I woulda done."

"Sure you do, Ophy. You're a meticulous woman. You wouldn't have made fresh stew if there was leftover stew less than a week old in your freezer." He pushed the freezer bag across the counter so she could read the label. "See there? Says, 'January thirteen. Rabbit Stew.'"

She looked at it, then looked slowly up at Ray. "So what? What's this got to do with anything?"

Ray sighed and took his time lighting another cigarette. "Ophy, darlin', when Mort froze, the contents of his stomach froze, too. Mort's last meal was this rabbit stew he ate here with you on the night of Wednesday the thirteenth. Fact is, Mort was dead four days when you called me on Sunday morning."

Dawn said, "Oh, Mama."

Misty said, "You saved the stew? Oh, Mama."

Ophelia said, "He hit me. He hit me for thirty years and I just couldn't—"

Ray held up a hand to stop her. "I'm gonna tell you what I think happened. I'd appreciate it if you all would just not say a word till I'm finished. Then, if you're a mind, you can talk."

Everyone, including Naomi and I, nodded our heads. May June smiled and nodded, winking at Ray.

Ray looked at his cigarette as he talked. "I reckon you all got tired. Tired of Mort hitting your mama, tired of changin' his pants every time he messed 'em, and tired o' takin' his abuse while you did your best for him. Come last Wednesday night you had your fill, and he did somethin'. Maybe he hit you again, or maybe he threw his supper across the room, or maybe he was just bein' ornery like usual, but it was the last straw.

"You gave him some shine to mellow him out, or maybe he demanded it and you gave in. It warmed him up and he stepped outside. Have a smoke, pet the dog, whatever.

"I doubt you planned it, but the opportunity was just too much to pass up. You all realized that you wouldn't have to wait for him to die and you wouldn't have to shoot him. All you had to do was close and lock the door. So that's what you did.

"He pounded on the door for a while and then he pounded on the side of the trailer." Ray looked at me. "That's why there weren't no wood splinters in his hands or arms."

"It was probably hard listenin' to him scream and holler and pound on the trailer, and I doubt any one of you coulda stood it alone," he said to Ophelia and her daughters. "But you were together. Three against one, and you propped each other up just like you have since you girls was little. Finally, Mort crawled into his pickup truck and drank himself to sleep.

"When you went out to check on him in the morning, he was froze, and you just put him in the back of the truck and drove him over to Shadow Gorge to that old Rambler. I can't figure if you knew about the Rambler or it's just the first one you came across. And I don't know how you got him down the gorge into the car, but I'm guessin' you wrapped him in a blanket and drug him down the side, unwrapped him and set him in there in the same position he died in, still froze like that rabbit stew yonder.

"You called me on Sunday because you knew it wouldn't look right, him wanderin' off and freezin' without us lookin' for him again."

His cigarette was only about a half inch long, and he stubbed it out in the ashtray, trying not to burn his fingers. "All that cryin' this mornin' wasn't grief, was it? It was fear and maybe a little regret. You were scared you were gonna get caught." He sighed again. "I about got it right? Anything you wanna add?"

Ophelia started to say something, but Amber jumped in first. "You can't prove none of that."

Ray nodded slowly. "That's right. But you just made it so I don't have to, hon. Not for my own mind, at least. I guess a judge would want more, and I don't rightly know how to give it to 'im." He looked directly at Ophelia. "You didn't have to kill him, Ophy. You coulda walked away. Women do it all the time. We woulda helped you."

Ophelia started to cry. "Who woulda took care of him if I

left? He was helpless as a child. Thirty years I give 'im, and the only way he touched me was with his fist. Thirty years." She sat in one of the kitchen chairs and looked at the floor, shaking her head. Amber patted her shoulder.

Ray nodded his head toward the door, and Naomi, May June, and I moved that way. He followed us and paused before we went out. "You all gonna stay here?" he asked the women.

Misty looked up defiantly from her mother. "There's some life insurance from the mine. We was thinkin' about movin' to Cincinnati."

Ray nodded. "That might be best," he said.

He walked with us to the car and folded himself into the front seat. Naomi pleaded fatigue and asked me to drive home. No one had much to say on the way back to Baird. Naomi and May June talked about Cincinnati. I listened to the radio and wondered if my funeral homily had been appropriate after all. Ray smoked and looked out the window much as he had on the way up the mountain.

Somewhere around the Viper Cutoff I heard him sigh as he flipped his umpteenth cigarette butt out the window. He said something under his breath and I saw him subtly shake his head. Then as he settled back in the seat and closed his eyes, he said it again, and this time I heard him.

"Hill people."

With this story, Dean Feldmeyer continues his series featuring Dan Thompson, an Appalachian minister with a checkered past and compassionate heart. His 1994 debut novel, *Viper Quarry,* was nominated for an Edgar for Best Paperback Original; Thompson also appears in *Pitchfork Hollow* (1995). Feldmeyer's books draw on his own work as a Methodist pastor in Ohio.

Barbecued Bimbo

Susan Rogers Cooper

I threw my duffel bag on the bare mattress of the bed, barely missing the bloodstains. Two unidentifiable bugs screamed and scurried off. I took a quick look around the "luxurious" efficiency apartment—a folding lawn chair in one corner, the webbing frayed and broken in spots, the single bed with its bloodstained bare mattress, a two-burner stove so thick with crusted food the burners weren't visible, and a small refrigerator I didn't have the heart to even open.

Anyone in their right mind would have walked out the door that minute, but it was three A.M., I had no transportation, and it was raining. My next thoughts were less than generous ones about my agent and the things I'd like to do to her if I could get my hands on her.

She'd said things like "headliner," "Kansas City's newest club," and like an idiot, I'd bought it.

After six years in the biz, opening for guys whose idea of funny was making bodily function noises and seeing how many times they could use the f word, I was offered a job at a new club as a headliner. One week at Stet's in K.C. Half my airfare and accommodations included. Looking around the efficiency apartment, I concluded that this room was the better part of the deal.

I'd gone straight from the airport to Stet's. I'd had to pay for all of my airline ticket and the taxi from the airport to downtown—I'd be reimbursed. Nobody, though, had mentioned that Stet's was something other than Kansas City's newest comedy venue. It was mostly a barbecue joint.

Stet himself was a thick-necked redhead with a protruding belly and not enough teeth left in his head to chew his own barbecue, and he was less than impressed with my offer of my airline ticket and taxi receipt. All the time we talked was on the run as he moved from one end of the restaurant to the other, telling me my duties.

"Two acts a night, okay? Eight and midnight, okay? Resta the time you wait tables. You get to keep your tips—"

"I don't wait tables—"

"Yeah you do, okay? Look," he said, trying to hand me an apron and a tray, "go clear off number four and see if number seven needs more iced tea, okay?"

"No, really," I said, attempting to keep from actually touching the apron and tray. "I don't wait tables. I do comedy. Okay? That's what I do—"

"She's too good to wait tables," the only waitress in the place said as she walked by us, arms laden with full trays and sarcasm dripping off her tongue like saliva from a *Texas* barbecue rib.

"Stow it, Allison," Stet said to her over his shoulder as he walked to a table near the cash register that seemed to serve as his office and brandished a piece of paper. "Got a contract right here, signed by your agent, okay? You work seven nights, two shows a night and wait tables in between, okay?"

Staring at the bloodstained mattress of the "luxurious" efficiency apartment, I knew I had two choices: hop the next flight back to Austin (lawsuit came instantly to mind) or live with it.

My cellular phone (it and nationwide service a Christmas present from my best friend, Phoebe Love) rang inside my purse. I picked it up, halfway hoping it was my agent and I could tell her exactly what I thought of her. But I knew the only person who would be calling me at three A.M. was Phoebe.

"Hello?"

"How's K.C.?"

"Don't ask."

"That bad?"

"Worse."

"Are you sitting down?" she asked.

"That's not a viable alternative at the moment," I said.

"If there's any possible way, I would prefer that you sat down before I said any more."

I sighed my usual long, suffering sigh when dealing with Phoebe. She has a tendency to be overly dramatic.

"Just tell me."

"Well, I was talking to Pucci earlier today—"

"How nice for you," I said as sarcastically as possible. Pucci was a detective with the Chicago force I'd met a while back. He and I had an off-again, never on-again kind of relationship. We'd sucked face once or twice, but he wasn't my type.

"He's in Kansas City right now."

"Oh, God, you didn't tell him I was here!"

"Yeah, I did."

I glanced at my reflection in the fly-spattered mirror over the bed. My hair was growing out but it was still the color of rancid wheat. I had circles under my eyes, but a little makeup could do wonders—

"There's something else, Kimmey," Phoebe said.

I didn't like her tone. "What?"

She sighed. "Kimmey, listen, Pucci's . . . well, he's in love."

"Huh?" I sank down on the mattress, oblivious to the stains.

"He's met this girl—woman—and they're in Kansas City to see her family. Kimmey, I think it's serious."

I sucked in air. "Well, that's great," I said, putting my smiley voice on. "That's exactly what he needs. I'm really happy for him. This is just great. I mean it, I think this is just . . . great."

"You're babbling, Kruse."

"No, really. Pucci needs someone in his life. I turned him down. This is just rebound, right?"

"She's twenty-two and her name is Tiffani—with an i."

"I'm going to gag."

"Thank you, I already did."

"You didn't tell him where I'm working—"

Another sigh. "I'm sorry. I told him where you were before I found out about Tiffani with an i."

"And?"

"He laughed."

He already knew about Stet's. He already knew how humiliated I was going to be over the next seven days.

"I have to go now, Phoebs. Thanks for calling."

"Kimmey, you okay?"

I forced a laugh. "I'm fine. Really. I'm happy for him. Really. 'Bye."

"How many Republicans does it take to screw in a lightbulb?" a familiar voice said behind me.

I felt my body freeze.

"Two. One to mix the martinis and one to call the electrician."

The giggle that came at the punch line did not come from me. I turned slowly around, knowing I'd be facing Sal Pucci. He smiled his wicked smile. It accomplished nothing. I shot back with my patented Kimmey Kruse "I Loathe You with Every Fiber of My Being" smile. "Hey, Pucci," I said.

"Hey, Kruse."

The giggle came again from the vicinity of his left arm. Tiffani. With an i. Pucci made quick introductions. I figured if she was twenty-two, I must still be a virgin. She was closer to Pucci's five feet six inches than to my five feet nothing. She was wearing flats, obviously catering to Pucci's male ego. She had dark brown hair, entirely too much of it and entirely too shiny. Her eyes were milk-chocolate brown and as big as a Walter Keane waif's. She was thin everywhere except her chest. Her boobs and my hair color had a lot in common. She was wearing skintight jeans, the legs of which seemed to go on forever, and a red T-shirt that stopped an inch above her belly button. Because of the size of her breasts, however, the shirt stood entirely too far away from her skin as it hung down. She had full, pouty lips and a little upturned nose. She was pretty—in a perfect sort of way.

She gave me her hand to shake and I noticed immediately it was limp and damp. I smiled. "Hi, Tiffani, nice to meet you."

"I've heard so much about you from Sal," she gushed, leaning into Pucci. He beamed at her. "He says you're a good friend."

"Right," I said, keeping my smile firmly in place by gritting my teeth.

"Hey, Kruse, you taking table eleven or what?" I heard from behind me.

"Oh, Stet, let her be," Tiffani said, slapping playfully at my erstwhile boss. "She's an old friend of Sal's. We need to catch up. Okay?" she said, batting her lashes and pushing out her lower lip.

Stet turned an unhealthy shade of red and smiled. "Sure, Tif, honey. Whatever you want."

Tiffani let go of Pucci's arm long enough to pat Stet on the cheek. "You're the best, Stetti, but then you always were, huh?" She giggled and Stet laughed.

When he walked off, Tiffani said; "He used to be married to my mother. He's Daddy number four." She giggled again.

Pucci said, "Come on over to our table, Kruse. Take a load off your feet."

"And miss all my tips? Y'all have fun," I said, and walked over to table eleven.

I tried not to look over at Pucci's table, where Tiffani was handfeeding him bits of brisket and barbecued chicken. I'd already done the eight o'clock show and was an hour away from the twelve o'clock show. I took a long time cleaning table eleven, anything to keep away from Pucci and Tiffani with an i.

Twenty minutes before I was to go on for my last show of the evening, I felt a hand on my arm as I was leaving with an order from table six. I stopped in my tracks, knowing the feel of the hand that touched my arm. "What?" I asked, letting my irritation show. It was never difficult with Pucci to let my irritation show.

"You mad at me?" he asked, looking more childlike than I'd ever seen him.

"Why would I be mad at you?"

"Well, you and I—well, we—"

I shrugged his hand off my arm. "You and I nothing, Pucci. Like Tiffani with an— Like Tiffani said, you and I are just friends. And even that definition is stretching it."

The little boy look left his face, replaced by the all-too-familiar Pucci leering grin. "You're jealous!" He cackled. "My God, Kruse, you're jealous!"

I laughed in his face. "Of what? Don't be a jerk, Pucci. Anymore than you can absolutely help."

I left him standing there and went to the kitchen to turn in the order for table six. I could hear him laughing behind me.

My hand was on the swinging door into the kitchen when I heard voices raised from beyond. It wasn't hard to recognize Stet's blurry bass, and I was pretty sure the other voice—syrupy sweet—belonged to Pucci's Tiffani with an i. When I unabashedly listened to the conversation, I knew for sure it was Little Miss Big Boobs.

"I tole you not to come back here!" Stet said.

"Oh, Stetti, don't go on like that," she said.

"Your mama know you're in town?"

"Why don't you just call her and let her know—unless you're afraid of that new young stud of hers," Tiffani said. "Take that new cop of yours—he's another cop, right?" She giggled. "I just love our boys in blue—"

"Just take him and get out of here. I don't want you hanging around, Tiff. I mean it."

There was a silence, and I cracked open the swinging door and peeked around the edge. The kiss little Tiffani with an i was giving ex-stepdaddy Stet wasn't exactly daughterly.

Stet pulled away. His voice was gruff. "Get away, girl. I don't need you doing this to me now—"

I felt a hand on my back, and the other waitress, Allison, said, "Are you going in or coming out? Whichever, just move!"

I went through the swinging doors and handed Stet my order for table six. Tiffani, ignoring Allison, looked at me and smiled. She came up and touched my arm. "You and I are going to have to get together, Kimmey. I want to hear just everything and anything you can tell me about my Sal." She beamed at me and moved through the swinging doors.

Stet looked after her, his face flushed, the order ticket for table six forgotten in his hand.

I followed Tiffani with an i out the swinging doors and went to the rest room to wash my face and try to compose myself for my next show.

I stayed up too late that night, lying on my brand-new air mattress on the floor of the "luxury" efficiency apartment, worrying about whether or not to tell Pucci what I saw. Finally I called Phoebe.

I got a grumpy "Hello?" in response to the fourth ring.

"Something came up tonight and I don't know what I should do about it," I told her by way of greeting.

She sighed. "What?"

So I told her about seeing Pucci and meeting Tiffani with an i. I described her in gory detail. ". . . and if those boobs are real, it's only because plastic has been reclassified as organic."

"Breast implants aren't made of plastic," Phoebe the rational said.

"That was just a desperate attempt at humor, Phoebe. You see how low I've sunk? But that's not the real point anyway. The real point is I saw her laying a lip lock on her ex-stepdaddy, old Stet baby."

There was a small silence, then Phoebe said, "Interesting. What kind of lip lock?"

"The open-mouth-insert-tongue kind."

"That is a decidedly unwelcome picture," Phoebe said.

"Tell me about it. I actually saw it. Now, my question is: Do I tell Pucci?"

"No."

"No?" I was disappointed.

"As much as you'd obviously like to, I don't think that

would be wise. Not if you ever want anything to come of your relationship with Pucci—"

"Relationship? Are you out of your mind? I have no relationship with Pucci and I don't want anything to come of anything with that man!"

"Right." Another space of dead air.

"Phoebe?"

"What?"

"Will you tell him?"

She sighed. "You want me to tell him that you saw his lady love kissing her stepfather?"

"Yes."

"No."

"Why not?"

Again she sighed. "Kimmey, just let this run its natural course. Pucci is not a stupid man—"

"Says you—"

"He'll see her for what she is—sooner more likely than later. It's best that he thinks he's in control. If you tell him—or if I tell him something that came from you—it will seem like you were in control of his relationship with Tiffani—as well as his relationship with you."

"He has no relationship with—"

"Yeah. Right. I wish you'd just hop into bed with that guy and get this over with."

"That is probably the most disgusting thing you've ever said."

"You have no feelings for Pucci whatsoever?"

"None."

"Then don't ever mention his name to me again."

"Fine."

"Fine."

"Good night."

"Good night."

I came on shift at three P.M. Stet's opened at five and it took two hours to get the pits going and the food ready for the evening rush. I had six more days, then I'd be free to fly to New York, find my agent, if the address I had was still good, and kill her.

I'd barely put my stuff in my temporary locker in the hall outside the kitchen when I heard a familiar voice.

"Stet, you're a hard man to get ahold of. Have you seen Tiffani?" Pucci asked.

I peeked around the corner of the kitchen door.

"Not today," Stet said.

"What time she leave here last night?" Pucci asked.

"Thought she left with you," Stet said.

"No. She said she had to stay and talk to you about her mother. I went on back to the hotel after the last set."

"She didn't come in here to talk to me about her mother or anything else," Stet said, turning away, his voice obviously close to anger.

Pucci grabbed Stet's arm and turned him around. "Look, man, she never came back to the hotel. I didn't know how to get ahold of you—I don't even know her mother's last name! Call her mother and see if she went over there."

"Oh, for criminey's sake," Stet said, but dutifully went to the phone on the kitchen wall and dialed a number. Into the phone he said, "Reba? That you, honey? Stet, yeah, baby, how are you?" He laughed. "Look, sweetheart, you know Tiff's back in town? . . . Well, she's with her new boyfriend, okay? And he said she said . . . Oh, yeah, he's a cop . . . I dunno." He turned to Pucci. "You cute?"

Pucci grabbed the phone from Stet's hand. "Mrs. . . . Reba. Hi. Sal Pucci. Yeah. Look, have you seen Tiffani? She said . . . No, I went back to the hotel last night and she said . . . No, she said she had to . . . No, she never made it back to the hotel. Did she call you? You have any idea where . . . Okay, Mrs. . . . Reba, yeah, thanks."

Hanging up, Pucci asked Stet, "You didn't see her during or after Kimmey's midnight set?"

"No, I didn't see her but the one time early on when she was with you and the comic."

Pucci sighed and headed for the door into the dining room. "Mind if I hang around awhile in case she shows up?"

"Naw, go ahead. I'll have one of the girls bring you some coffee," Stet said.

Pucci grinned. "Just make sure it's not Kruse."

Smart man, I thought. I waited until Pucci was in the dining room before I ventured into the kitchen.

"Go out in the yard and clean pit number two, okay?" Stet said, handing me a wire brush and a bottle of cleanser.

"No," I said, trying to hand them both back. "Wait tables, okay. But there's nothing in the contract—"

He walked to the table by the register and picked up my contract. "Paragraph six, section three. Okay?"

He turned and walked into the kitchen, saying over his shoulder, "Have Allison come in here and get that cop some coffee, okay?"

I headed into the yard behind the kitchen that held two large barbecue pits. Allison was scrubbing pit number one. I told her about the coffee; she gave me a dirty look, but turned and walked back in the kitchen.

I headed to the other pit, thinking of ways I could torture Myra, my agent, before I actually killed her. Both pits were large, but number two was the biggest—four feet long, two feet wide, it could hold a side of beef and five chickens on its rotating spits.

I pulled at the cast-iron lid, trying to lift it. The lid itself probably weighed as much as I did. I turned around and saw Pucci standing by the door, coffee in his hand, a stupid grin on his face.

"Are you just going to stand there like a jerk or are you going to help me?" I asked.

His grin got bigger. "Oh, I just thought I'd stand—"

I gritted my teeth. "Get over here!"

He came, setting his coffee down on pit number one. The grin never left his face. With his help it only took a second to get the lid up. The other minute and a half we wasted staring at Tiffani with an i's dead body curled into a fetal position, her head resting precariously on the chicken spit. The shiny red hole in her temple showed dried blood, with a pool congealing in the hollow beneath the grating.

"I gotta open in twenty minutes, okay?" Stet said, addressing the Kansas City cop who had all of us—Stet, Allison, Pucci, and I—sitting at a long picnic table in the center of the dining room. "I got chickens to cook, beef and ribs to get on. Man, food ain't gonna be ready as it is—"

"I suggest you close for the evening, Mr. Barnes," Jerry Sims, the cop, said. "Out of respect for the dead."

Stet stood up, puffing out his chest. "Stet's ain't never been closed since the day we opened back in 'sixty-three!"

There was a commotion at the front door and all eyes turned in that direction. A woman of indeterminate age was doing battle with a uniformed cop at the front door.

"Reba, honey!" Stet yelled. To Sims he said, "That's the girl's mama. Let her in, for God's sake."

Sims motioned to the uniform, who gladly gave up the fight. Tiffani's mother flew into the room, curly blond tresses floating out behind her. "Where's my baby?" she screamed in a high-pitched whine.

"You are?" Sims asked, notebook in hand.

"I'm her mama, you idiot! Who do you think I am? Gawd!"

"What's your *name,* ma'am?"

"Reba Bullard." She frowned. "No, I changed it back. It's Reba Swanson now. Used to be Reba Bullard." She smiled coyly at Stet. "Used to be Reba Barnes, too."

Tiffani obviously got her desire to hide her age from her mother. Although Reba Barnes Bullard Swanson—in whatever order—had a face that showed at least fifty if not more years, she was dressed like a teenager in black tights, an oversized Nirvana T-shirt, and Reeboks. Several gold chains hung from her neck and wrists, and she had multiple earrings in both ears. Her blond hair was big—loose curls hanging down to the middle of her back. Part, if not all of it, was definitely as phony as her daughter's breasts.

"Mrs. Swanson," Sims said, "I'm afraid your daughter's been killed. Murdered."

"Well, damn," Reba said, sinking down next to Stet and resting her head on his shoulder. "You mean she's dead, huh?"

"Yes, ma'am."

"Oooooh," she said, and burst into tears, holding onto Stet for dear life.

Pucci sat next to me. He hadn't moved a muscle since

he'd run in to call the cops minutes after he and I had found Tiffani's body. That had been almost an hour ago. He'd answered Sims's questions in a frightening monotone, and I sat next to him, hoping my presence would be at least some comfort.

Reba's performance seemed to snap him out of it. He turned to me and raised an eyebrow. I wanted to hug him, but refrained. Instead I told him something I'd been meaning to pass on since I'd heard his conversation with Stet earlier in the day.

I leaned over, keeping my voice low. "I heard Stet in the kitchen tell you he hadn't seen Tiffani since the two of you were standing with me last night. He lied."

Pucci raised the eyebrow again, then turned slowly and looked at Stet. Turning back to me, he said, "Tell me."

So I told him of the conversation I'd overheard the night before.

Sims broke in. "Ms. Kruse, if you have something to say, I'd like to hear it."

I felt like I was back in Miss Gamble's sixth grade class. I looked at Pucci and he nodded his head once. Fighting the urge to stand up and recite, I told those gathered what I'd overheard the night before. Like my recitation to Pucci, I left out the lip lock.

When I'd finished, Pucci added that Stet had told him he hadn't seen Tiffani since earlier the night before and had not talked to her alone.

Stet was staring daggers at both of us. Sims turned to Stet. "Well, Mr. Barnes?" he asked.

"Well, what? So I talked to the girl. She was my step-daughter, for crying out loud. I had that right. I figured if she'd run out on Sal, I didn't want to get mixed up in it so I didn't say nothing to him. So shoot me."

"You intimated in your conversation with her that she had a thing for cops," I said.

"Yeah, I may a said that," Stet said.

"What did that mean?" I asked.

"Who is this little girl?" Reba asked, holding onto Stet's arm and glaring at me.

"She's that comic—" Stet started.

"I told you that was a bad idea," Reba said, hitting Stet playfully on the arm. The woman really needed to work on consistency in her roles. She didn't seem to be able to stick with her grieving mother shtick.

Sims said, "Ms. Kruse asked a valid question, Mr. Barnes. What did that mean?"

Stet looked at Reba. Reba shrugged. Finally, Stet said, "Well, Tiffani liked cops. She liked to marry 'em."

Allison made a sound next to me. I glanced at her but she quickly glanced away.

Pucci's eyes got big. "Okay, fine, she was married to a uniform in Chicago. That's how I met her—"

"Oh, she was married in Chicago?" Reba asked. "I din know that. Where's her husband?"

"He was killed in the line of duty—"

Allison made another noise beside me. Again I looked her way. She had her head bowed. Tears were dripping into her lap. I put my arm across her shoulders, but she pulled away.

Reba shook her head. "My poor baby. She just never had no luck with men. That makes three of 'em up and got killed. You'd think she'd give up on cops."

The sound coming from Allison turned from quiet crying to what I at first thought were sobs. When she threw her head back for air, I realized she was laughing.

All eyes turned to Allison. Reba squinted at her, pulled some glasses out of her purse and put them on. Looking at Allison, she said, "Oh, my God! It's you! Jimmy McAllister's little sister!"

Allison abruptly stopped laughing. "Used to be," she said. "Back when he was alive. Pre-Tiffani."

Sims looked at Allison. "I remember Jimmy McAllister. Out of the 406, right?"

Allison nodded.

"Got killed in the line of duty one night at a burglary at a grocery store, right? Walked in on the guy—" Sims said.

"Or something," Allison said. She leaned back in her chair.

"That's 'zactly what happened to her second husband,"

Stet said. "Joey Germaine. They was living in Cleveland. Joey was a cop and he walked in on a burglary, too—"

"Just like Dave Maher. In Chicago," Pucci said. "Mom and pop grocery store. They found him shot in the head two hours later when he didn't respond to his radio."

Sims and Pucci exchanged glances, and Sims nodded for Pucci to follow him. They went into a corner and conferred. After a few minutes they came back to the table. Both sat down. "Ms. McAllister," Sims said, addressing Allison. "How well did you know Tiffani Maher?"

Allison smiled. "We used to be best friends in high school. That's how she met my brother. He was older than me and already a cop when Tiffani and I were still in school."

"I forgot you and Tiffani was friends 'fore she married Jimmy," Reba said, smiling. "It's all coming back to me now."

"What is, Mrs. . . . whatever the hell your name is?" Allison said, leaning forward and glaring at Reba. "Is it all coming back to you that you raised a she-devil of the first degree? But how could Tiffani have turned out any other way, with you as a mother?"

Reba, mouth open, turned to Stet. "Stet, you gonna let your help talk to me like that?"

Stet cleared his throat. "Now, Allison—"

"Ms. McAllister," Sims said, "where were you last night?"

Allison smiled. "Here. Working. Ask Stet."

Stet nodded his head. "Yeah. She was here working till two A.M. We close up at one but the girls gotta clean up, okay? So they stay until about two, right, Allison?"

"Kimmey," Pucci asked, "were you here late cleaning up?"

I shook my head. "No. I got home around one-thirty. Allison said she'd clean up and I could go on home. Stet and the receipts were gone by the time I left."

"So exactly how long were you here all alone, Ms. McAllister?" Sims asked.

Allison waved away the question. "I have no idea. Twenty

minutes, an hour. Who knows? The place was its usual mess. But rather than worry about what I was doing last night, I'd think you'd wonder how a woman like Reba here could be living at the Tri-Star."

Sims looked at Reba. Referring to his notes, Sims said, "Mrs. . . . Swanson—"

"Call me Reba, honey."

"Mrs. Swanson, you live in the Tri-Star Towers? That's an expensive place."

Reba shook out her blond locks. "It's real nice. My girl bought it for me."

"How was your daughter paying for an expensive condo like that?" Sims asked.

"Well, honey, she had all that insurance money—"

"Why would she pay for it?" Allison demanded. "She hated your guts. Why would she pay for you to live in style?"

"You just shut your mouth! Stet, that girl's talking trash to me again."

"Allison, now—"

"Shut up," Allison said, glaring at Stet. "I'm talking to the queen bimbo. What were you holding over her head that she'd pay out the nose for you?"

Reba stood up, squaring her shoulders. "I've just suffered a great loss and I ain't about to stand here and take garbage from trash like you, Allison McAllister. So you can just go piss up a rope."

She swung around and headed for the front door.

"Mrs. Swanson," Sims said, grabbing her arm. "I'm sorry for your loss, ma'am, but I don't think you should leave right now—"

"I don't give a diddly what you think. I'm not staying here and putting up with her sassy mouth!"

"I think Ms. McAllister posed an interesting question, Mrs. Swanson. Why was your daughter paying for your condo at the Tri-Star?"

"Because she loved me and wanted me to be happy, that's why!" Reba said, glaring at Allison. "Don't believe a word that girl says. She was always queer for her big brother, and got real mad when my Tiffani married him. Not that he was such-a-much."

Allison stood up so hard her chair fell over backward. "You disgusting old cow!" she screamed. "Don't you even breathe my brother's name! You hear me? You're not good enough to have even known my Jimmy!"

Sims sat Reba back down in her chair and walked over to Allison, picking up the chair that had fallen over. "Sit down, Ms. McAllister."

Allison sat.

"Ms. McAllister, did you see Tiffani Maher last night after closing?"

"No."

Stet seemed to have removed himself from the entire scenario. I thought it was time to bring him back in. "Excuse me, but when Stet said he didn't see Tiffani last night, which we now know is a lie, he also forgot to mention something else."

"You're fired, Kruse!" Stet said.

"Thank you," I said fervently.

"What's that, Ms. Kruse?" Sims asked. He was looking at me closely—and so was Pucci. I felt a stupid need to protect him from my words, but I didn't know how to do it.

"They were kissing," I said.

There was a silence in which Reba slowly turned to Stet. "Not again," she said. She slapped her ex-husband in the face. "You bastard!"

"I didn't kiss her—she kissed me!"

"Jesus, Kimmey, a little peck on the cheek—" Pucci began.

I shook my head.

"A little smack on the lips—" Pucci tried.

I shook my head.

"Stet didn't do nothing to my girl. Ask Allison there about her precious Jimmy's funeral," Reba said. "Ask her about hitting my Tiffani and calling her names right there in front of God and everybody!"

Allison was silent. Sims looked from Allison back to Reba.

Reba, voice high, grating, and a little out of control, said, "She said right there at the graveside that Tiffani better leave town 'cause if she got her hands on her she'd kill her. Didn't you say that, you little tramp?"

I was turning my head to glance at Allison when I felt her arm go around my neck.

She pulled me to my feet, my neck in the crook of her arm. I choked and tried to pull away—but then I felt the pressure at my temple. Cold, metallic pressure.

"Oh, Lord!" Reba yelled. "She's got a gun!"

Reba and Stet jumped up from the table, backing away.

"Everybody just stay put," Sims said. He and Pucci moved closer to the table.

"Don't," Allison said. "Just stay back. I have nothing against Kimmey and I don't want to hurt her, but I will if you don't just stay back."

My eyes were getting blurry. I pulled at Allison's arm, making a croaking noise.

"You're choking her, Allison," Pucci said, his voice soft. "Let up on the pressure. The gun's enough."

The pressure let up. I would have fallen to the floor if Allison hadn't grabbed me by the waist, pulling me against her, putting the gun back to my temple.

Very calmly Allison said, "Ask the old bitch again why Tiffani was paying for her fancy condo. Remind her I have several bullets left in this gun and I will happily shoot her in the leg if she doesn't answer *right now!*"

Reba began blubbering. "I tole you! My little girl was just taking care of her mama! That's all."

I felt the pressure on my temple release. The sound of the gun in the enclosed room was deafening. Reba screamed. Stet grabbed her, catching her before she fell. The gun was back at my temple, the barrel hot against my skin, before Pucci could move more than a few feet.

I heard Allison laugh behind me. "Damn, I missed. That's just a flesh wound. Tell her, officer. Tell her next time I'll aim better if she doesn't tell the truth."

I could hear Reba sobbing and screaming in the background. "Girl, you shot off a chunk of her flesh!" Stet yelled.

"Get something to stop the bleeding—" Pucci started.

"No. The old bitch can bleed to death for all I care. And she will—unless she tells the truth."

Allison jerked me around until we were both facing the sobbing Reba. "Now!"

Reba looked from Allison to Stet, then to the two cops standing side by side. "I saw her do it," Reba finally said. "Saw Tiffani shoot Jimmy. I was working at a little store then—between husbands—and it was late and the store was closed. So Tiffani made me take her and Jimmy's body over to the store and then we tripped the silent alarm."

"What's she been paying you with?" Allison demanded.

"Well, now, working for the city and all, Jimmy had a nice life insurance policy, and Tiffani got her widow's pension and some extra 'cause they thought Jimmy was killed in the line of duty. And then, of course, with Joey, she got more. A lot more."

"Why'd she shoot Jimmy, Mrs. Swanson?" Sims asked.

"I'm bleeding real bad here. Please." She looked imploringly at Allison. Allison nodded her head, and Stet took off his shirt to stanch the flow of blood.

"Why'd Tiffani shoot Jimmy?" Sims asked again.

"It was an accident," Reba whined. "They was fighting. They was always fighting, them two! And that little girl had a temper since she was a baby! She grabbed his gun, I think just to scare him. But Jimmy tried to grab it away from her and it went off. It was really just an accident."

"But the guy in Cleveland and the cop in Chicago weren't accidents, were they, Reba?" Allison said. "Little Tiffani decided being a cop's widow wasn't a bad gig, huh?"

"Now, that's not true," Reba said, whining. "My Tiffani just had a run of bad luck."

"Allison," Pucci said, his voice soft, "where was Tiffani when you told Kimmey to take off?"

"In the kitchen. She was going to sneak off with Stet for another quickie, just like when she was a kid, but Stet, as stupid as he is, wasn't stupid enough to get mixed up with her again. He'd already left. I told her, though, that Stet asked her to meet him in the kitchen. When Kimmey left, I went in there and confronted her. Told her I knew she'd shot Jimmy. She just shrugged her shoulders. Denied it like it wasn't worth talking about. It didn't mean a thing to her. Not a thing. I wanted her to tell me why. Say she was sorry. I wanted her to beg me for forgiveness. But she just shrugged. So I shot her. Then I took her out back and put her body in the barbecue pit."

Pucci held out his hand. "Give me the gun, Allison. I understand about Tiffani. She hurt me, too. But Kimmey hasn't done anything to you. Kimmey's innocent. You don't want to hurt another innocent person, not like Tiffani hurt your brother. Kimmey's got a big brother, too. Think what you'd be doing to him."

My body was being held so close to Allison's that I could feel the sob before I heard it. "He was my big brother!" she said. "My best friend."

Slowly, Pucci walked up to her. "I know. That's how Kimmey and her brother are. Always have been. Best friends. I wish I had something like that. Sometimes I'm jealous of Kimmey and her big brother. Phil. Her big brother Phil. He's always protected her and checked out the boys she dated. And took her punishment when her mom and dad were mad. Phil would say, 'Kimmey didn't do it. I did.' That's what a big brother's for, huh, Allison?"

I could feel the sobs wracking Allison's body. The arm around my waist, which only moments before had been a prison, now felt like a caress.

"Phil's always worried about Kimmey on the road. He calls her every night, checking on her. Bought her a cellular phone for safety, because he worries about her."

Pucci was moving closer, closer. Allison's chin was resting on my head, both arms around my waist, the gun pointing limply at the floor. Pucci pulled the gun from her hand and I turned around, putting my arms around her.

Sims came forward and cuffed Allison, calling for the

uniform at the door. Pucci handed Sims Allison's gun, and he and I stood back, watching the cops march her off.

I hope Allison never finds out the only Phil in my life is a lady lawyer named Phoebe, and she's not even a blood relation.

———————

In this outing, Susan Rogers Cooper continues her series featuring acerbic stand-up comic Kimmey Kruse and an unusual locale for a corpse. Kruse also appears in *Funny as a Dead Comic* (1993) and *Funny as a Dead Relative* (1994). Reflecting her southwestern roots, Cooper's other two series feature chief deputy Milt Kovak of the Prophesy County, Oklahoma Sheriff's Department, and housewife and novelist E. J. Pugh of Black Cat Ridge, Texas.

Honeymoon

Nancy Atherton

"Still raining," Will confirmed, climbing onto the cush-
ioned window seat.

"It's gotten colder, too," Rob added, clambering up to
kneel beside his brother.

"How do you know it's colder?" I asked.

As one, the twins leaned forward to breathe on the
diamond-paned bow window, then point at the condensa-
tion, giving me their best "Elementary, dear Mummy" look
in order to remind me that I wasn't dealing with just any
six-year-olds.

I lay my head against the back of the couch and sighed.
The boys were right. It was a lousy day. In the four long,
rainy hours since breakfast, Will and Rob had exhausted
card games, board games, fort-building, toy trucks, cookie-
baking, hide-and-seek, and me. I could have summoned
their father from the study to lend a hand entertaining the
troops, but it was Bill's turn to enjoy a child-free day.
Besides, it had been my bright idea to spend the Easter
holidays at our cottage in England, so I couldn't grumble

too loudly about the dreary—and entirely predictable—April showers.

Rob wheeled around to face the sofa, where I stared at the raftered ceiling, praying for inspiration. "What about a story?" he proposed.

"I'll get Reginald," Will offered. Reginald was the powder-pink flannel bunny who'd presided over the story-telling hours of my own childhood. He was still hale and hearty—in the pink, as it were—and the boys saw no reason why he shouldn't go on performing the same service for them.

"You're on," I said, and as Will ran upstairs to fetch Reginald from the master bedroom, and Rob trotted over to flop beside me on the couch, I thought smugly that my two little geniuses had come up with the answer to a tired mother's prayers. If I worked it right, a half dozen of their favorite Aunt Dimity stories would keep the boys happy and in one place for at least a couple of hours, and I could reel off those familiar tales in my sleep.

A moment later Reginald landed in my lap. "Wake up, Mummy," Will demanded, bouncing up onto the couch. "Reginald says it's too early for naps."

"What would you know about it, anyway," I muttered into one powder-pink ear as I turned the bunny to face me. Reg's reproachful gaze met mine, and he won. As usual. I sat up a bit straighter and tried to pretend that I was the kind of wide-awake, bouncy, peppy mommy every six-year-old craves. "Okay, you guys, what'll it be? *Aunt Dimity Buys a Torch? Aunt Dimity's Cantankerous Cat?* How about—"

"No," Will interrupted decisively. "We don't want an Aunt Dimity story."

"Reginald is shocked," I observed. "Look. He's turned pink with embarrassment."

Ignoring me, Rob said firmly, "We want to hear about your honeymoon."

Some mothers might have been dismayed by the request. Honeymoons are, after all, supposed to be private, personal, and intimate—not the kind of thing one discusses in front of the children. Unfortunately, Bill and I had had the kind of honeymoon one could discuss in front of maiden aunts and aged clerics, so there was no reason not to tell the twins all about it. Well, maybe not *all* about it. "You want to hear about the Cavanaughs?" I asked.

Nodding vigorously, the boys chorused, "We want to hear about the *murders!*"

Bill and I would have been happy to spend our honeymoon in our English cottage. It was a charming little place made of honey-colored stone, set in the rolling hill country of the Cotswolds, in the west of England, and nothing could have been more romantic.

But my father-in-law, William Willis, Sr., was as old-fashioned as he was kindhearted, and he had other ideas. He sent us to Switzerland, to spend ten days at the Immelhof Hotel, the grandest of the grand old hotels in Lucerne, and since the trip was his treat—and since Bill and I would rather dance barefoot on tacks than hurt Willis, Senior's feelings—we'd accepted his gift without a murmur of complaint.

And, to tell the truth, the Immelhof was a lot of fun. The staff treated us like royalty, and the decor was just this side of eye-popping. Lucerne was a medieval town, but the Immelhof was pure baroque, a riot of gold leaf and gleaming marble, painted ceilings and gilded furnishings. The fact that our suite had a balcony overlooking the sparkling waters of the Vierwaldstätter, with the conical peak of Mount Pilatus rising in the distance, didn't hurt, either.

That first night, over supper in the hushed and richly appointed dining room, Bill and I were staring up at the ridiculously elaborate chandelier, trying to decide whether it was exuberant or just plain garish, when we were distracted by a genteel cough. I lowered my gaze to see Henri, the obsequious desk clerk, standing at our table. Henri was a short, balding man in his mid-fifties whose round face matched his round belly. At that moment his normally placid features betrayed mild distress.

"Madame, Monsieur," he said in a deferential murmur, "I do beg your pardon for disturbing your meal, but a fax message has arrived for Monsieur." With a punctilious half bow, he offered Bill a silver tray bearing a pale gray envelope and an inlaid silver letter opener. Bill used the letter opener, then returned it to the tray, and Henri whisked it away with another bow and a heel-click straight out of a 1940s costume drama.

"They have fax machines here?" I whispered, envisioning the quotidian devices embellished with as much gold leaf as the chandelier.

"You're in Switzerland, Lori," Bill reminded me, "where good taste is never allowed to interfere with good business. The Immelhof has a complete communications center for the convenience of traveling businessmen."

"But you're not a traveling businessman," I protested. "You're a honeymooner. What kind of thoughtless crumb would bother you with business on the first night of your honeymoon?"

"My father," Bill answered. "He's the only one who knows where we are."

"Oh," I said, momentarily nonplussed. "Well, it had better be important," I added petulantly. Bill and his father ran a law firm back in Boston. Willis & Willis looked after the trusts and wills of a select clientele of Very Rich People, and atoned for their sins—in my opinion—by running a free legal clinic and mentoring needy law students who did scutwork for the firm in exchange for room and board. While I appreciated the importance of Bill's work, I was, I thought, understandably piqued to find it horning in on our wedding trip.

I folded my arms to wait while Bill read the note, saw concern crease his brow, and felt my heart turn to ice. "What is it, Bill?" I asked anxiously. "Is William—"

"Father is fine, Lori," Bill assured me hastily. "He's written to tell me that one of my clients has passed away."

I breathed a sigh of relief, then felt apprehension rise again as a host of images flashed across my mind: file folders and paperwork and Bill with a black armband in a musty library, intoning the contents of a will to a bereaved, upper-class family. "Does this mean we'll have to go back to Boston?" I asked in a very small voice.

"Not at all." Bill waved away my worries. "Father's

looking after my clients while I'm away, and Finbar's will is very straightforward. Everything goes to Liam."

"Finbar?" I said doubtfully. "Liam? You're sure we're not talking about Dublin?"

Bill explained. "Finbar Cavanaugh was the eldest of the Cavanaugh brothers. Until yesterday he was the president and chief executive officer of Cavanaugh Textiles." He nodded toward the fax. "Father says here that he broke his neck in a riding accident. Forgot to tighten the girth, whatever that is."

I looked with loving pity on my sedentary new husband. "The girth is the strap that goes around the horse's belly," I informed him. "It holds the saddle on." I thought for a moment, then frowned. "God rest Finbar Cavanaugh's soul and all that, but forgetting to tighten the girth is pretty dumb. It's the kind of mistake a novice would make."

Bill's eyebrows rose. "Really? How strange. Finbar was hardly a novice. He was a world-class rider. It's true that he was getting on in years, but—"

"Maybe he was getting forgetful, too?" I suggested.

"Maybe." Bill shrugged. "It's the way he would've wanted to go, at any rate. Hunting was Finbar's passion. He owned a stables, and he'd won more cups and ribbons than he knew what to do with. The whole family is like that. Sports-mad, Father calls them."

"How many of them are there?" I asked, picturing a sprawling Irish brood.

Bill counted on his fingers. "Finbar, Liam, Eamon, and Bridey. Bridey's the youngest and the only girl. The only Cavanaugh who ever married, too. Her husband died some years ago—"

"Skateboarding?" I asked dryly.

"Heart attack," Bill replied with a wry smile. "Bridey has one child, a son, Niall. Father says Niall's the one who found Finbar's body."

"Grisly," I said, with a shudder.

"You're right," Bill agreed. He folded the message and stowed it in the inside pocket of his sport coat. "And I'm not going to let it spoil our dinner." He raised his glass of Taittinger and gave me a smile warm enough to melt the polar ice caps. "I have more pressing business to attend to at the moment."

I tapped his glass with mine, and all thoughts of the sports-mad Cavanaughs receded to a far distant corner of my mind.

They refused to stay there. Two days later, as Bill and I sank into chairs on the glass-enclosed veranda, our feet throbbing from a morning spent exploring Lucerne's medieval walls and towers, Henri hove into view once again, his round face apologetic as he bore down on us with the silver tray, the letter opener, and another pale gray envelope addressed to Bill.

"I am so very sorry to intrude, Madame, Monsieur, but again I have received a message for you, Monsieur Willis. You will forgive me."

"Of course." Bill looked less sanguine than he sounded as he opened the envelope and sent Henri on his way.

"Next time, we elope," I stated firmly.

Bill took my hand and toyed with it absently while he read. "I don't believe it," he said finally. "I simply don't believe it."

Willis, Senior, had written this time to inform Bill that Liam Cavanaugh had died the day before. A shotgun had blown up in his face while he was trapshooting at his gun club. The Cavanaugh family was definitely having a bad week.

"Trapshooting?" I said. "Horseback riding? What were the Cavanaughs trying to do? Form their own Olympic team?"

Bill sat back in his chair and slipped out of his shoes. "I told you they were sports-mad. Liam was one of the finest shots in the United States."

"Was he getting on in years, too?" I asked.

"He owned to sixty, but I happen to know he was sixty-four." Bill wriggled his tired toes luxuriantly. "Steady as a rock, though, and not at all forgetful. He knew how to handle a gun. At least, I thought he did."

I rolled my eyes. What Bill didn't know about guns would fill an encyclopedia.

Bill sighed as he bent to pull his shoes back on. "Ah, well, Eamon's next in line to inherit. He'll be able to indulge himself in a few more World Cup races now."

"He's a yachtsman?" I asked. "What about Bridey? What's her sport of choice? Bungee-jumping? Hot-air ballooning?"

"Bird-watching," Bill replied.

"That's more like it," I said. "If I were you, I'd suggest that the other members of this rapidly dwindling tribe take up something equally unadventurous, like, say, portrait painting or writing poetry."

"As a matter of fact, Bridey's son is a writer," Bill said thoughtfully. "Not poetry, though. Niall's a sort of journalist."

"Sort of?"

"He writes mainly about his own relatives. Sells articles on their exploits to various sporting magazines. The family chronicler, I suppose you could call him. He was doing a piece on Liam when the accident happened."

"Well, Niall's safe, at any rate," I pointed out, "and his bird-watching mother is, too. I've never heard of anyone writing himself to death, and I'm pretty sure the killer chickadee scare was a hoax. But Eamon Cavanaugh had better watch his step on that boat of his."

"Indeed." Bill grinned, and stuffed the fax message into his pocket while he scanned the room for Erich, the uniformed waiter who presided over the Immelhof's elegant veranda. "Now, why don't we order some cream buns and tea, then retire to our room for a little afternoon siesta?"

"Without the Cavanaughs?" I asked, eyeing him suspiciously.

Bill stopped scanning, reached for my hand and kissed it. "Just you and me, Lori."

"Forget the cream buns," I murmured, and we headed up the grand staircase for the most pleasantly exhausting siesta I'd ever taken.

Eamon's yachting accident occurred the day before we were due to leave Lucerne. Bill and I had spent the morning riding the cogwheel mountain railroad from Alpnachstad to the top of Mount Pilatus, and the early afternoon at the Historisches Museum, oohing and aahing over the armor, uniforms, costumes, and coins, and we were looking forward to a lazy hour or so on the veranda, watching crazed wind-surfers zigzag in front of the ferries chugging across the Vierwaldstätter. All we wanted was a chance to rest up for the evening. What we got was Henri, armed with what I was beginning to regard as his instruments of torture.

"Eamon was hit in the head by the boom?" I exclaimed, incredulous.

"That's the long spar at the foot of the sail," Bill put in quickly, to demonstrate that he wasn't a complete ignoramus where at least one sport was concerned. "And, yes, that seems to be what happened. Went over the side and drowned."

"In Boston Harbor?" I said. "Wasn't he wearing a life jacket?"

"Apparently not. According to Niall—"

"Niall was there?" The chill mountain air seemed to get a bit chillier.

Bill nodded. "He came down to help his mother arrange the funerals, and went out with his uncle Eamon for an afternoon sail. He was belowdecks when it happened. Didn't even know Eamon had gone overboard until it was too late."

"I see." I ran a hand through my perpetually disheveled curls. "And Bridey gets the family fortune now?"

Again, Bill nodded. "She'll have control of Cavanaugh Textiles, as well, but I doubt that she'll keep it. She was never interested in the family business. Father says she's planning to sell out and open a bird sanctuary in Florida. She's got a spot all picked out in the Everglades. She and Niall are going down to take a look at it after the funerals."

I stood abruptly. "You have to stop her."

Bill looked at me, puzzled. "Stop her? Why? What could possibly happen—" He broke off and squinted into the middle distance. Slowly, he too rose to his feet, and our eyes met as we both said, "Niall."

* * *

"And, sure enough, when Bridey's airboat was checked out, they found a few loose screws that would've sent her spinning into the nearest clump of mangroves." I looked down at the twins, who had by now rearranged themselves into their favorite listening positions. Will was on his back, his legs resting on the back of the couch, his sneakered feet poking straight up in the air. Rob's soft, dark curls were in my lap, and Reginald was on his chest.

"But how did you know it was Niall?" Rob asked. He knew the answer as well as I did, but the question was part of our story-telling ritual.

"Niall was the writer," Will answered, right on cue. "So he knew about everything."

"That's right," I said. "He knew enough about riding to saddle Finbar's horse—the wrong way. He knew enough about guns to put too much gunpowder in Liam's shotgun shells. And he wasn't belowdecks when Eamon went over the side of the yacht, he was at the helm, and he knew enough about steering a boat to bring it around just as Eamon was stepping out to trim the sails."

"But he didn't get Bridey!" Rob crowed.

"No, he didn't," I confirmed. "Because Daddy called Grampa and Grampa said"—here I grabbed Reginald for his star turn as Willis, Senior—"'Tut tut, my dear boy, I have already notified the proper authorities.'" The boys giggled with gratifying abandon while Reg took a bow.

"And then . . ." Bill's voice sounded behind me and I turned my head to see him smiling softly from the doorway. The boys scrambled upright on the couch as their father strolled into the living room, continuing the story. "And then the police found the nice lady with the telescope who'd seen Eamon's yachting 'accident' from the balcony of her condominium."

"And that busted the case wide open," Rob said, relishing the opportunity to impress us with his tough-guy imitation. "And greedy old Niall went straight into the slammer."

"And Bridey went down to the swamps, to save the scarlet ibises." Will enunciated the traditional closing line of the tale with a satisfied smile, though I was fairly certain that he hadn't the slightest notion what a scarlet ibis was.

Bill paused before breaking the moment of silence that followed every story. "Okay, you two," he said briskly, "how about if I take you over to visit with Emma and Derek and Ham for a few hours?" Emma and Derek were our neighbors. Ham was their dog. Will and Rob adored all three. The boys bounced to the floor and were halfway to the coat rack in the hall before they stopped and turned back to us.

"You can come too, Mummy," Will offered.

"No, thanks." Bill answered for me as he leaned over the couch to give me an upside-down hug. "I think your mother and I will enjoy a little afternoon siesta while you're away."

"Like on your honeymoon?" asked Rob.

Bill nodded solemnly, but the warm glow in his eyes told me that he'd thought of yet another answer to a tired mother's prayers. "Yes," he replied, nuzzling my neck, "exactly like on our honeymoon."

In this story, Nancy Atherton's characters from her Aunt Dimity series solve several murders long distance while honeymooning in Switzerland. Atherton's books featuring the benevolent spirit include *Aunt Dimity's Death* (1992) and *Aunt Dimity and the Duke* (1994). A Brooklyn, New York, resident, Atherton works as an editorial freelancer.

Vivian by Moonlight

Medora Sale

A fugitive sound made Felicity pause with her knife poised over the mound of parsley on the board. She reached out and turned off the radio. Nothing. With an expert sweep of the blade, she piled the parsley up one more time and reduced it to a moist heap that bled green essence over the maple block.

"Something smells wonderful in here." The voice came from behind her, and she dropped her knife with a clatter on the tiles.

"Oh. It's you," she said, reaching down to pick it up again. "You're early. You startled me." She put down the knife and gave the blond woman standing in the doorway a kiss. Black and blond hair whirled together for a moment and parted. "Just a minute. Let me wash my hands before I get parsley juice all over your silk shirt." Felicity leaned forward and murmured in her mother's ear, "Did you bring him? What's he like?"

Vivian nodded and winked; Felicity went over to the sink to scrub the green blood of the parsley stalks from her hands. "Felicity darling," said her mother, raising her voice to be heard over the running water, "I'd like you to meet my friend, Peter." She reached into the darkened hall and, with the air of a magician drawing a very tasty-looking rabbit out of a hat, produced a tall, tanned young man, all blond hair and regular features. "Peter, love, this is my daughter, Felicity."

Peter Fitzgerald felt like a man who has just put his foot through a rotten plank. Trapped, uncomfortable, and stupid-looking. He was staring like an awkward adolescent—he could tell—while his jet-lagged brain coped with a factor he wasn't expecting. Two women. Nowhere—not from Vivian, nor from the background stuff he'd dug up—had he found the slightest hint of the existence of a daughter. That's the trouble with doing research at a distance, Peter my friend, he said to himself, and tried to compose his features. Felicity stepped back to examine him, picked up a towel and smiled.

"Don't worry," she said coolly. "The sight of me hits everyone that way. Mummy was a mere child when she married, and they left the page about birth control out of her instruction manual."

"Not funny, Felicity darling. Especially the fiftieth time."

"It's better than having them think you're on your fourth facelift." Felicity picked up a wooden spoon and gave the heavy iron pot on the gas cook top a stir. "Looks okay," she said to no one in particular, scraped the parsley up and dumped it in.

"Smells great," said Peter, backing hastily away from a topic that had the smell of an unstable explosive.

"Don't expect Mummy to be able to cook," said Felicity. "I was forced to learn in self-defense. She can't cut up an onion without slicing off a finger. I remember a time when the entire Opera Committee writhed in agony through five hours of Wagner after one of her meals. Of course, that might have been the music, not the cooking . . ."

"Felicity, darling, you may think that's funny, but I find it very hurtful. And rude. It's not my fault I can't cook. Your father never let me near the kitchen," she said, turning to Peter with a wry smile. "This was all designed for him, and it cost us a fortune. He loved cooking. He and Felicity spent hours in here trying all sorts of new dishes. I would have been in the way."

"Like now," muttered Felicity.

"It's a beautiful house," said Peter hastily, running his fingers appreciatively over the granite countertop.

"Thank you," murmured Vivian Moore. "It belonged to my husband's parents, and it's become my greatest consolation." She drew in a deep breath that caught soblike in her throat. "Along with Felicity, of course. I've spent a lot of time trying to get everything in it just right. Come and have a look." She nudged him gently away from her daughter until they were back in the entrance hall, standing in the open door to the living room. "That sketch above the fireplace, for example . . ."

"It looks sort of Picassoish," said Peter cautiously.

"Can you tell?" She almost purred her satisfaction. "It is. The minute I saw it I *knew* it would be perfect for—"

"That's right. A real, honest-to-God Picasso." Felicity's dry tones interrupted Vivian from the kitchen. "Or that's what the man said."

Curious, Peter drifted over to the pen-and-ink drawing and studied it with a practiced eye.

"This is my favorite room, I think," said Vivian, walking through a double doorway at the back of the living room. "It has a wonderful view of the garden," she added, nodding at the heavy draperies that covered all the windows.

"You run all this without servants?" asked Peter.

"It's not that big. And we don't need help just for the two of us. Isabel comes in twice a week to keep us from being slaves to housework." Vivian laughed a silvery tiny laugh, but her expression flicked from coy to chilly. "I must get out of these clothes," she said abruptly.

A small table with gracefully curved legs and rococo ornamentation caught Peter's eye. It gleamed at him with the soft patina of centuries of polish on beautiful wood. "I like that," he said, running his hand lightly over it. "Is it old?"

Vivian's expression thawed again. "Charles found it for me in Maryland. On a business trip. It's pretty, isn't it?"

"And the next most expensive thing left in the house after

the Picasso," said Felicity, who had materialized in the doorway again. "If you want to include it on your valuation sheet," she added. Her chef's knife swung back and forth between her fingers, providing a counterpoint to her sour voice.

"Really, Felicity! That's rude."

"I'm sure Peter can take a joke."

The two women faced each other, a study in contrasts. White angry blotches were spoiling Vivian's lovely face, matched by the scarlet patches of rage spreading over her daughter's. They were momentarily speechless, furious combatants regrouping their scattered forces for the next attack. There was something unreal about the whole episode, and Peter wondered for a moment if this little exercise in dissonance was being staged for his benefit. He smiled to indicate that he could indeed take a joke; Vivian patted him on the hand and the atmosphere lightened.

Felicity began humming to herself, a snatch of melody from the *Lucia di Lammermoor* mad scene. Its peculiar suitability made Peter shiver. "Besides," she added carelessly, "the house is half mine, remember, and I can be rude if I like."

"I refuse to have this conversation again. I'm going to shower and change," said her mother. "I'm hot and tired and grubby from the plane. Bring my suitcase up with you, will you, Peter dear?"

Peter ran his hand through his hair and contemplated Vivian Moore's retreating back. "It was kind of your mother to invite me to stay for a few days."

"I doubt she did it out of kindness," said Felicity. "That's not her style. She wanted you back here, and so she set out to convince you you had to come. Right? You'd better hurry," she added. "She'll need those suitcases in a second."

When Peter walked into the kitchen again, Felicity was sprawled on a window seat on the far side of the kitchen, reading a paperback. On the table in front of the window sat a mug of tea and a pile of cookbooks. "Hello," she said, without looking up. "There's beer in the fridge, wine behind that door, and hard stuff in the cabinet in the dining room. Through there," she added, pointing to a swinging door. "What state is Mummy in? Vis-à-vis dinner, that is. An hour? two hours?"

He considered Vivian Moore as he had left her, in a tumble of sweaty sheets, sprawled soundly asleep in her giant bed. How in hell was he supposed to know when she was going to wake up and want dinner?

"Two hours, I guess. She's, uh, taking a nap."

"One hour," said Felicity. "I hear her moving around. If you're going to clutter up my kitchen, though, you can make yourself useful. Open a bottle of wine. Red. And Mummy would probably like a Margarita about now." She took a plastic container out of the refrigerator. "Salad, I think, and a nice loaf of crusty dark bread to go with the lamb stew." She began to tear up an assortment of green and reddish leaves into a salad bowl.

Peter obediently slipped through the swinging door into the dining room. Lost in the middle of the large room was a modest dining table, new-looking, of the kind that comes in pieces in a big flat box. It had been put together by inexpert hands. It struck Peter as a little too bright in color, and too hard and glittering in finish. It would look tawdry beside the table from Maryland. Four chairs of the same family huddled miserably around it. Peter shook his head. The drinks cabinet was a cousin to the table and chairs—shiny and bright, with doors that didn't quite meet properly. But the sideboard across the room took his breath away. He glided silently over to inspect it. It was a big piece, heavy and darkened with age; its drawers were filled with silver that looked both old and valuable. He examined a fork and replaced it, and then opened the cabinet doors. The shelves were empty.

"You won't find the tequila in there," said a dry voice behind him.

"I noticed that," said Peter, straightening up and looking at her with cheerful insouciance. "Tell me," he said. "Why did your mother neglect to mention your existence to me? Surely she must have known that if I came here, I'd meet you."

Felicity shrugged. "Who knows? She finds me a trial at times. We don't, uh, value the same things, shall we say, and she gets tired of explaining me. Don't you have relatives you don't talk about?"

Peter shook his head. "Not really. I don't have many relatives. There's my big sister, Susanna, of course. But we kind of lost touch after she moved to Portland, so I suppose I don't talk about her much. I'm not embarrassed by her." All of which was—in its own way—true.

Felicity watched in silence as he gathered up the necessary bottles and walked back into the kitchen.

"What was that little passage of arms with your mother about?" asked Peter innocently, leaning over the island and filching a bit of endive from the salad bowl. "Isn't this her house? From the way Viv talked, I thought—"

"Well, it is, in a way. Under Daddy's will, we're stuck here together till I get married. Unless either one of us wants to give her share to the other one."

"That's awkward."

"For whom? You?" Felicity giggled and poured olive oil into a cup. "I don't think Daddy could bear to think about Mummy as a rich widow, traveling around the world in search of an appetizing new husband." She turned to look at him with eyes sparkling with amusement—or malice. "Last year Daddy went on a business trip to Australia."

"Last year?" said Peter, surprised. "I thought he died at least ten years ago."

"Mummy does fiddle with the facts sometimes to make a better story. You'll get used to it," said Felicity with a gentle smile. "Anyway, you should have seen the one that Mummy brought home that time. He was cute. Tall and blond. Just like you, actually. And very susceptible—which I guess you aren't. The poor thing turned to slobbering mush whenever she looked at him." She paused to add a pinch or two of herbs to the oil. "But you know, she got bored with all that mindless adoration. He left here in tears. Whimpering like a puppy." She shook her head and added balsamic vinegar to the oil. "Of course, he had been under the impression that Mummy was a very rich widow. Which she wasn't at that point. And he'd abandoned some piddling little job in a bank somewhere in Nowherestown when he latched on to her."

"What happened to the poor bastard?" asked Peter casually.

"Who knows?" said Felicity simply. She turned and leaned against the counter. "He hung around for a couple of days, calling and making a nuisance of himself. Then Mummy had him removed. Because Daddy was about to come home, and he might not have understood."

"Removed? What exactly does that mean?" asked Peter. The answer to his question was forestalled by a loud crash. "What was that?"

"Nothing. Mummy's a pitcher. You know. Something gets in your way and you pitch it as far as you can. Then other people pick it up for you. They say that I got in her way once when I was toddling around in diapers, and I have a scar behind my ear to prove it. I've never looked. Did you leave your suitcase on the floor?"

"I can't remember. I suppose I did."

"Then it's probably your suitcase. I hope there wasn't anything too fragile in it."

"Peter? Are you down there?" Vivian's clear voice floated down the curving staircase. "Could you bring me a drink? Felicity knows what I want."

"Sure thing," he called.

Felicity opened the refrigerator, took out a chilled pitcher, filled it with ice, and handed it to him. He poured and squeezed and stirred with the assurance of a pro. Felicity watched the performance closely. "Salt rim?" he asked.

She shook her head. "Where did Mummy find you? Behind a bar? Not that it matters," she added, catching a fleeting look of annoyance on his face before he managed to repress it.

"I've tended bar in my time," he admitted. "And done a lot of other things as well. Someday when you have ten, twelve hours to spare, I'll tell you my life story. In the meantime, can I get you anything?" he asked, reaching into the refrigerator for a beer for himself.

Felicity shook her head. He shoved two glasses into his pockets, grabbed the pitcher and his beer, and fled up the staircase.

Vivian Moore was seated in front of the mirror in her dressing room. She was wearing a pair of pale gold silk panties and a yellow hairband in her glossy blond hair, with a towel draped over her shoulders. Otherwise she was clad only in her pale, beautiful skin. How old was she? Forty? Thirty-five? Surely not less than that, not with that sharp-tongued, scary twenty-year-old in the kitchen claiming to be her daughter.

"Put my drink where I can reach it," she said, and spread a thin film of moisturizer over her face.

The tone was a trifle peremptory, but he did as he was told, and settled quietly into a comfortable chair, waiting for whatever might happen next. Money might not buy happiness, he reflected, but it did get you comfort and convenience. And space. And someone's money—Daddy's presumably—had bought those neatly sculpted breasts, well-shaped hips, and long legs in the first place.

"Thank you, Peter," said Vivian, rather belatedly. "Has Felicity been entertaining you?"

"She has," he said. "I was watching her make a salad."

"That's all she does these days," said Vivian. "Cook, I mean. She'd like to work in a restaurant, but really." She made a comic grimace in the mirror. "With a trust fund the size of hers, spending your days and nights chopping onions and peeling vegetables seems a waste of time."

"Why doesn't she open a restaurant, if she has so much money?"

"Because I wouldn't dream of letting her, Peter darling. She'd go broke in six months."

"I'm impressed. You have a lot of control over someone that independent." Not to say bloody-minded, thought Peter.

"True—she is independent, but she doesn't get her hands on the money until she marries someone I'm willing to sign off on."

"So she'd be quite a catch for someone you liked."

Vivian hesitated. "Yes and no," she said. "She's a sweet girl, a *rich* sweet girl, but she's a bit neurotic about men."

"Neurotic? Like—frigid?"

"Not precisely. There have been a couple of unpleasant incidents. . . ." Her voice trailed off.

"For whom were the incidents unpleasant?" he asked. "Her? Or the men?" There was no response. "I see. What does she do? Shoot them?"

Vivian smiled. "Oh no. She'd never shoot anyone. She doesn't like loud noises. It's just that she can be difficult once you get to know her. No. More like, once she gets to know your little weaknesses, you can never be quite sure what Felicity's going to do next. When she was fourteen, she reduced a very sweet boy to tears at a club dance. It took him ages to recover." Vivian picked up a small key and unlocked a drawer in the vanity table.

The drawer was divided into velvet-lined sections, each one filled with jewelry that glittered and winked in the light from the makeup mirror. She pulled out and rejected a diamond necklace and bracelet in favor of a pair of long gold earrings. "Actually, it would have been hilarious if it hadn't been so awkward at the time." She shut the drawer, locked it, and threw the key into a pile of panty hose in the drawer beneath it.

"Are you warning me off, Vivian?" asked Peter lightly. "Because I do get very contrary when people try to push me around."

"Certainly not. Why would I do that? Could you get me those things over there?" she added, pointing to a riot of scarlet and white clothing draped over the back of the other chair in the mirrored, windowless room.

"You haven't actually seen your room, have you?" said Vivian, whirling around in front of the mirror to inspect the finished product.

"Do I have a room?" asked Peter. "I hadn't wanted to ask in case it was a problem."

"Don't be silly. It's not a huge house, but we have masses of space. I'll give you the fifteen-second special tour, and then we must go down and eat." She walked from dressing room to bedroom and opened the elaborate window coverings a crack. "You can see the garden from here. And that's our own tiny forest behind it. We're very private and quiet. I once saw an enormous hawk catch a rabbit for his dinner right in the garden."

He glanced out, and then turned his attention back to the room. He picked up a picture of Vivian in a riding habit, standing beside a sturdy hunter, the four-legged kind, with her left hand lying casually on its saddle. The reins were in the firm grasp of a man with his back to the camera, who appeared to know what he was doing. And that was more than you could say for Vivian, thought Peter. He could almost smell the terror emanating from her. The picture was in a heavy silver art deco frame.

"It's a striking piece," he said, examining the frame.

"That was me ages ago, when I could actually go for a long morning canter without getting so stiff I couldn't move for days." She swept by him as she spoke, the fine fabric of her loose jacket fluttering in the breeze she herself had made, and walked down a passageway lined with windows that connected her room with the one next to it.

Peter stopped to examine the back garden. There were no rabbits. No hawks. But Felicity was sitting on the flagstone terrace with a glass of wine and a book. She looked cold.

"This was my husband's room," called Vivian, sharply recalling him to his duties as houseguest. It was very utilitarian: comfortable-looking but sparely decorated. A photograph of Felicity at twelve or thirteen hung on one wall, and a couple of very good modern prints on the others. A paperback thriller with a bookmark in it sat on the bedside table, beside the lamp, a carafe of water, and the clock radio. A pair of binoculars rested on the windowsill, as if their owner had set them down a minute before to answer the phone or get himself a coffee. Peter shivered. His grandmother had kept her late husband's room like that. Darkened, with his brushes and clean underwear ready should he walk in at any time. As a child, he had imagined the ghostly figure of his ancestor coming in every night to select clean socks and shirts, and had refused to go near the second floor after dark. But his grandparents had been married for forty-five apparently happy years. He couldn't imagine Vivian as the shrine-to-his-memory sort.

"Come along then. Dinner won't keep forever," said Vivian, briskly shattering his reflections as she swept across the room and into the hall. "This is Felicity's," she continued, throwing open the door. It was a large room, very organized and tidy-looking, like its owner. "And the bathroom," she announced, opening the door onto a giant bathroom and closing it again.

She walked right past another door and opened the last one. "And this is the guest room." She winked. "You share a bathroom with Felicity."

Peter recognized his suitcase on the floor by the bed. "What's in here?" he asked, turning the handle of the door Vivian had passed by.

Before it was open wide enough for him to glimpse its contents, Vivian reached smartly over and slammed it shut. "Don't open that," she said. "It's just a closet, full of junk. It'll all land on your head and we'll have a lawsuit on our hands. One of these days I'll tidy it all up. It's supposed to be locked. Felicity must have opened it looking for something."

The full moon was rising over the trees that made up Vivian's little forest to the east. The curtains were open, and her bedroom glittered in its pale cold light. The scene reminded Peter unpleasantly of a time in his childhood that abounded in stories about ice queens and trolls and mountain fastnesses lit by glowing icy-white gems. The claustrophobic images from those books filled his nightmares. Susanna, however, had loved them. Grudgingly, she would read *The Little Engine That Could,* or *Jack and the Beanstalk,* and other such infant fare. But every other night, with a touch of childish sadistic pleasure, she would drag him down into the moonlit caves of his deepest fears in the interest of what she called justice. Odd that Vivian—or her house—should remind him of his gentle sister's darker edge.

Peter listened patiently while Vivian tossed and twitched, turned once, and finally fell into deep, helpless sleep. He eased up the covers and slid gingerly out of bed. When his feet hit the floor, she muttered something and then fell back into sleep. He scooped up his pajamas and padded silently over the broadloom. As he walked by the table, he picked up the photo in the silver frame and transferred it to the hand holding the pajamas.

Between the Scylla of opening the squeaky door that led directly from Vivian's room to the hall, and the Charybdis of using the one from her husband's room that might alert sharp-eared Felicity across the way, he opted for Felicity. With misgivings. But nothing stirred. He moved at speed for the guest room. His suitcase was just discernible on the bed, with a dark heap of his clothing beside it. He took a flashlight from its corner and dressed, except for his shoes, which he stuffed into his pockets. Without turning on the lights, he searched every drawer, shelf, and corner of the room by flashlight. His search turned up nothing but a small amount of dust. He slid the silver-framed picture into the capacious inner pocket of his jacket and opened the door.

He moved into the hall like a mousing cat and stopped to consider his options. The locked closet intrigued him, but it was uncomfortably close to Felicity's bedroom. On the other hand, if he hit a creaking stair on his way to the ground floor, Felicity would be out of bed like a shot and he'd have lost his best chance. The closet it would be.

It was a very simple lock. Probably all the doors on the floor could be opened with the same key. Peter took a bunch from his pocket, selected the most probable, and started in.

When it finally caught and turned, it went with a whole-hearted snap, loud enough to awaken everyone in the house. Loud enough, he was convinced, to set the neighbors' dogs barking. He froze, listening for the creak of bedsprings or the subtle, microscopic movements of floorboards. Nothing.

He opened the door and turned on his flashlight. Without any surprise, he saw that it lit a steep set of stairs going directly up to the third floor. He moved up them with infinite care, avoiding the center of the step, setting each foot gently down. Only the third step from the top betrayed him with an answering groan as it took his weight. He leaped off and stood absolutely still, his heart pounding, until he was sure he had elicited no response from the sleepers below.

The arc of his flashlight picked out a large, white-painted room. The two end walls were perpendicular; the front and back sloped almost to the floor. Gable windows with deep window seats were set into them, and long storage cupboards filled in the awkward space in the eaves. There was a bed, made up, a table, chairs, a dresser, and a television set. Two closed doors hinted at a closet and a bathroom. In palmier days, before Mr. Moore's demise, this would have been the maid's room.

Peter repeated his systematic search of the room, halting every minute or so to listen for movement in the house. He checked the drawers, the closet, the bathroom, with no result, and then turned his attention to the bed. He tore off the bedclothes and let his flashlight examine the bare mattress. His hand shook as he took out his bunch of keys; with a sharp blade on the miniature knife set he kept on his key ring, he ripped out a piece of material from the mattress cover. He lifted the mattress, picked up a small object, and tucked it into his pocket. He remade the bed very neatly and crept as quietly as he could to the guest room. He removed a telephone from his suitcase and punched in a set of well-known numbers. "Susanna? I'm in the house. I can't speak up. Turn off the TV and listen. He was here. I found Tony's medal under a mattress. Don't get your hopes up. I'm going back up there to see what else I can find." Without another word, he tucked the phone away and headed back upstairs.

He opened the door to the first of the low cupboards in the eaves, dropped down onto his belly in the dust and wriggled halfway inside.

"I doubt if you'll find much to interest you up here," said a voice.

"You never know," said Peter mildly. His voice echoed

inside the empty cupboard. "I like attics. They're interesting." He started to ease himself out.

"Don't move." A heavy weight settled on the middle of his back. "That sharp point just under your rib cage is my knife. If you don't believe me, I'll stick it in just a little bit."

"Don't bother," said Peter hastily. "I believe you." He waited for an uncomfortable moment or two. "The stair creaks," he added casually. "I was afraid that might disturb you."

"It wasn't the staircase so much as the floorboards. They sort of groan when people walk over them. Not loud, but you can hear it in my room. We had to get rid of the maid because of that." She eased her weight off his back a little. "I can't decide whether to call Mummy or the police," she continued in a thoughtful tone.

"Don't worry about me," said Peter. "Call the police, if you like. They're sweeter than Mummy. But why bother?"

"Why do you say that? Why shouldn't I call the police if I find a thief in the house?"

"A thief? Me? Not at all. A guest. A curious guest with insomnia who likes exploring attics. Why would I come up here if I were going to rob you? I admit that Vivian's jewelry is mostly fake, but the silver in the dining room is worth a few bucks."

Heavy footsteps shook the stairs to the attic. A warm baritone voice filled the space under the rafters. "Good heavens, Felicity, what do you have there?"

"It's a man, Daddy. His name is Peter. Peter Fitzgerald."

"Whyever are you standing on him, darling? That's hardly the way to treat a guest, is it? Unless he's a very old friend?" There was a long, silent, stubborn pause. "I thought not. Come here, sweetheart." The pressure on Peter's back eased and then disappeared. "I apologize for my daughter. She's excitable and has a tendency to overreact. Do let me help you up." He reached a hand in Peter's direction. "Charles Moore, Mr. Fitzgerald. Peter."

"Mr. Moore?" repeated Peter as he scrambled to his feet. "I thought you were dead."

"Hardly," said Mr. Moore. "Felicity darling, do turn on the lights. Moonlight may become you, but I find it difficult to see by. Tell me, Peter, did Vivian play the grieving widow to lure you up here? She loves that role."

Suddenly the room filled with light. Peter blinked, and then turned to inspect his rescuer. Mr. Moore was leaning against the table, his hands in his pockets, with a fawn-colored sweater tied casually about his neck. Everything about him—his haircut, his shoes, his shirt, his beautifully tailored, casual pants—screamed money and a restrained but excellent dress sense. "I rescued her," he went on casually, "from a sadly undistinguished career in the theater. She was very grateful at the time, but the poor thing does miss the excitement. And it comes out in odd ways from time to time. But we forgive her, don't we, Lissy? We forgive her."

Felicity Moore was sitting cross-legged on the bed, glaring at Peter. She declined to respond.

"Do come downstairs," said Mr. Moore. "We'll have a drink and a little chat. I have a small proposal to put before you."

Moore put the kettle on and set out a tray with lemons and rum and honey. "Something to warm us up. It may be spring, but I'm chilly, and I suspect you are too, Peter. We usually keep the heat turned off up in the attic. A little economy gesture in these difficult times. But it does get awfully chilly."

"I hate hot toddies," said Felicity. Her words were addressed to her father, but her baleful glare was fixed on Peter. "I think they're sickening."

With a swish of silk, Vivian walked into the kitchen and sat down at the rustic pine table with her back to the windows. The cold light from the full moon riding high in the heavens lit up her hair and silvered over the deep blue of her dressing gown. "Stop making such a fuss, Felicity. Just don't drink it. Has anyone explained to Peter what's going on? I thought not." She shook her head.

"We had planned to let you get to know us a little better before springing it on you," said Moore apologetically, "but.

since you seem to be curious about the situation, well—this is what it's all about."

"Let me see if I get this, Charles," said Peter. "Your parents left you this house and contents, and a whopping chunk of money to be divided between you and Felicity, hoping to cut Vivian, whom they loathed, out from at least half the loot. Now, being worried about Felicity's misanthropic disposition, they added an uncomfortable rider that no one gets a penny until Felicity marries with your approval. At this point you would sign off on her marriage to a boa constrictor if that would cause the money to be released. Little ole Vivian lured me back here to marry Felicity, and then bow gracefully out with my ten percent or whatever. Since you're selling everything you can, you must be getting desperate. Why not get rid of the Picasso?"

There was an awkward moment of silence.

"Oh," said Peter. "Fake. I wondered about that. And the table?"

"There are some things in the house that I am not willing to sell. Not yet, anyway," said Moore.

"And if I get all huffy and won't go along?"

"No problem," said Moore. "There are lots of men out there who'd be happy to pick up ten thousand for a few days work."

"That's my cut? Ten thousand?"

"Yes. As a divorce settlement. A contract can be drawn up as soon as tomorrow with guarantees." The three Moores gathered closer to each other, fixing their eyes on his face.

"Ten thousand," he mused. "That's not much. I'm very good on a horse. Is that worth more?"

Charles Moore froze. His wife and daughter looked as if a ghost had just wandered into the room.

"It's a useful skill around here," said Moore cautiously. "But not essential."

"I would think," said Peter casually, "that with my name and face, *and* expertise, I'd be worth closer to half a mil."

"Let's get rid of him," said Felicity suddenly. A smile crept across her face.

"I would imagine," said Peter, "that there's a limit to the

number of young men named Peter that you can plant under the trees—it takes a long time for that kind of disturbance to disappear into the landscape. One of these days someone will wonder what happened to us all. And that someone is going to start digging up your forest floor."

"I doubt that," said Charles smoothly. "Peter the first didn't have much family. And we investigated you. You have a history of going off for long periods of time. It will take a while before someone starts to worry, and by then you will be replaced by a third Peter. The neighbors get a glimpse of Felicity's young friend, Peter, from time to time, and their curiosity is satisfied."

"You're wrong on one point," said Peter. "Peter the first—a.k.a. Peter Jenkins—had a mother who worried about him. And she communicated her worries to her younger brother, who happens to be in law enforcement. You see, young Peter was named after his uncle, who had a strong interest in his nephew's welfare. And so after he disappeared I took some leave—"

"You're a cop?" hissed Vivian. "But we checked . . ."

"Not very efficiently. You weren't hard to fool." Peter's tongue felt thick and his words fuzzy. There had been something in that drink, and he had swallowed it like a lamb. "Have you never heard of the sacred responsibility between brother and sister's son?" The three vultures across from him divided into six. He closed one eye to bring them in focus. His other eye fell in step with the first and he could not force it back open. His head crashed onto the table and blackness intervened.

"They needed to find someone who wasn't local to marry their terrifying daughter and then be willing to divorce her without taking half the cash with him. Or, God forbid, talking her into staying married to him. It was quite a technique—Vivian concentrated on being seductive, while Felicity reminded you that her mother was a flake, and you wouldn't want to live with either one of them. It would have worked with the right kind of guy, I suppose. But not my poor nephew Peter. He was an idealist. A romantic. He must have turned them down flat, and so they locked him in the attic while they decided what to do with him."

"Are you sure?"

"I found his father's ring under the mattress. And a scrap of paper with a note on it in the cupboard—I left that for you guys. And Vivian had a picture of him holding her horse. It was taken from behind, but it was him, all right. You might find more stuff up there in the attic." He slipped back down in the bed. "Go look. My head hurts and I need some more sleep." His eyes closed. "The disturbed earth of the grave stands out very clearly if you look down from the second floor."

"Right, Lieutenant. It's a good thing we got your message, or they would have planted you back there along with him."

His eyes flew open. "What message?"

"Some woman called and said you were in big trouble. She referred us to Palm Beach, and they knew what you were up to. Told us where you were. The woman's name was Susanna."

"My sister? She always knew when I got in too deep for my own good," said Peter, and fell asleep.

Canadian author Medora Sale introduces a mysterious stranger into an even stranger household in this story. Sale's novels feature architectural photographer Harriet Jeffries and police inspector John Sanders and include *Murder on the Run* (winner of the Crime Writers of Canada's Ellis Award for Best First Novel in 1988), *Murder in Focus* (1989), *Murder in a Good Cause* (1989), *Sleep of the Innocent* (1991), *Pursued by Shadows* (1992), and *Short Cut to Santa Fe* (1994).

A Parrot Is Forever

Peter Lovesey

⸺

That eye was extraordinary, dominated by the yellow iris and fringed by a ring of spiky black eyelashes. In the short time I had been watching, the pupil had contracted to little more than a microdot.

"It's magnificent, but it's a lot larger than I expected," I told the young woman who was its keeper.

She said, "Macaws are big birds."

At this safe distance from the perch, I said, "I was expecting something smaller. A parrot, I was told."

"Well, a macaw is a member of the parrot family."

This member of the parrot family raised itself higher and stared over my head, excluding me, letting me know that I was unworthy of friendship at this first meeting.

"No doubt we'll learn to get along with each other," I said. "I'm willing to try, if the bird is." I took a tentative step closer.

Too close for the macaw, because it thrust its head at me and gave a screech like a power drill striking steel.

I jerked back. "Wow!"

The keeper said, "It's a pity. Roger was just getting used to us. Now he has to start over again."

First lesson: you address parrots as you would humans. The impersonal "it" was unacceptable. This was Roger, a personality.

Roger. About right for this rebarbative old bird. Roger is one of those names redolent of wickedness. Jolly Roger, the pirate flag; eighteenth century rakes rogering wenches; Roger the lodger, of so many dirty jokes. The glittering eye and that great, black beak curved over the mouth in a permanent grin would make you believe this Roger had been everywhere and tried everything.

"He's called 'Sir Roger,' according to his papers," said the young woman, wanting to say something in the parrot's favor. "We were taught a dance at school called Sir Roger de Coverley. I expect he's named after that."

Fat chance, I thought. My uncle George, the parrot's former owner, was never a country dancer. He was a diamond robber. A long time ago, in May 1954, Uncle George and two others held up a Hatton Garden merchant and stole twenty-seven uncut diamonds valued at half a million pounds. Half a million was a fortune in 1954. The advantage of uncut stones—if you steal them—is that they are difficult to identify, so it was also a clever heist. The only blemish on this brilliant crime was that the three robbers were rounded up within a week and given long prison sentences. But the diamonds were never recovered. Two of the robbers died inside. Uncle George served twenty-six years. After his release, he seemed mysteriously to come into money. He emigrated to Spain, the Costa del Sol. It was a wise move. He lived another fifteen years, without ostentation, but comfortably, in a villa, in the company of a señorita half his age.

In my ultrarespectable family, Uncle George was a taboo topic. My father rarely mentioned him, and never spoke of the robbery. I only learned of it after Dad died and I was going through his papers. There was a newspaper clipping about the release from jail of the old diamond robber.

Now my uncle was dead. He'd gone peacefully last Christmas, in his own bed, at the age of seventy-nine. It seemed he'd known his time was coming, and he had made appropriate arrangements. This blue and yellow macaw was bequeathed to me.

In January I had received a solicitor's letter advising me of my legacy. At first I thought it was a practical joke. I was told I must wait six months while the parrot served the six-month quarantine period that applies to all imported animals—as if I was impatient to meet this creature! I hadn't asked for the parrot. I knew nothing about parrots. I was an actor, for pity's sake. How would I fit a blue and yellow macaw into my life? The solicitor informed me when I phoned him that he understood parrots make fine companions. As for my acting career, he'd heard that the late Sir Ralph Richardson had kept a parrot, and it hadn't held him back.

I was in a spot. Only a complete toe-rag would deny an old man's dying wish. My uncle must have been devoted to the parrot to make arrangements for it to be shipped to England. But oh, Uncle George, why to me?

True, I was the only surviving relative, but I have another theory. Uncle George may have seen me on cable television in the part of a wisecracking villain in some corny crime series. It ran for some weeks. I think he identified with the part.

The crushing irony of all this was that the rest of the estate, consisting of the Spanish villa and all its contents and enough pesetas to provide many years of comfortable living, all went to the señorita Uncle George had shared the last years of his life with. The parrot came to me, I guessed because Isabella said she'd strangle it if Uncle George didn't get rid of it.

So here I was at Bird & Board, the aviary close to the London airport. Roger had completed his quarantine and now I had arrived to claim him.

"This is the box he travels in," the young woman informed me, opening the welded mesh grill that was the door of a sturdy plastic pet container. It was the sort of box used for cats and dogs, the only concession to Roger's comfort being a wooden perch fitted some three inches off the floor and much chewed by his sharp beak. "He doesn't like it much. Would you like me to put him inside?"

"Please."

Roger had seen the box and was already getting agitated, swaying and ruffling his feathers. The moment the keeper started putting on a pair of leather gauntlets, there was a flexing of wings and a series of bloodcurdling screams that started off all the other birds and created bedlam.

"They can be noisy," she said, as if she were telling me something. "Hope you're on good terms with your neighbors." Skillfully avoiding the thrusting black beak, she grasped the big macaw by the neck and legs, lifted him off the perch, and placed him in the box. "He'll calm down presently," she shouted.

And he did. She draped a cloth over the front and the darkness subdued him.

She asked me, "Have you kept a parrot before?"

"No."

"You've got treats in store, then. If Roger gets unbearable, you can always see if one of the tropical bird gardens will take him."

"Would you?" I asked hopefully.

"Couldn't possibly. We deal only with birds in quarantine."

"So I'm lumbered."

"Try not to think of it that way," she said compassionately, then added, "That will be a hundred and fifty pounds, please."

"What will?"

"Roger's account—for staying here. We can't do it for nothing, you know."

"Some legacy!" I said, getting out my checkbook.

"If you do sell him," she told me, "don't sell him cheap. They're worth a few hundred, you know."

"So I'm finding out," I told her as I wrote the check.

I carried the pet container to the place where I'd left my car. Heaven knows, Roger had given me no grounds for friendship, but I muttered reassuring things through the ventilation slits. I continued to speak to him at intervals all the way along the motorway. At Heston I stopped at a garden center and bought some heavy-duty leather gloves.

When I got home and opened the pet container, it was some time before my new houseguest emerged. Having seen the size of his beak, and read a little about the damage one peck can inflict, I didn't reach inside for him. In fact, I was extremely nervous of him. After waiting some time, I left the room to get myself a coffee. When I returned, Roger had stepped out to inspect his new quarters.

If nothing else, he had brought some much-needed color to my home. His back and wings were vivid sky-blue, his chest and the underside of the wings purest yellow, his crown and forehead dark green. Spectacular—but at what cost?

I'd gone to the trouble of making a perch out of beech wood and installing it in my living room. What I hadn't appreciated was that Roger wasn't capable of getting up there unaided. His wings were clipped. I wasn't ready yet to handle him, even with the leather gauntlets. But I didn't need to bother, because he made his own choice. After a cursory inspection of the room, he decided to occupy the sheet feed of my printer, which projected at a convenient angle and left just enough room for his long blue tail feathers. He reached it by scaling the wastepaper basket and the top drawer of the desk, using his beak and claws.

Once on his new perch, he established his right of residence by hunching his shoulders, lifting his tail, and depositing a green dropping on the script of my next TV part, which I'd left behind the printer. I felt the same way about the script, but I replaced it with an old newspaper.

There was sunflower seed and corn in the feeding bowl attached to the perch. I succumbed and moved the bowl close to the printer. The parrot appeared to have no interest in food. He watched me keenly from my office machinery, I suppose to see if I had plans to eject him. To foster confidence, I removed the pet container altogether and put it in the spare room.

There is no doubt that parrots are exceptional in their ability to communicate their feelings to humans. They have eloquent eyes that dilate and contract at will. The skin around the face can blush pink. With the angle of the head, the posture of the shoulders, and the action of the claws, they can express curiosity, boredom, sorrow, anger, approval, domination, and submission. All that, before they let go with their voices. Mercifully, Roger hadn't yet screamed in my home.

That night, I left him perched on the sheet feed. In the morning, although he still hadn't touched the food, he seemed interested to see me. Genuine trust was slow in developing on both sides, but he began to feed, and the day came, about a week later, when he succeeded in maneuvering his way across the furniture to the back of a chair I was seated in. Neither of us moved for some time. It was a distinct advance.

One morning the following week, perched on the printer as usual, Roger put his head at an angle, dilated his eyes and extended a claw to me. With some misgivings, I extended my arm. He gripped it at the wrist and transferred himself from the sheet feed to me. Acting as a living perch, I walked slowly around the room. When I made to return him to the printer, he clawed his way higher up my arm until he was on my shoulder. He had decided I was not, after all, the enemy.

I suppose the discovery was mutual.

If all else fails, I thought, I can now audition for a part in *Treasure Island.*

In a couple of months I learned to handle Roger, and he transferred to the purpose-built perch. He had a small silver ring around one of his legs, and I could have chained him to the perch, but there was no need. He behaved reasonably well. True, he used his beak on things, but that is standard parrot behavior. The worst damage he inflicted was to peck through my telephone cable. Sometimes it's an advantage to be incommunicado. At least a day passed before I realized I was cut off. I discovered the damage only when Roger fooled me with a perfect imitation of the phone's ringing tone. I picked up the receiver and the line was dead. This was the first inkling I had that he was capable of mimicry. In time, when he really settled in, he would greet visitors with, "Hello, squire," or "Hello, darling," according to sex. He must have been taught by Uncle George. He had no other vocabulary and I didn't want to coach him. I think it undermines the dignity of animals to make them ape human behavior.

As you must already have gleaned, Roger was winning me over. I found him amusing, and appreciative of all the attention I could give him. There were moments when he would regard me intently, willing me to come forward and admire him, utterly still, yet beaming out such anticipation that I was compelled to stop whatever I was doing. The unblinking eyes would beguile me, seeming to penetrate to the depth of my being. As I went closer, he would make small movements on the perch, finally turning full circles and twitching his elegant tail. If I put my face against his plumage, the scent of the natural oils was exquisite.

One evening I returned late from a rehearsal and had a horrible shock. Roger was missing. I dashed around the house calling his name before I noticed the broken window where the thief had got in. I was devastated. My poor parrot must have fought hard, because there were several of those spectacular blue tail feathers under his perch.

The police didn't give much comfort. "We've had parrots stolen before," said the constable who came. "It's just another form of crime, like nicking car radios. They know where to get rid of them. A parrot like yours will fetch a couple of hundred, easy. Did they take his cage as well?"

"He doesn't have a cage. He lives on that perch."

"How did you get him here in the first place?"

"In a pet container. It's in the back room . . . I think." Even as I spoke, I knew it was gone. I'd been through the spare room and the box wasn't there. I should have noticed. Well, I had, in a way, but it hadn't registered in my brain until now. The bastards hadn't just taken Roger; they'd had the brass to take his box as well.

"We'll keep a look out," said the constable in a tone that gave me no confidence. "Would you know your own bird? That's the problem. These blue and yellow macaws all look the same."

I felt bereft. It was clear to me now how important that parrot had become to me. I was angry and guilty and impotent. I'm a peaceful man, or believed I was. I could have strangled the person who had taken Roger.

Each day, I called the police to see if there was news. They'd heard nothing. Almost a week went by. They advised me to get another bird. I didn't want another bird. I wanted Roger back.

I had to move the empty perch into the spare room because the sight of it was so upsetting. My work was suffering. I messed up an audition. I couldn't learn lines anymore.

On the sixth day after Roger was stolen, a Sunday morning, my phone rang.

It was Roger.

Reader, don't give up. I haven't gone completely gaga over this parrot. Roger hadn't picked up the phone and dialed my number. Somebody else had. But I could hear Roger at the other end of the line. He was giving his imitation of the phone ringing.

The person who had dialed my number didn't speak. I said, "Who is this?" several times. Roger, in the background, was still mimicking the phone. It *could* have been a second phone, but I convinced myself it was not.

I guessed what it was about. The thief was checking whether I was home. He was thinking of breaking into my home again, perhaps to steal something else.

The line went dead after only a few seconds. Not a word had been spoken by the caller.

I was frustrated and enraged.

Fortunately, there is a way of tracing calls. I dialed the message system and obtained the caller's number. It's a computerized system and you aren't given the name or address.

I thought about going to the police and asking them to check the number, but I hadn't been impressed by the constable who had come to see me. He didn't regard a missing macaw as a high priority.

Instead I waited an hour and then tried the number myself. It rang for some time before it was picked up and a woman's voice said, "Marwood Hotel."

Thinking rapidly, I said, "Is that the Marwood Hotel in Notting Hill Gate?"

She said, "I've never heard of one in Notting Hill Gate. We're the Marwood in Fulham. Gracechurch Road."

Fulham was just a ten-minute drive from where I lived. I told her I'd made a mistake. I put down the phone and went straight to the car.

Gracechurch Road was once a good address for the Edwardian middle classes. Now it stands under the shadow of the Hammersmith Fly-Over. The tall, brick villas have become seedy hotels and overpopulated flats.

My approach wasn't subtle. I went in and asked the woman at the desk if the hotel welcomed pets.

She said in the voice I'd heard on the phone, "Provided they behave themselves."

"A parrot, for instance?"

"I don't know about parrots," she said dubiously.

"You have one here already, don't you?"

She said, "I wouldn't want another one like that. It makes a horrible sound when it's excited. Fit to burst your eardrums."

"Blue and yellow? Big?" I said, my heart racing.

She nodded.

I asked, "Does it belong to the hotel?"

"No, the foreign gentleman in number twelve. The top floor."

"When did he arrive?"

"About ten days ago."

"With the parrot?"

"No, he brought that in one day last weekend. In a box. He says it's only temporary."

"Is he up there now?"

She checked the board where the keys were hung. "He should be. If you want, I can ring up."

I said that on second thought I'd call back later. Simply going upstairs and knocking on the door would not be a wise course of action.

She didn't see me double around the side of the house to the back. These old buildings converted into hotels often have fire escapes, and this was no exception. It was the most basic sort, a vertical iron ladder fixed to the brickwork, with access to the large casement windows on each of the three upper floors. With luck, I wouldn't be visible to anyone inside.

This was a chance I had to take. I climbed about fifty rungs to the top floor. The window was a hinged one and it was open. Easy to open wider. There were extra rungs directly under it. All I needed to do was transfer sideways, put my leg over the sill and let myself in. First, I listened for sounds of movement from the room.

I could hear nothing.

I'm not much of an acrobat, but I succeeded in getting my legs through the window and scrambling into the room.

A voice I knew said, "Hello, squire."

Roger!

For me, that reunion was on a par with H. M. Stanley meeting Dr. Livingstone.

Roger was perched on the footboard of a double bed. He recognized me. He lifted his claw—a signal that he wanted to transfer to my arm and so to my shoulder. Elated, I took a step toward him. There was a sound behind me. I was not conscious of anything else, except a crushing blow to the back of my head.

I don't know how long I was out.

When the world started up again for me, I was lying on the bed with my hands tied behind me. The foreign "gentleman" had his thumb jammed into my eye, forcing it open. He spoke some words I didn't recognize.

My head ached. My vision was blurred, but clearing. He looked evil. His shoulders were huge.

I said, "I don't want trouble. I just want my parrot back."

He said with a strong Spanish inflection, "You own this parrot?"

I told him who I was.

He spoke again. "This parrot Roger, he is stupid. He tell me nothing. Nothing."

I said, "He's just a parrot. What do you expect?"

"You ask what I expect. I expect you have talked to this parrot, yes? He tell you where diamonds are kept."

I said, "I don't know what the hell you're talking about."

He raised his arm and slapped me across the face with the back of his hand. My lip split.

He shouted, "Your uncle had many diamonds, yes? Why he send you this parrot when he die?"

I said, "Just who are you?"

He grabbed my hair and forced my head back. "Now you are here, you will talk to Roger. Then he tell you some number, some number of box inside bank."

Box inside bank: I was beginning to understand. "A safe deposit number?"

"Si."

"He docsn't speak numbers."

"Do it. Speak numbers now." Still grasping my hair, he hauled me off the pillow and toward the foot of the bed where Roger was still perched, looking uneasy, swaying slightly, just as he had when I'd first seen him at Bird & Board.

Feeling incredibly stupid and helpless, I started chanting numbers to my parrot. "One. Two. Three. Four."

Roger watched me in a stupefied silence.

"Five. Six. Seven."

"This no good," said the man. "Try three, four numbers together."

I said, "One two three. One two four." My lip had swollen. I could feel warm blood trickling down my chin.

Roger looked away.

"One two five."

I continued speaking sets of numbers, trying to think how this would end.

I said, "Roger is nervous. You've made him nervous. They don't speak when they're nervous."

This seemed to make some impression. Roger played his part by drawing his wings tight to his body and making a groaning sound deep in his chest.

The man produced a pocketknife and cut whatever it was that pinioned my wrists. I sat on the edge of the bed and wiped some blood away from my face. I needed to think. He was far too big to take on.

He said, "Now you try again."

I said, "I'd like to be clear what this is all about. You want a safe deposit number, and you think the parrot will speak it, right?"

He pondered how much to tell me. Then he said, "George, he had diamonds. Isabella, his woman, she search the villa. No diamonds."

"You were sent by Isabella?"

"Si. She think maybe there is one deposit box in his bank in Malaga. No name. Only number, *comprende?"*

"Yes."

"Isabella say George he was crafty old gringo. He teach the parrot this number and send it to you."

"I don't think so," I said. "I hardly knew him at all."

This didn't impress my captor. "Stupid old man, he do this to cheat Isabella."

"You're Isabella's friend?"

"Brother."

I doubted if that was true. I said, "I've had Roger for almost a year now. He's never spoken numbers to me. Basically, all he can say is 'Hello.'"

Isabella's "brother" struck me across the face a second time.

Roger screamed and spread his wings.

He took a swipe at Roger and just avoided being pecked.

In extreme situations, the brain works faster. I said, "If you'll listen, I have a suggestion. You see the little silver ring attached to his leg? There's something written on it. Very small. I don't know if it's a number. We can look if you like."

"The ring! *Si!"* His face lit up. He reached toward Roger, who dipped forward and tried to peck his hand.

There was no chance of Roger letting him examine that ring.

He said, "You hold him."

I said, "He's nervous."

He said, "You want me to kill you and the parrot?"

I spoke some encouraging words to Roger and held my wrist close to him. If ever I needed my parrot's cooperation, it was now. After some understandable hesitation, he put out a claw and transferred to my wrist. Continuing to speak to Roger as calmly as I was able, I fingered the ring with my free hand.

I told the man, "I need more light. I can't read this."

He said, "You come to the window."

I stroked Roger's back and stood up. The man led me toward the light. He said, "No tricks. You show this number to me. You hold the parrot and show me."

Roger was amazingly compliant. He let me finger the ring again. In the better light, I gazed earnestly at the completely blank ring and started inventing numbers. "It looks to me like a three, a five, a nine. Is that a nine, would you say?"

The Spaniard moved to the only position convenient for viewing the ring. He didn't dare come within range of that vicious black beak. He had his back to the open casement window through which I'd climbed.

It was my opportunity. I was poised to give him an almighty push, but Roger forestalled me. He screeched, opened his wings and reared at the man—who rocked back, lost his balance and pitched backward out of the window. It was a long drop, three floors to a concrete yard. I didn't look out to see the result.

I don't believe Roger understood the consequence of his action. My theory is that he thought he was being taken to the open window. In the year I had owned him—as I discovered later—his wing feathers had grown and he was perfectly capable of flying. He wanted to test those wings. For him, it was the best escape route. When the man blocked his exit, he acted.

I'm not proud of my actions after that, but I ought to set them on record. I grabbed my parrot and pushed him into his pet container, which was just inside the door. I carried the box downstairs and drove off without speaking to anyone.

The inquest on the Spanish guest at the Marwood Hotel resulted in an open verdict. Identification was impossible, because he was found to be using a false passport. It was assumed by most people that this was a sad case of suicide.

Within a week I, too, changed my identity. I moved away from England, sacrificing my TV career for an early retirement to the tropics. For obvious reasons I am not disclosing the name of this island paradise. The climate is a lot better than I'm used to, and it suits Roger well. I have a fine stone house, a large swimming pool, servants, and a speedboat.

Maybe you are wondering where I got the funds. Roger discovered the seven large uncut diamonds. They were hidden in the hollow wooden perch fixed in the pet container he so disliked. He'd pecked through the wood before I got him home from the Marwood Hotel. So Isabella's "brother" had them in his possession for a short time, and never knew it. Sorry, Isabella—I'm certain they were meant for me. They were my legacy from Uncle George. Along with Roger, who is sitting on my shoulder as I write these words.

He's got life running as he wants it, I think.

———

A not-so-jolly Roger the Parrot proves a mixed blessing for the protagonist in this tale from British author Peter Lovesey. Lovesey's current series features former Detective Superintendent Peter Diamond *(The Last Detective, Diamond Solitaire, The Summons)* and the hilariously lecherous and inept Bertie, Prince of Wales *(Bertie and the Seven Bodies, Bertie and the Tinman, Bertie and the Crime of Passion).* His Sergeant Cribb mysteries are well-known from the PBS *Mystery!* series. Lovesey, winner of the British Crime Writers Association Silver Dagger and Gold Dagger for *Waxwork* and *The False Inspector Dew* respectively, was a 1991 Agatha nominee for Best Short Story for "The Crime of Miss Oyster Brown."

Married to a Murderer

Alan Russell

". . . murderers get sheaves of offers of marriage."
—George Bernard Shaw

Danielle Deveron thought of herself as an *outmate*. She liked the expression, because in the word there was an element of outcast, as well as the notion of being mated. It was accurately descriptive, she thought, of those carrying on a relationship with a prisoner.

Not that Danielle thought she had much in common with other outmates. Most of *them* she considered pathetic, women with no self-esteem. As she saw it, their relationships with prison inmates offered them little more than a perverse nunnery. Danielle was sure her situation was different. Her wealth, reputed to be in the neighborhood of fifty million dollars, was only a part of what Danielle believed distinguished her from the other outmates. Perhaps she'd read too much Fitzgerald, who insisted that the very rich "are different from you and me." Or perhaps she was just being realistic.

Her money had brought Danielle to the prisoner. Helen

Bernard had been the inadvertent matchmaker, guilty Helen who'd always been somewhat ashamed about her own vast wealth. Helen believed it was her duty to sit on philanthropic boards and work for the betterment of society, and was always dogging Danielle to become involved with one do-gooder organization or another. Usually Danielle escaped such duties by writing a check. In the end that's what they always wanted anyway. But on this occasion, Horseface Helen had piqued her interest. She had wanted Danielle to accompany her on an afternoon outing to San Carlos Prison.

Prison. Not some luncheon, or fashion show, or gathering of serious-looking people talking about addressing some pervasive wrong. Danielle had never been to a prison before. And what truly intrigued her was that Helen was scheduled to meet with a murderer. In her thirty years on the planet, Danielle had never met a murderer. She had dated the gamut of males, including poets, stockbrokers, race-car drivers, royalty, near royalty, surgeons, CEOs, and even a junior senator from the state of Colorado, but she had never spent any time with a murderer (or at least with anyone who boasted of having made a killing in anything other than the market).

What did they see in their first look? There was an immediate attraction for both of them that went beyond the physical. Clay Potter had been on death row for a dozen years. He was thin and pale, had sunken cheeks and a consumptive cough that caused a lock of his long dark hair to fall up and down on the bridge of his nose. There was a scar running along his right cheek. His arms, exposed to his elbows, were a canvas of tattoos, displays mostly of naked women, but his painted ladies, even in their exaggerated forms, disappeared in the presence of Danielle. Preternaturally pale, her milk complexion set off her dark lashes and blue eyes. Her pressed, shoulder-length golden hair glittered.

Gold, he thought. The hair, the woman. She personified his dreams and his fantasies of wealth. He had always had visions of what it must be like to be wealthy, and had pursued lucre, Jason after the fleece, Jason willing to fleece, or worse. Clay's problem was that he had never been able to distinguish fool's gold from the real thing.

The attraction wasn't one-sided. Clay didn't have the looks of the pretty boys Danielle usually associated with, but there was something about him that beguiled. She remembered attending a party replete with movers and shakers. There were familiar faces everywhere, household names from the entertainment industry, superstars from the sporting world, but the person that drew the most murmurs and looks was a mobster. "He's arranged murders," were the whispers.

Clay had done more than arrange murders. He had committed them, Danielle thought, though as might be expected, he still proclaimed his innocence. His pronouncement was made to the two women without any enthusiasm, words from a tired old script, words that had been uttered too many times to audiences that never listened or believed. Anyone who works in the criminal justice system knows that most inmates proclaim their innocence as a matter of course. Though lockup wasn't anything new to Clay, he tried to explain to Danielle and Helen that murder was.

"I've always been a B and E man," he said, explaining that meant "breaking and entering." It was just his bad luck to have broken into the wrong house. Everything had been quiet, he said, too still. It was one of those Hillsborough mansions, the kind where there should have been noises. He had been cruising the neighborhood, looking for some easy pickings, when he stopped at this one house. "Just a feeling," he said. He said his suspicions should have been aroused by the off-line burglar alarm, but he had encountered lots of homes where people had deactivated their systems just because they didn't want to be bothered with them.

"I'm an opportunist," Clay said. Was he warning Danielle? "I take advantage of circumstances."

He told them how he quietly went through the house, relieving it of rare coins, stamps, jewelry, and silverware. He took his pickings from the den, dining room, and family room. Clay said he was not a confrontational thief, wasn't the kind to hold a gun on the occupants. He liked his houses unoccupied, and he began to wonder whether anyone was home. He decided to sneak a peek into the master bedroom, and that's where he saw the blood and what looked like bodies.

"I panicked," he said. "I ran out of the house. I was so scared I even forgot my booty. I drove away fast. Unfortunately, my car didn't fit the neighborhood profile. That's why I got stopped by the police. If I'd had another car, I wouldn't be here."

Unsaid, but directed to Danielle with a telling look, he proclaimed the injustice. And somewhere in the look was also the hint that he should have been driving a new European sedan with the kind of shaded glass that hides its occupants from admiring eyes.

"The police didn't hold me," Clay said, "but after the murders were discovered, they picked up one of my prints on the gold coins I left behind. Taking off my gloves was felony stupid, but I never expected it would get me convicted of felony murder."

His initial statement was what hung him, Clay told them. He had tried to deny ever being in the house, and later, when he recanted, the prosecution made much of his changing stories and admitting to "fabricating." The jury, faced with four bodies (two of them children, aged eight and twelve), and having a hardened criminal at the scene of the murder, sentenced him to death. The Golden State had decided not to let Clay see his golden years. His death was scheduled in six months.

"My lawyer says you've helped others," Clay said, addressing Helen with his eyes and words. "I don't have many cards left to play, but the one survivor in the family was an older son that was away at college. He and his parents weren't getting along. Apparently he had a drug problem. That's what they call it when you have money. You're a junkie otherwise. The day before the murders, there was a big family fight. The parents said enough was enough, and that they wouldn't be supplying the kid with any more money."

Clay theorized that the night after the fight, the son had left his university apartment, driven home, turned off the burglar alarm, and then bludgeoned his family to death. Their son was the one who would have benefited from their deaths, Clay said. And who would benefit from his as well.

"That little preppy did whatever he could to help build the state's case against me. He hired some private dicks, and they dug up the dirt on me."

"Was there a lot of dirt?" Danielle asked.

Clay shrugged. "I was never any angel, but they made it sound like I was up to my ears in it. Their tactics didn't only work on the jury. They worked on me. I felt dirty, especially when preppy showed up every day in his thousand-dollar suits. He was always quick with his silk hankie too. Pulled it right out of his fancy suit like a magician, and started with the waterworks.

"Maybe if I'd had one of them suits, and a fifty-dollar haircut, and a Swiss timepiece, I wouldn't be in here."

Helen was too polite to disagree, but in her own mind she thought sheep's clothing would not have helped Clay Potter. He looked like a criminal. No. He looked like a murderer. When driving home later, Helen made a point of apologizing to Danielle.

"This wasn't what I expected at all," she said. "I often assist with prisoner's aid. But this is not the sort of case I would involve myself in. There are not the extenuating circumstances here which would warrant my involvement."

Danielle only half listened. She knew Helen liked to throw herself into frays that made her feel good about herself. Helen needed her noble causes, relished helping the disadvantaged and the downtrodden, especially if they were victims of persecution or prejudice. But assisting an unlucky criminal or—more to the point—an inventive murderer, was not something that would benefit society, and more importantly, Helen.

"I might help him," Danielle said.

"What?"

"Yes. I might."

Danielle didn't promise him anything at first, and he didn't ask. Visiting a prison, talking through a reinforced window, isn't the usual way men and women get to know one another. But there was an intensity to their talks that neither could have imagined. They only had minutes with each other, but those were the kind of minutes many couples never experience. There wasn't music, or food, or a movie between them. There wasn't physical contact, or shared passions. There was only death around the corner, death and the discoveries between them.

A week after they met, Danielle offered Clay her financial support. Her money, she said, would buy him the best lawyers, the best tacticians. If her wealth could buy him another day's life, it was there for him.

There for the taking. Clay was usually good at that, but he wasn't sure how to respond in this case. Now that everything was being offered, he felt off balance. He had heard about things like this happening, but only in fairy tales. He felt like the frog being kissed by the princess. Clay had always enjoyed stealing from the rich because he thought it brought him closer to them, almost made him one of them. And now everything was being offered on a golden platter. She was his last wish come true.

"I couldn't just take," he said.

"It's not taking," she said. "It's sharing."

"Like we were married?"

"Till death do us part."

"What would your friends say?"

"About what?"

"You know," he said, then struggled for the words, "if we were to get married."

"They'd say," she said, " 'Married to a murderer.' "

Neither of them spoke. The words hung between them. Each felt a thrill. He, that this one in a million (no, make that one in fifty million, he thought) woman could be at his side, and she, at the audaciousness of his notion.

Married to a murderer. Each of them thought about that. Marriage suited their desires, though each wanted different things. He wanted respectability, and she wanted notoriety. Both perceived the other as being powerful, as belonging to worlds they had only imagined.

"Will you marry me?" he asked.

"Yes," she said.

They didn't wait. Time was not on their side. Their nuptials set off a media frenzy. Why would one of the richest and most desirable women in the world marry a murderer? Danielle didn't offer answers, so the media tried to find their own. The life and times of Clay Potter were examined. If Danielle Deveron saw something good, and noble, and attractive in the man, then the reasoning was that there must be something there. Witnesses surfaced that remembered a different Clay Potter than was evidenced on his rap sheet. Even before his new team of lawyers went to work, the press began to call for a reexamination of his murder conviction.

"There is a God," said Clay Potter. And he knew there was an angel—his wife.

While desperate motions were filed, man and wife continued in their jailhouse courtship.

"People whisper behind my back," Danielle confessed. "Everyone is talking. And mostly what they say is, 'Married to a murderer.'"

"They're wrong," said Clay, his voice rising, red suddenly appearing in his ashen face. "They're wrong."

He coughed long and hard, the coldness of his years of imprisonment, and the harshness of the lies directed at his wife, making him burn with anger. Danielle consoled him. He didn't understand that she hadn't been complaining. Quite the opposite. Being married to Clay set her apart, made her something novel. Others might have five diamond rings, and Learjets, but she had something they didn't: she was married to a murderer.

They were quite the odd couple, but to all appearances, Danielle and Clay savored their moments together. Despite all the tumult going on around them, despite the clamor for a new trial, neither of them expected that Clay would be alive for very long. In some ways they found a freedom in his execution date. "Carpe diem," Danielle often said. Clay didn't know the Latin meaning, but he did like the excited look on her face.

The reprieve call never came from the governor. But Clay's lawyers found enough extentuating circumstances to allow for a retrial. Clay was ecstatic. He had been proclaiming his innocence from the day of his arrest, and now, at long last, people were beginning to believe him.

Clay's retrial was blessedly short. On further review of the so-called evidence, Clay was found innocent. In the arms of his beautiful wife, Clay left the courtroom. He told the media that he had never been happier, but he coughed all the while he made the pronouncement. It was clear to all that Clay was very sick, his body wasted from his long confinement. Many wondered whether his freedom had come too late.

His death was announced a week later, and the press treated it like a Greek tragedy. Center stage was the widow in black, poor little rich girl Danielle Deveron, but the public was not quick to rid itself of their early take on the story. Behind the widow's back, Danielle still heard the whispers: "Married to a murderer."

The words were all too familiar to Danielle. They had been Clay's last words to her. He had made his pronouncement minutes after his last dose of medication. Clay had been obedient and adoring almost to the end. It was only when he took that final swallow of medication that he finally awakened. His face had undergone a remarkable transformation, beginning with a cherishing gaze, to a questioning glance, to a piercing stare, and then, at the end, a horrified look. He was staring at death, and something else, something that must have appeared even uglier to him.

From the first, they had both seen what they wanted to see, both seen what wasn't there. For a time, each had thought the other perfect for their needs. Danielle had been married to a murderer, and her beloved was to die for his deeds. When it turned out Clay was innocent (just her luck, she thought), everything changed. This wasn't a man Danielle had wanted to spend a life with, but a death with. She had married a guilty man. She had married a murderer. She wanted that distinction, wanted the whispers. But even more, she had wanted his death.

"Married," Clay had gasped, trying to shout out his last words, trying to raise an alarm, "to a murderer!"

Then he died. Poisoned, but that was something only his widow would know.

Of their relationship, the public would always judge, "Married to a murderer."

They would never know, thought Danielle, how right they were.

———————

Alan Russell checks out of his usual venue of California resorts to introduce the oddest of odd couples: a society woman and a felon. Russell's books include *No Sign of Murder* (1990), *The Forest Prime Evil* (1992), and *Multiple Wounds* (1996). His *The Hotel Detective* (1994) and *The Fat Innkeeper* (1995) feature hotel security director Am Caulfield and reflect Russell's many years and offbeat experiences as a hotel general manager.

Bugged

Eve K. Sandstrom

I turned off the motor, got out of the car, and kicked the left front tire.

"Stupid thing!" I told it. "Quit the spooky stuff!"

I glared at the car, and my reflection glared back from the finish of the door. No more ordinary matron had ever lived than the one looking back at me. Slacks for comfort, long shirt to hide the broad beam the slacks failed to disguise. Salt and pepper hair, styled for simplicity, not beauty. Strictly dull.

Yet I had just been scared spitless by a 1965 Volkswagen.

"Act your age," I snarled at my reflection.

Harry came out of the garage then, wearing the faded plaid jackass pants he reserves for mowing the lawn. "There's nothing wrong with your age, honey," he said.

"Oh, never mind. I'm just mad at myself."

"Is something the matter with your car, Paula? You said you liked the gears."

"The car's fine, except for some spooks. I love the gears. I'd also love a drink. Spirits should exorcise the spooks."

I headed into the house, with Harry following.

"Spooks? What are you so mad about?"

"It's so dumb, I'm ashamed to tell you. But every time I drive this car past the west end of the golf course—you know, the place where they found Phyllis Wilkins—I get this feeling—and it's not imagination, it's a physical sensation—that someone just pulled on the back of the driver's seat."

Harry stared at me, then went to the cupboard where we keep the bourbon. "Well, naturally, all of us feel kind of spooky about that end of the golf course since—"

"No. I've driven by that place a thousand times in the past year. I never had that feeling in the Buick."

Harry got down a jigger and a glass and made a bourbon and water. Light, the way I like it. As he handed it to me, he put an arm around my shoulders and squeezed my arm. I could tell what was coming. Another crack about my age. My "time of life."

Harry's mother had a menopause that kept her family in an uproar for ten years. None of them ever seemed to realize it was the only interesting thing that ever happened to the woman. But Harry's been eyeing me suspiciously since I turned forty. So I spoke before he could.

"Harry," I said. "Shut your damn mouth."

He grinned. "You're so sexy when you're mad," he said. Then he patted me on the fanny. Harry and I aren't over the hill yet.

The Volkswagen—a classic Bug—had come into our lives two weeks earlier. Mike, our younger child, had joined his sister Susan at college that fall. Luckily, he had found a good part-time job. With two kids in the state university, both too smart not to go to college and both too dumb to win scholarships, that job was important to our family's finances.

But it meant that Mike needed transportation. So my three-year-old Buick went off to college, too, and we bought the Volkswagen for me to drive. Public transportation does not exist in Plains City, U.S. of A.

We rejected the idea of having Mike take the VW for two reasons. First, although the car's mechanical status was okay—somewhere between "collector's item" and "jalopy"—

it was old. Very old. Its original wheels had been chiseled from stone. Neither Harry nor I trusted it enough to let Mike drive it from Plains City to College Town and back.

But the second reason was mine, and I kept it to myself. The Volkswagen made me feel young again. I had a Bug when I was in college. Behind the wheel of my new used Volkswagen, I was no longer a middle-aged matron worrying about keeping two kids in college. When I drove it, I was again a carefree college girl, headed for a fraternity party, with my whole life ahead of me.

Or at least I felt like a young mother, because I had hauled Mike and Susan a lot of miles in the old '65 VW. I knew what it felt like when a hand tugged on the back of the driver's seat.

The first time I felt the tug, just as I passed the golf course, I nearly snapped out, "You can just wait until we get home." Then I realized that I was alone, and I was passing the place where Phyllis Wilkins had been found. My scalp quivered. The hair-standing-on-end bit.

I laughed it off. But it happened again that evening. A tug on the back of the seat. I felt it every time I passed that spot.

Was the fact that our new used car was a Volkswagen the reason for my fixation? Because a Volkswagen might have been involved in Phyllis's death.

Phyllis Wilkins had been an attractive woman in her forties, a newcomer to our little town. Our most eligible local widower, Dr. Lionel Wilkins, had met her on a visit to relatives in Virginia. Her southern charm had—well, charmed him, and he swept her right off her feet. Or vice versa. I think most of the women in town were somewhat miffed at Phyllis's appearance, since we had all mentally matched Lionel with Agatha Draper, the nearest thing our town has to a grande dame.

But once we met Phyllis, we were charmed, too. Phyllis was energetic and imaginative. She became active in our local organizations, and for the first time in a long time, women's activities began to be fun.

Even those of us who love Plains City have to admit it's isolated. Our population is just under 20,000, and the nearest large town is 120 miles away. We have to make our own fun.

There's not a lot of opportunity for career women in Plains City either, simply because there are not a lot of jobs here for anybody. My husband inherited his father's insurance agency, and he's always made a decent living. But the low pay scale for women, particularly for those of us who didn't finish college, has produced a large group of women who find an outlet in volunteer organizations. We all know each other, we belong to the same clubs, and we've worked on the same old projects for years.

Phyllis blew into town like the winds of change. Her ideas may not have been new to her, but they were to us, and we loved them. At the time she was killed, she'd just been nominated as president of a new group, the Community Action Coalition, which was to combine women's and men's clubs in joint projects.

Phyllis must have been the victim of an insane killer. That was the only explanation any of us could think of for an apparently motiveless crime.

She had been a devoted jogger, running every evening after dinner. The previous September, before dusk, Phyllis had jogged off down Ash Street on her usual route. When it began to rain about eight P.M., her husband drove out to look for her, thinking she'd like a ride. He couldn't find her. He went home, expecting to discover that she'd beaten him back. No Phyllis. He called people, did all the things we do when someone's been misplaced. At midnight he called the police. They weren't too concerned. You can't call a grown woman a missing person after only a few hours, even when she left home in the rain in her jogging togs.

The rain stopped during the night, and an early-morning golf foursome found Phyllis's body on the fourth green, at the west end of the country club course. Phyllis had been beaten to death, hit in the head several times with a heavy object. The autopsy report said she had not been raped.

The police had questioned Lionel, of course. Phyllis's death so soon after their marriage—and the wills they had made leaving everything to each other—made him the obvious suspect. But there was nothing else to link him with the crime, and he definitely could not be connected with the car that seemed to be involved in the case.

The car had been described by a five-year-old neighbor. She had seen Phyllis near the streetlight at her corner, talking to someone in a blue Volkswagen, the old beetle kind that even a child could identify. Tracks near Phyllis's body indicated a small car had been there. It could have been a Volkswagen, police said.

No arrest had been made.

So, I thought, perhaps it was the Volkswagen that reminded me of the murder and made me feel that silly tug on the back of the seat. Or maybe, I thought again, I'm really cracking up.

My hair continued to leap to attention every time I passed the golf course, but I wouldn't have said any more about it if it hadn't been for Harry. And maybe for one too many bourbons before dinner at the country club.

The country club is the one decent place to eat out in Plains City, and it's a minor luxury we refuse to give up for the sake of education. That night the club was so crowded we had to wait in the bar. But there were people we knew and liked waiting with us, and we had a drink, then bought the other couple a round, and they felt they had to repay us, and I slipped my third drink to Harry, because I didn't really want it. Big mistake.

A few minutes later we were joined by the Plains City grande dame, Agatha Draper. Agatha is a tall, cool blonde with an unflappable pageboy. She has run all the women's clubs in town for twenty-five years. She was born with money, made a suitable marriage to a docile husband who died young. She has one son, Hayden, a tall blond like his mother.

Poor old what's-his-name, the husband, apparently hadn't contributed a single dominant gene to his progeny. While Hayden fell somewhere behind the Ladies' Cultural Guild and the Mayor's Ad Hoc Committee on Traffic Safety in Agatha's affections, he was the picture of her physically. But only physically. The mental strength that beautified our parks and encouraged the few arts Plains City offers seemed to have missed Hayden. A year earlier Agatha had dropped a few hints that led us to understand that Hayden was in a mental hospital. His prognosis wasn't too good, I had deduced, because Agatha had just sold his car.

Our 1965 Volkswagen.

But Hayden's old car had no possible connection with the death of Phyllis Wilkins. It was green, not blue, and it had a well-worn set of Goodrich tires, not the Dunlaps the police had said were on the wanted car.

Agatha's forceful personality always makes men nervous, but that doesn't excuse what Harry said that night. His extra bourbon and water doesn't excuse it either.

"Why, hello," Harry said when Agatha joined us. "It's the lady who sold us the haunted Volkswagen."

Agatha raised a well-bred eyebrow. Then Harry put on a confidential whisper and told everybody in the bar about me and the Volkswagen and our adventures driving by the golf course.

Everyone in Plains City had been fascinated by our very own murder, of course. They loved having a new twist on it. They all began to buzz. So I was horrified when the head waitress called out, "Dr. Wilkins," and Lionel unfolded his lanky form from a booth at the other end of the room. I hoped he hadn't heard us.

I tried to be a good sport, but I could have killed Harry. I guess Agatha was annoyed, too. The next day she offered to buy the car back, "if it is in any way unsatisfactory."

That was quite a concession from Agatha. She runs her business affairs as efficiently as she runs her clubs. She's the kind of woman who takes an auto mechanics class just in case the garage should try to cheat her. The garage wouldn't try it twice.

I assured Agatha that the car wasn't at all unsatisfactory, that we liked it, and that we certainly planned to keep it.

"I wouldn't object to buying it back," she said. "Hayden is coming home next Thursday, and he always had an absurd sentimental attachment to that car."

My deduction about Hayden's prognosis had been wrong. "I'm glad he's coming home," I said, "but we want to keep the car."

Hayden and my Susan had been in school together from

kindergarten through high school, and he was a nice enough kid. If he'd had a different mother, he might even have had a chance.

Harry had caught a vigorous hint that I didn't think the haunted Volkswagen story was funny, but the next Sunday evening the bartender, Bud, brought it up. "How's the Volkswagen?" he asked. His broad, crooked grin was innocent. "Still haunted?"

"Sure is, Bud," I said. I was still trying to be a good sport. "But a bourbon and water ought to de-spook it."

As I spoke, a blond man at the end of the bar turned around, and I saw that it was Hayden. He looked great. He was about two inches taller and four inches broader than he had been at high school graduation, and his hair was about six inches shorter than the shoulder-length do he'd had when I'd last seen him.

"Hello, Mrs. Carlson," he said. "How's Susan?"

"She's fine. Doing her practice teaching this semester. We're glad to see you home."

"Thanks. It's good to see you." I thought he emphasized the "you." Then Hayden went on. "Mother said you bought my old car. What's this about it being haunted?"

Agatha's blond pageboy loomed up behind him, and I tried to joke it off. But no luck. Hayden pressed for the story. Bud egged him on. It was less awkward to tell it than to refuse.

And Agatha Draper got mad, in her own ladylike way. Before I got to the bit about this being too, too silly, Agatha took Hayden's arm. "Come," she said. "This is morbid. Let's go into the dining room."

Hayden didn't look as if he found it morbid. He was grinning broadly. A rabbit ran over my grave about then, and I shivered.

Hayden patted my hand. "Don't worry, Mrs. Carlson," he said. "I think this killer has gone inactive. Don't you, Mother?"

He laughed merrily and went off beaming.

Harry and I stared after them, and I gave another shiver.

Harry snorted. "I think they harvested the nuts at the funny farm a few days too early," he said.

That was the night before my accident.

I was leaving work when it happened. As a belated entrant to the job market, I had found a job to suit my limited talents. I am a church secretary. They don't pay much, but I can't do much.

Peace Church is located in one of the most beautiful places in our town, atop one of our few hills. Pines and poplars dot the front lawn of the church, and the church perches above, looking like a postcard as you drive down the valley.

But most people enter and exit the church from the rear, even though that side of the building is a blank wall, with no windows and only one metal door. That's the side where the parking lots are. Worshipers and staff members park in three little rice paddies, connected by winding drives. And the longest, steepest, and most winding drive leads down to State Highway 59, the busiest street in Plains City.

The minister makes Monday his day off, so I had been on my own all afternoon. I came out at four P.M. and locked the door behind me. I climbed into my little green VW, fastened my seat belt, and started up. I always park in the shade at the back of the lot while the weather is still hot, so I didn't have to back out of my parking slot. I simply drove straight toward that long, steep, narrow, winding, crooked drive.

As the car started down the hill, I automatically hit the brakes. The pedal went clear to the floor. I couldn't believe it. I was hitting the brakes hard, but the car wasn't slowing down.

I was rolling faster, still stomping the brake through the floorboard, when I entered the first curve. A right-hand curve. Thank God and VW engineers for a short turning radius. I made it.

A sharp left followed. I swung the wheel back and hung on. The asphalt slid rapidly by. The VW and I were completely out of control. The foot-high stone wall that bordered the drive loomed close, then floated away. The wall, I thought. Maybe I could crash into it. No, it was too short. I'd go right over, and the hillside was even steeper than the drive.

Somehow I made that left-hand curve. But now I had entered the final straightaway, a long slope with a stop sign at the bottom and big trucks whizzing by on the highway beyond.

Waiting for a traffic break was always a problem there. This time I would be the traffic break.

I could feel the car gathering speed, rushing faster and faster toward the street. I was definitely going to crash.

At least I had my seat belt fastened. The thought was absurd. A seat belt was not going to make any difference when I hit a semi. But my right hand felt to see if the belt was right, and it accidentally touched the hand brake between the seats.

I yanked it up. The green bug gave a groan and several squeals. It skidded down the final twenty-five feet of the drive.

And it stopped. It stopped with its little nose almost touching the stop sign, with the big trucks whizzing by a few feet away.

I leaned my head on its little gray steering wheel and I said, "I love you." Then I got out, climbed back up the hill and called the garage. And called Harry. And shook all over.

Both Harry and Ernst Horst were there fast. Ernst Horst runs the only garage in Plains City that will handle foreign cars. The next surprise came from that cheerful young man.

"Hey, oh," Ernst said. "I heard you bought Hayden's old car. It's an old 'un, but it had putty good care. Can't have been in too bad a shape. Wonder what happen to dem brakes."

He hoisted the front end with the wrecker, ignoring the traffic snarl he was causing, and took a look.

"Hey, oh," he said. "Trust dat Mrs. Draper. She took the new tires off and sold you the old set. She never misses a chance. But look at dat!" He whistled and pointed with a screwdriver. "The brake indicator switch. She's loose."

Harry and I looked. It didn't mean a thing to either of us. But Ernst's eyes were getting big. He looked back up the hill.

"Mrs. Carlson," he said, "you didn't have no brakes at all. And I ain't no detective, but it looks like to me dat somebody scratched this with a wrench or something."

Either you had a real amateur working on dis car, or somebody's got it in for you."

The whole thing seemed ludicrous to me, and to Harry as well. "Don't be insulted, Paula," he said, "but I think you're only special to me. What could anybody have against you? The only obnoxious thing you ever do is make a few wisecracks."

That time the wisecracks failed me.

When a police officer came to investigate the traffic snarl, neither Harry nor I said anything to him about the car being haunted. The officer talked to Ernst, but he apparently didn't take his suspicions any more seriously than we did. He recognized the car as quickly as Ernst had, however.

"You bought this car from Hayden Draper, didn't you?" he said, scribbling on a clipboard. "We investigated Volkswagens that were sixty-sixes or older about a year ago. I remember Draper's custom upholstery job."

I couldn't resist opening my big mouth. "Why were you looking at Volkswagens?"

The policeman looked at me sideways, but I plunged on. "I mean, was it about Phyllis Wilkins? I mean, I remembered that a Volkswagen was supposed to . . ." I let my jaw clatter to a stop. For once old big mouth was flustered.

But the officer nodded. "Yeah, that was the case. This car was one we eliminated, of course. Wrong color and wrong tires. And Mrs. Draper said Hayden and his car were out of town. But we thought it was a car manufactured before the high seat backs—you know, the neck rests—were required."

"How come?" Harry asked that one.

"The only firm witness we had was a five-year-old. She told us she saw the back of a head, and the driver was a guy with shoulder-length hair. There's no way a child that short could have seen the back of a head if the car had a high seat back." He frowned. "I guess the case is dead. We investigated every VW in five counties. It had to be somebody from out of the area."

I think Harry and I were both relieved to hear that Hayden had been investigated and cleared in the Wilkins

case. After the odd way he had acted the previous evening—
well, I didn't want to suggest him to the police, but it had
left me feeling funny.

So I got into Harry's car, and he drove us to the country
club for dinner. I didn't argue. The last thing I felt like
doing was going home to cook, but being nervous was
making me hungry. If they'd filled the nibble bowls with
golf balls instead of peanuts, I think I could have eaten
them.

Over cappuccino—cappuccino at the country club is
about as uptown as Plains City gets—Harry asked me if I
wanted to get rid of the Volkswagen.

"Absolutely not," I said. "I need transportation. You
need transportation. We don't need another bank note,
which is what a different car would mean."

I was still resolute the next day, when Ernst delivered
the repaired car to the church. "Hey, oh, Mrs. Carlson,"
he said. "She's all okay. You scared to drive her down the
hill?"

"Yes," I said, "but I'm going to do it anyway. Hey,
oh."

And I did. No problems, though I'll admit I tried those
brakes a dozen times before I started into the first curve.

That was Tuesday, the night Harry goes to Lions Club. I
was still nervous, I guess, because I decided I didn't want to
eat dinner in front of the television set. I called an old
friend, Connie Prince, and arranged to meet her for dinner
at the club. That's why I happened to take the Volkswagen
to the country club parking lot at night, something I had
never done before.

Connie and I met at seven and had a leisurely dinner. We
caught up with each other's kids and left about nine P.M. I
walked Connie to her car, still talking up a storm, waved her
off, then turned toward my own little Bug.

And it wasn't there. In the spot where I had parked my
green Bug was a Volkswagen, true. But it was a weirdly blue
one.

After a startled moment, I caught on. It was the lights in
the parking lot. Mercury vapor lights, they're called. They

change the color of a lot of things, and they were making my green VW look an odd sort of blue.

To a five-year-old, that color could have been blue.

It was too much to be coincidence. The old tires that Ernst had mentioned, replacing a new set. The low seat back, with no head rest. The blond driver with shoulder-length hair, a style that Hayden Draper had worn a year earlier. Hayden's peculiar behavior. And now a blue car where there had been a green one.

I didn't believe in a supernatural explanation for the ghostly tugs on the back of the seat, but there was nothing spectral about my conclusions. Whether Agatha alibied her son or not, Hayden must be responsible for the death of Phyllis Wilkins.

But what motive could Hayden have for doing such a thing? Could the death have been an accident? Was Hayden crazy enough simply to stop on the street and pick up a friend of his mother's and hit her in the head? Was Hayden some kind of a sex maniac, even though Phyllis hadn't been raped?

I didn't believe it.

My impulse was to run home to Harry. He might be able to convince me I was wrong. But if I wasn't wrong, we'd have to do something. And how could we tell Agatha her son was a killer?

Maybe I should keep quiet. After all, Agatha had had Hayden committed, and the doctors had let him out. They surely knew what they were doing. But what if Hayden had entered treatment voluntarily? Would he need permission to leave? I'd have to find out. And how could I investigate something that didn't appear to be any of my business?

This worry session took only thirty seconds or so, because I was still standing in the parking lot like the world's leading dummy when something moved in the shadows beside the fence.

I jumped. Then I saw it was only Agatha Draper.

I didn't have the nerve to grab the lead cow in our small town herd by the horns, but Agatha went straight to the point.

She motioned toward the car. "How did you learn that this car was involved in the Wilkins case?" She was terribly calm. "You've known for weeks, haven't you?"

"No, Agatha, I just figured it out. Do the doctors think it's safe for Hayden to be—out?"

"Hayden?" Agatha shrugged. "Hayden doesn't matter. What matters is that I won't be blackmailed."

"Blackmailed? Who's blackmailing you?"

"You, Paula. You were working up to that, weren't you? With your silly stories about haunted automobiles. It's not going to work."

She reached into her oversized canvas tote bag and brought out an old-fashioned six-shooter. She examined it, cocked it, and pointed it in my direction.

I was so amazed that I just stood there with my jaw flapped open. I guess I should have run when she was taking out the gun, but I just couldn't take the whole thing seriously. Agatha Draper, club woman, pointing a pistol. At me. I almost giggled.

"Get into the Volkswagen," Agatha ordered. She was still her usual efficient self. It was this calmness that made the whole thing ridiculous. Agatha was waving her pistol around and giving orders in the same tone she had used as she presided at a thousand committee meetings. Agatha had used those meetings to train all the women in Plains City. We couldn't think of being rude to Agatha. She was a real lady.

So I got into the car on the driver's side, still feeling giggly, and Agatha got in on the passenger side, slinging her heavy tote bag into the backseat.

"Now drive onto the service road." The gun was still pointed in my direction.

"Agatha," I said, "I'm tired, and I want to go home."

"Drive down the road."

I heaved a sigh, just the way I do when Agatha railroads something through at Study League, but I started the car and headed it onto the road the greens keepers use.

"Turn left," Agatha said.

We were driving toward the fourth green, where Phyllis Wilkins had been found. My hair was beginning to stand up.

Agatha was still very calm, still pointing the pistol toward me. It didn't waver. I was trying to think of some polite way to tell her I didn't like this.

Agatha began to talk, in her usual ladylike manner.

"I'm very well-prepared tonight," she said. "I even arranged some bracelets for you to wear." Turning slightly sideways in her seat, she reached into the tote bag and pulled out some bicycle clips—the elastic kind that fasten with Velcro.

"What are those for?" My voice nearly cracked.

"To tie you to the steering wheel."

"What for?" This time I yelped.

"To hold you still so that I can kill you."

"Kill me! Look, Agatha, I don't want to hurt you. I don't want to blackmail you. All I need to know is that Hayden won't hurt anybody else."

"Hayden? Why do you keep talking about Hayden? Hayden has nothing to do with this."

She was silent a moment. Then she laughed harshly. "Did you think Hayden was responsible for the death of that wretched woman? My unworldly son wouldn't have the nerve, much less the community spirit, to take care of Phyllis Wilkins. Hayden was like all the rest of you— completely taken in by that woman. She knew nothing about the situation in Plains City, yet she tried to take over. She even campaigned to become president of the Community Action Coalition.

"Now what would Phyllis Wilkins have known about the sort of community action we need here? She was just a stranger.

"For a hundred years the women of this community were relegated to a minor role in civic affairs. The Art Guild, the Study League—time wasters! But the Community Action Coalition! That is bringing together Plains City's movers and shakers, men and women. As president of that, I could build a real base—even run for political office. I could show the stupid men in this town what an intelligent person can do with some real power!

"But that idiotic woman would have ruined it, if I hadn't had the community spirit to take care of the situation."

Jealousy. While everyone else was envying Agatha Draper, she'd been jealous of Phyllis Wilkins.

We were approaching the fourth green, and Agatha waved toward a clump of trees. "Pull the car up here," she said. "The trees will hide us from the street. Turn the lights off and put the car in neutral. But don't stop the motor."

She was still using her calm, committee chairman voice, and she was still holding her pistol steady. So I obeyed, but I was beginning to rebel. If she would only look away. I felt certain I was as strong as she was.

But I wasn't any more vigilant than she was. She held the pistol steady in her right hand as she lifted the bicycle clip up near my right hand with her left.

"Keep your hands on the wheel," she ordered, "and hold the end of this under your thumb."

"Don't be ridi—" I began. But something hard and small suddenly was jammed against the right side of my head.

It was the barrel of the pistol.

At that moment I faced the fact that I was going to die. I think I quit breathing. I was cornered.

So I held the end of a bicycle clip under each thumb while she pulled the bonds tightly around the steering wheel and my wrists.

Then Agatha opened the door of the car, and the inside light came on. I saw my chance. As soon as she got out, I could pull the Velcro loose with my teeth and drive off. Nothing easier. A moving car would be a hard target for the pistol.

It must have been mental telepathy. Agatha reached back into the car and turned the strips. It was a painful process for me, but she arranged the fastenings so that they were behind the steering wheel, where I couldn't fit my pin head to bite them.

She took her tote bag out of the backseat. For the first

time I caught the significance of the golf gloves she was wearing. No fingerprints.

Agatha reached into the bag and pulled out a piece of plastic garden hose. Was she going to beat me?

"What's that for?"

"Oh, this is a piece of hose I cut off the roll in your garage," Agatha said. "You really should lock up more securely. I brought it to attach from the exhaust to your wing window. For your suicide."

"Suicide?" I tried to act calm. "Come on, Agatha, the joke's over. Let me loose." The bike clips were really tight. "Nobody will ever believe I committed suicide."

"Oh, I think they will. You've had such strange ideas lately. A haunted car, for example. And after you're unconscious, but before you're actually dead, I can take the clips off your hands and let the circulation get back to normal.

"It's a better plan than tampering with your brakes. I didn't think you'd have the sense to pull the hand brake. Most people don't realize there are two separate systems."

I began to strain against the Velcro strips.

"Jump around and scream all you please," Agatha said. She picked the tote bag up and closed the door. Looking through the window, she said, "No one can hear you, no matter what you do."

I realized that she was right. We were a quarter of a mile from the clubhouse, and the street in front of us had a forty-five mile per hour speed limit and no sidewalk. No one was going to go by slowly enough to hear a honk or interpret a scream.

I made my mind up not to die easily.

I yanked at the clips that held my hands, pushing with my feet at the same time. Something in the floorboard gave. My feet had automatically found their positions on the brake and clutch.

I still had a weapon. The car. If I could get it in gear.

I pushed the clutch in with my left foot and kicked my right shoe off. I pulled my leg all the way up and back, until the ball of my foot was on top of the stick shift. It wasn't ladylike.

I wiggled the gearshift back and forth gently. Yes, it was in neutral. It had to be or the motor would have died earlier.

If I drove forward I would wham into the trees. I had to get the car into reverse.

In a Volkswagen you have to push down, left, and back to get into reverse. Down, left, and toward yourself. My foot slipped, and I pulled a muscle, but the gearshift moved the direction I wanted it to. I jiggled it a little, and it seemed tight.

I knew I would have only one chance. When Agatha figured out what was going on, she wouldn't hesitate to use her pistol instead of staging the suicide.

I put my foot back on the floorboard, still keeping the clutch in with my left foot. Thank God Agatha hadn't ordered me to put the hand brake on. I pressed down hard on the gas and let up on the clutch. The car leaped backward.

I heard a scream, then felt two thumps as the car bumped over something. First the back wheels, then the front ones.

I yelled, "I've killed her!"

I didn't know if the thought made me happy or sad.

The car was still shooting backward. I threw the brakes on and engaged the clutch. The car stopped, and I squinted through the gloom. Finally I made out a lighter form against the dark grass. It didn't seem to be moving.

I shifted into first with my foot. Turning the wheel with my pinioned hands, I started back to the clubhouse. I drove slowly because it was dark, and I couldn't get my hands loose to turn on the lights. But I had to get help for both of us.

Agatha proved to be too tough to kill, though she did have two badly smashed legs.

Hayden came by yesterday to tell me that as a condition of her plea bargain, she has been committed to a high-priced mental hospital. I feel sure she'll have it organized to suit her in no time at all, with the grounds thoroughly beautified and an active cultural program. I didn't tell Hayden that.

"I sure feel awful about all this," Hayden said.

"I guess I owe you an apology, Hayden. At first I thought—I mean—I wouldn't have gotten into that mess if I had realized that your mother was the one—the one to be afraid of."

Hayden nodded. "I feel bad too. See, I realized that she had gotten rid of my new tires. I even knew she hated Mrs. Wilkins. After the cops came by to question me about the Volkswagen, I kidded Mother about being the killer. I could tell it got her goat, so I kept it up.

"She always had a hundred ways to put me down, and I guess I wanted to get even. But I never seriously thought she had anything to do with Mrs. Wilkins's death. I liked Mrs. Wilkins."

I nodded, and Hayden went on. "Besides, I can't blame you for thinking I was nuts enough to kill somebody. I think Mother managed to convince everyone that I'd been in a mental hospital for the past year."

"Where were you?" Might as well live up to my reputation for bluntness.

"In a commune, Mrs. Carlson. We renounce all worldly possessions. I think that's what Mother couldn't take."

Ernst Horst had a little surprise for me too. He dropped by without being summoned. "Hey, oh, Mrs. Carlson," he said. "I heard dat the back of your seat been giving funny jumps when you pass dat golf course."

"Now, Ernst, don't laugh. I know it's just my imagination."

"Maybe not, lady. Let me look at dat front seat. You should have told me about it."

I followed him into our garage, where Ernst got down on his knees and fiddled with things under the driver's seat. Then he got up, smiling triumphantly.

"Hey, oh," he said. "You chust had a loose spring. Must be some sort of bump in the road near the golf course." He gestured. "Problem solved."

I haven't had the nerve to tell Ernst that I still feel someone grab the back of the seat whenever I pass the fourth green on the country club course. The funny part is that it doesn't scare me anymore.

———————

Journalist and Oklahoman Eve Sandstrom examines spooky car trouble in this tale of suspicious death and Farvegnugan. Sandstrom's mystery novels feature husband-and-wife sleuths Sam and Nicky Titus in *Death Down Home* (1990), *The Devil Down Home* (1992), and *The Down Home Heifer Heist* (1993).

Accidents Will Happen

Carolyn Wheat

I have to go. She knows I have to go. I told her—what, fifteen minutes ago? Why doesn't she come? I watch the second hand moving from little mark to little mark on the clock, a jumpy little movement, ticking away the seconds I lie here in agony, my seventy-five-year-old bladder about to burst.

Why doesn't she come?

Because she likes it when I can't hold it. She likes it when she gets to clean me up and say in that syrupy cracker voice of hers, "Accidents will happen."

Only it won't be an accident. It will be deliberate, not on my part, but on hers. She's taking away my dignity, second by second, as she makes me lie here squeezing my legs shut like a toddler being toilet-trained.

A toddler who isn't going to make it to the potty unless she gets that bedpan over here in one more minute.

Two more minutes have passed. I'm shaking with need. Oh, God, I'm so glad no one from my past can see me now. Professor Hofsteader, reduced to counting the seconds before she pees her bed.

Thanks to that peroxided little bitch in the greens. They don't wear white anymore. They wear sickly green pants

228

and shirts, look like they work in a gas station instead of a nursing home. God knows why.

She's here. Thanks be to God.

I leak a little as the bedpan slides under my frail hips. I can't help it; I have to go so badly, and the sight of the bedpan makes it even worse. It's just a few drops, but of course she sees it and giggles. "Don't worry your head none, Teacher, everybody knows accidents will happen. I'll change the bed in no time flat."

I was not a schoolteacher, you cretin, I was a full professor. I taught graduate courses in art; my paintings hung in the Great Hall at the state university. I taught students who went on to win prizes, whose work is shown in museums.

She changes the bed with a sweet little put-upon smile that says she's earning her crowns in heaven by being so extra-nice to a bitchy old lady. It never seems to cross her tiny little mind that she wouldn't be changing it at all if she'd come when I first rang the bell.

And she could have. That's what galls me the most. If she couldn't get to me because someone on the floor was having a heart attack, or worse, I'd understand. If this only happened once in a while, when one of the comatose patients died, I'd understand. I am not an unreasonable woman, after all.

But it happens on average four times a week. Four nights out of seven I lie in agony, counting the seconds, praying my sphincter muscles are stronger than I think they are, plotting ways to kill that little bitch.

How can I kill someone when I can't even go to the bathroom by myself?

I don't know, but I'm going to. I swear to God I'm going to.

"Why, your radio is tuned to that awful religious station again, Gladys. How on earth does that happen so often?" Mavis, the day nurse, switches back to public radio. She knows how much I love *All Things Considered;* how classical music soothes me—and how much I loathe the rantings of Reverend Billy Don Shoemaker. I have told her more than once that the night nurse changes my station and then leaves it, so I can't change it back. She even leaves it on all night, low, not too loud, but still, there I lie in bed, the hellfire voice of Billy Don in my head instead of Vivaldi and Garrison Keillor.

Oh, I want her dead so badly. As badly as I have to go on those nights when she puts me through the hell of the old. The hell of helplessness, the hell of depending on the kindness of strangers who are not kind, strangers who enjoy the infliction of pain and indignity on those who used to be their betters.

Yes, their betters. There, I said it. I was better than Bobbie Sue Mason, and I don't care who knows it. She is ignorant; I was educated. She has no sense of beauty; I was an artist. She is young and has no compassion; I was—

Well, perhaps my compassion was nothing to brag about. But I would not condemn my worst enemy to the torture she puts me through, four times a week on average.

I would not.

But I would kill. I would indeed. But how?

There is medication. I could hoard my sleeping tablets and slip them, one by one, into the coffee she drinks all night. Coffee whose smell enters my nose and speaks to me of the days when I was alive. Speaks to me of all-night coffeehouses in Greenwich Village, of little cafés on the Rive Gauche, of long nights in Barcelona—of artistic discussions and cigarettes smoked with lovers, and—

And youth.

When she first came on the floor, I asked Bobbie Sue for a sip, just a taste, of her coffee. The smell took me back, even though hers was an indifferent brew held in a plastic cup instead of the nectar of the gods I used to drink out of little demitasse cups.

She screwed up her face into a pose meant to make me think she was actually considering the possibility, then said, "Sugar, I can't give you somethin' the doctor might have told you you shouldn't have. You know better'n that, you bein' a schoolteacher and all."

I corrected her. God help me, I corrected the little snip, told her I was a professor of art at the state university. Even added a little lecture on how difficult it was in those days for a woman to achieve full professorship, and how my year at the Sorbonne of course made a difference in the faculty's tenure vote.

I might as well have been talking to a cat.

Except that a cat wouldn't have held a grudge, wouldn't have referred to me as "Professor" in a drawn-out little simper whenever I couldn't hold my water, as if underlining ever so slightly the difference between the dignity I had then and the complete lack of dignity I possess now.

I must kill her. I must.

How?

"Darlin', I know just what to do about that radio business," Mavis the day nurse says as she waltzes into my room and rids me of the Reverend Billy Don with a flick of her middle-aged wrist. She has the other hand behind her back and pulls out a long wire made out of a bent coat hanger. She hands it to me with a flourish that invites praise. I do not completely understand what she means for me to do with it, but then she shows me. I can reach the dial with it. If I'm patient and careful, I can turn the dial and retrieve my public station. If I'm less patient, less careful, I can at least hit the power button and turn the cursed thing off.

Of course, she manages the wire with ease, being a healthy strapping woman whose muscles obey her commands. I bend my twisted fingers one by one around the thin wire and, when I finally have a grip that will hold it, I inch it toward the radio.

"There, now, Gladys. You're almost there," Mavis says in a brisk tone. "Now bring the wire close to the dial and give a little push."

The wire is shaking in my hand; it feels as heavy as a gun. But I am determined. If I can do this for myself, I will gain some tiny control over my life—and every bit helps me feel as if I were still alive.

I am exhausted with the effort. I give the "little push" Mavis recommends—and I succeed in knocking the radio right off the shelf. It lands on the wheeled bed table next to the IV drip and the nurse's bell push.

I want to cry. But Mavis—dear, unsentimental Mavis—just picks the radio up, puts it back on the shelf, and says, "You'll get the hang of it in no time, Gladys."

I watch her set the wire in place behind my bed frame. It was made from a white wire hanger; it blends with the painted metal of the bedstead and the white of the cords. All I have to do when I want to use it is reach behind me and unhook it from the cord that connects to the bell push.

I thank Mavis profusely, but at the same time I wish she could supply me with my own bedpan instead. Some needs are more pressing than others; I believe I could live with the Reverend Billy Don if only I knew I'd get the bedpan when I needed it.

I must have dozed; I wake in a fog of oversleep to hear voices outside my room. It is Bobbie Sue and Dr. Fiske.

". . . really do think Miss Hofsteader ought to be diapered before bed, Doctor," Bobbie Sue is saying in a voice she doesn't bother to keep low. She wants me to hear, oh yes, she wants me to drink in every nasty word she's saying.

"I don't know, Nurse," the doctor says in reply. I go limp with gratitude, but at the same time there is a hint of doubt in his voice. "I hate to put a patient in diapers unless it's absolutely necessary. It tends to make them regress even more quickly."

"But Doctor," Bobbie Sue says, and I can picture her tossing her peroxided curls at him and giving him her little pout, "she's had three accidents this week already."

I hold my breath. Dr. Fiske lets out a sigh of resignation and says, "Very well. If she has another one, we'll discuss this again."

No. My soul cries out, *No.* If I truly had lost the power of control, I would submit, not graciously perhaps. Growing old with grace has not been my strong suit. But I would bow to the inevitable and present my shrunken body to be swaddled like a baby's. If I had to. If I was truly unable to control myself.

But I can control my bladder. For a reasonable period of time. I just can't do it for the unreasonable period Bobbie Sue Mason makes me wait.

Why don't I just tell the doctor I don't need diapers? Why don't I just tell him how long Bobbie Sue waits before she brings the bedpan?

You who ask those questions have never been old. You have never been stripped of everything you ever were, reduced to a grumbling bag of bones in a bed. You have never been called by your first name by boys and girls young enough to be great-grandchildren, without so much as a by-your-leave. You have never been denied coffee and fed mush and woken up so you could be given a sleeping pill you don't want and had your favorite radio station switched to something you cannot stand and be unable to switch it back. You have never depended upon the kindness of unkind strangers.

I have. So I said nothing to Dr. Fiske. Doctor, indeed. That boy was playing doctor with the neighborhood girls when I was ceremonially retired from the university, and he has the nerve to tell me I'm going to be placed in diapers if I have another "accident."

I see by the smirk on Bobbie Sue's face that there will be another "accident," probably tonight.

Bobbie Sue comes in, coffee cup in hand. She drinks a long slow pull, savoring it before my face. "I went to this new little coffee place," she says with a sly grin. "It's real cute, has all these fancy coffees. I believe the one I'm drinking is called a latte." She pronounces it wrong, of course, but by this time in our acquaintance I know better than to correct her. But I do conjure up a sense image of how that milky, strong brew would taste on my tongue. I do exactly what the little bitch wants—I envy her.

And to my intense surprise, she lowers the cup to my level and helps me drink. The smell curls around my nose and invites me to partake of its sensuous depths, to savor the rich taste of dark roast beans laced with steamed milk, topped with just a pinch of nutmeg.

That should have told me something right there. Bobbie Sue Mason is not by nature a nutmeg person. If she'd ordered that coffee for herself, she'd have poured a peck of grated chocolate on top and added cinnamon for good measure.

The nutmeg is for me.

I drink. I drink deep. I drink long. I finish the oversized plastic container and lie back with a sigh of contentment.

But later, I remember. Coffee is a diuretic.

I don't have to go so badly. Not yet. I can hold it a bit longer.

The Reverend Billy Don is asking me to make a commitment to the Lord. He says I am a miserable sinner and must repent. I find myself hanging on his every word, trying to concentrate on something other than my growing need.

I remember the wire.

I crane my neck as far as it will go and concentrate on the slender line hanging behind my bed. I focus my eyes on it and slowly edge my arm out of its blanket cocoon. I begin clenching my fingers in anticipation of grasping something thin and elusive. I reach toward it, feeling for the cold touch of metal.

My fingers are made of ice and iron. They no longer bend to my will. So it is three minutes by the clock, by the inexorable second hand, before I have the wire in my hand. I lift it carefully from the cord that holds it in place. I hold it as straight as I can, but it wobbles terribly as I reach for the radio.

I'm too tired, too weak, to work the dial. There will be no public radio. The best I can do is hit the power button and turn the ranting voice off.

I lie in bed exhausted, shaking from the effort of reaching for the radio and the effort of holding my sphincter muscles. I have to go so badly. How can she let me lie here like this, knowing the agony I'm in?

I rang the bell twenty minutes ago. Twenty long minutes I have lain in my bed, squeezing my thighs shut and counting the seconds as they tick by.

Every awful humiliation of childhood, my own and other people's, comes back to me. The time I peed at the county fair, waiting to use the outhouse. The time my little sister wet herself in church, all over her pink georgette dress. The time Sammy Perkins had an accident during a math test; the children behind him in the long rows of desks pointed and giggled as the puddle formed under his chair and his face turned red as a tomato.

If having an accident is a terrible, humiliating loss of dignity at four and five and six, what do you imagine it feels like when you are seventy-five?

In the hallway, I hear Bobbie Sue on the telephone, talking to one of her numerous boyfriends. ". . . on my floor used to paint the prettiest little pictures, and now she's so twisted up with arthuritis that she . . ."

Arthur-itis indeed. *I did not paint pretty little pictures, you idiot, I made art.*

I made art until my hands turned into claws and my shoulders refused to lift my arms. I molded clay and wielded a brush and mixed colors, and once I even welded metal into shapes that spoke of my relationship to the cosmos. I never created anything "pretty" in my life, though I like to think I added my share of beauty to the world.

I have to go so badly. I picture a flood coming out of me, a flood of used coffee. A veritable sea of urine, pouring out over the bed, the floor, sweeping the entire building away.

I reach for the bell one more time. I've rung it six times, but still the chattering voice on the phone tells me her majesty will not deign to answer until it is certain I will not be able to hold back the flood.

I am going to burst. I am shivering in the bed, my muscles working so hard to keep the dam from breaking. I have to let some loose. I have to open the floodgates just a little, no matter how awful it will be to listen to her giggle and her promise to "clean up this little accident in two shakes."

She *will* clean me up. That is the only salvation. She will strip the bed and pull new fresh sheets from the closet and put a new nightgown over my shrunken bones, and bring a pan and a sponge and wash and powder me like a baby.

At least the voice of the Reverend Billy Don will not be there to harangue me about the hereafter. I have no strength left to put the wire back where it belongs. I have hidden it under the mattress, but it is a near certainty that Bobbie Sue will find it when she changes my sheets. I sigh; Mavis's lovely present will be taken from me, along with my pride in spending my days and nights undiapered.

The floodgates open. I lie in bed with hot urine flowing down my thighs, into the mattress. The sense of relief is overwhelming, yet I sob a little for my lost dignity. Once more "the Professor" has become a baby. And after tonight I will be able to let myself go as often as I need to, for I will be diapered like an infant. I put my fingers to my eyes and blot my tears; how small and helpless I feel. How old.

What does it matter who I was, what I did? What matters is that I can no longer do for myself.

Perhaps a diaper would be a good thing. At least I'd no longer have the nightly battle, the counting of seconds, the desire to kill.

She comes in, looks down at the bed, with its giant wet spot giving me away. She looks at my face, red with tears and humiliation, and she giggles. "I guess that coffee wasn't such a good idea after all, was it, Professor?"

Then her head cocks to one side; her face wears a puzzled look. "Why, whatever happened to your radio? I could have sworn I left it on for you." She reaches for the power button and brings the unctuous voice of the Reverend Billy Don into the room.

She walks to the closet to get new sheets. She pulls out the metal pan and fills it with water and baby soap. Baby soap. There is baby powder, too, which she will sprinkle and then pat onto my shrunken, hairless, once-private parts.

She turns me expertly and pulls the sheets from underneath my body. I tremble that she will find my straightened wire hanger, but I managed to work it under the mattress, where she does not see it. I give it a little smile as I lie on my side, letting her pull the soaked sheet out from under me. Perhaps I can survive the night with one blessing intact.

She whistles along with the awful hymn the reverend's congregation is singing on the radio. She tosses the wet sheets onto the floor in a heap and slips a new, fresh sheet under me. I should be grateful—and I am, really I am—that she does not leave me in my puddle for hours on end. I have heard of such things, and occasionally I wonder why she confines her cruelty to making me wait too long. But then I hear the voice of the Reverend Billy Don and I realize she likes to think of herself as an angel of mercy. She likes reducing me to helplessness, but she would not put me in a position where my suffering would be an affront to her.

She places the big sponge in the warm water and glides it over my thighs. It feels good. God help me, it feels good to lie in bed while someone washes me in places no other human being has washed me since I was a toddler. Some part of me murmurs a prayer of thanks. She blots me dry and sprinkles baby powder—how nice it smells; I do love talcum—and then reaches for a diaper.

No.

No. I will not let her do this.

I have told myself that this is the last straw, that before I let them diaper me, I will drink all my sleeping pills at once and go where no one can take away my dignity.

But there is a better way. I look down at the wire that lies under my mattress and I see the better way.

"If you would be so kind," I begin, letting my voice quaver, "as to wash my back a little higher. I think some of the—wet may have—"

I break off with a blush that is all too real. She gives me a smirk of triumph—she has actually reduced me to asking her for something, to talking about "wet" like a toddler—but she reaches for the sponge and places her hands in the basin.

I slide the straightened hanger out of its hiding place and reach for the radio.

No, not the radio precisely. My goal this time is not the dial or the power button, but the cord that dangles behind the bed frame. I let the hook on the end of the wire grab the cord and then I give a great pull, put all my pitiful strength into the movement.

Bobbie Sue is humming her awful hymn, smiling a smile of triumph as she places the baby-pink sponge into the soapy basin that sits like an affront on the bed table behind my head.

The radio begins to topple on its shelf, wobbles and dances and finally tips right over, just as it did the first time I used my wire.

The radio falls onto the bed table with a splash.

With a splash!

"What an awful thing, Gladys," Mavis the day nurse says. She's talking a mile a minute and she hasn't even taken off her coat. She sets two cups of coffee on the bed table and shakes her head.

"I mean, I just can't get over you lying there in that bed, helpless as a kitten, while your nurse is dead on the floor next to you and nothing you can do about it. You must have felt just awful."

She takes off her coat and opens one container of coffee, which she holds next to my mouth. "I know I shouldn't let you have this, darlin'," she says with a smile, "but I also know how much you love a good cup of coffee. And after what you've been through, you deserve a little treat."

I take a sip. Pure heaven.

Before I can formulate a reply, Mavis is off and running. I swear, that woman's mouth could win a marathon. But for once I want to know every detail. "Dr. Fiske said he'd never heard of such a thing, a nurse electrocuted when a radio fell into the patient's bathwater. It just goes to show," she said, shaking her head and making a clicking sound with her teeth.

I wasn't sure what it went to show, but I added my own cliché to the ones piling up around us.

"Accidents will happen," I said, trying not to sound as pleased as I felt. I lay back on the bed and let another sip of coffee roll around my tongue.

———————

In this story, Carolyn Wheat takes a dark look at the relationship between nurse and patient. Reflecting her own experience as an attorney, she has published three mysteries featuring Brooklyn criminal lawyer Cass Jameson (*Dead Man's Thoughts, Where Nobody Dies, Fresh Kills*). *Dead Man's Thoughts* was an Edgar nominee in 1983. Wheat's short stories have appeared in the *Sisters in Crime* and *A Woman's Eye* anthologies.

MALICE DOMESTIC

Anthologies of Original Traditional Mystery Stories

1 **Presented by the acclaimed Elizabeth Peters.**
Featuring Carolyn G. Hart, Charlotte and Aaron
Elkins, Valerie Frankel, Sharyn McCumb,
Charlotte Macle_d and many others!

2 **Presented by bestselling author Mary Higgins
Clark.** Featuring Gary Alexander, Amanda Cross,
Sally Gunning, Margaret Maron, Sarah Shankman
and many more!

3 **Presented by Agatha Award-winner
Nancy Pickard.** Featuring Wendy Hornsby,
Dorothy Cannell, Deborah Adams, Camilla T. Crespi
and many more!

4 **Presented by Carolyn G. Hart.** Featuring Annette
Meyers, Rochelle Majer Krich, K.K. Beck, P.M.
Carlson and many more distinguished writers!

5 **Presented by Phyllis A. Whitney.** Featuring Joyce
Christmas, Eileen Dreyer, Peter Lovesey, Sharan
Newman, Jill Churchill and many more of today's most
skillful mystery writers.

616-04

Available from
Pocket Books

POCKET
BOOKS